# Praise for The Dutch Maiden

'De Moor's nature metaphors are of an an.........c power,
her reflections are as clever as they are distinctive, and how
she evokes the sultry, stormy atmosphere on the eve of
World War II testifies to her great storytelling ability'
*Frankfurter Allgemeine Zeitung*

'With Marente de Moor, Dutch literature has won a very
original writer, one with an apparently inexhaustible
imagination, and who will, hopefully, write many more
novels as exhilarating as this one'
*Trouw*

'An ominous atmosphere, moral dilemmas, raging passions—
all evoked by beautifully sculpted sentences'
*NRC Handelsblad*

'A masterfully written story that sparkles and effervesces,
demonstrating the richness of the language on every page'
*Limburgs Dagblad*

'A fascinating read: a gothic romance transplanted to 1930s
Germany. De Moor has lined up all the essential gothic
elements—powerful currents of sexuality, a rambling old
house, a possibly treacherous servant, a dark and brooding
man whose true affinity is with the wildness of nature—and
sent them on a collision course with concepts that come
from somewhere else entirely'
*The Herald Scotland*

**MARENTE DE MOOR** worked as a correspondent in Saint Petersburg for a number of years and wrote a book based on her experiences, *Petersburgse Vertellingen* ('Petersburg Stories'), which was published in 1999. She made a successful debut as a novelist in 2007 with *De Overtreder* ('The Transgressor'). For her second novel, *The Dutch Maiden*, she was awarded the prestigious AKO Literature Prize along with the European Union Prize for Literature. The novel has so far sold over 70,000 copies in the Netherlands and has been translated into ten languages.

**DAVID DOHERTY** studied English and literary linguistics in Glasgow before moving to Amsterdam, where he has been working as a translator since 1996. His translations include novels by critically acclaimed Dutch-language authors such as *Monte Carlo* by Peter Terrin and *The Dyslexic Hearts Club* by Hanneke Hendrix. He has also translated the work of leading Dutch sports writers Hugo Borst and Wilfried de Jong. David was recently commended by the jury of the Vondel Translation Prize for his translations of *The Dutch Maiden* and Jaap Robben's *You Have Me to Love*.

# The Dutch Maiden

MARENTE DE MOOR

# The Dutch Maiden

Translated from the Dutch
by David Doherty

WORLD EDITIONS
New York, London, Amsterdam

Published in the USA in 2019 by World Editions LLC, New York
Published in the UK in 2016 by World Editions Ltd., London

World Editions
New York/London/Amsterdam

Copyright © Marente de Moor, 2010
English translation copyright © David Doherty, 2016
Cover image © Nini and Carry Hess / Ullstein Bild
Author's portrait © Juergen Bauer

Printed by Sheridan, Chelsea, MI, USA

Library of Congress Cataloging in Publication Data is available
ISBN 978-1-64286-018-4
First published as *De Nederlandse maagd* in the Netherlands in 2010 by
Querido, Amsterdam

This project has been funded with support from the European Commission.
This publication reflects the views only of the author, and the Commission
cannot be held responsible for any use which may be made of the information
contained herein.

The publisher gratefully acknowledges the support of the Dutch Foundation
for Literature.

Twitter: @WorldEdBooks
Facebook: WorldEditionsInternationalPublishing
www.worldeditions.org

A braggart, a rogue, a villain, that fights by the book of arithmetic!
Why the devil came you between us? I was hurt under your arm.

Shakespeare, *Romeo and Juliet*, Act III Scene 1

# Part One

Dear Egon,

This letter requires no postage stamp and will surely not go unread, as I am entrusting it to my daughter, who will make sure you open it. I have long since given up expecting a reply from you but my heart rejoices at the thought that you will make the acquaintance of that which is most precious to me in this life: Janna, born in a period you dismissed as a failure. No doubt you will laugh, with the cynical snigger of someone who has forgotten what laughter is for, to hear that my daughter of all people has been possessed by the insane passion you call a life-enhancing art. Killing to enhance life: no one but you could dream up such a notion. My daughter has dealt me an unsettling blow. Could it be true that the ground where war has raged can only bring forth conflict? Janna was conceived at the site of the battle, an admission that leaves me somewhat shamefaced. Was this an act of desecration on my part? If so, it was not my intention. By then peace had returned to the land. The wounds had healed, the scars were gone, the grass had grown back thick and lush. The weather was mild and the air smelled fresh. The scent of life carrying on regardless.

The weather was not as warm as it had been then. In the wake of the battle, no one understood where that sudden heat had come from; was it the sun beating down or the fresh blood steaming from the soil? Perhaps I am mistaken and it was not the same field, but it was certainly a place ripe for planting new life in a warm-blooded woman—a woman who later, once the dust had settled, would withdraw into a fixed and deathly chill.

I went there with another purpose, of course. Do not think I have forgotten. Believe me, Egon, I searched high and low. I questioned farmers, blacksmiths, coachmen but none of them could tell me anything. I have explained all this to you, but you have never deemed my explanations worthy of an answer. I tried my best. I did not find your horse.

And now my daughter shares your passion for combat. I have tried to dissuade her. As you can imagine, I did not stand a chance. My own dear headstrong girl belongs to a breed you often see nowadays; she is a girl with no desire to become a woman. Do you understand that I am trying to make amends? First and foremost I am presenting you, the maître d'armes, with perhaps the best pupil you will ever have. Janna has real talent! Secondly, my friend, I offer you my doubts—the same doubts I kept from you when you had such need of them. Many men grow strong by feeding on the doubts of other men. Perhaps swordsmanship is the one essential art about which I understand nothing. These days, I am wise enough to admit that I cannot know anything with certainty.

But this is not all. Once you have finished gloating, it may please you to know that I have immersed myself in the art of swordsmanship. Not that I have ever held a weapon. A doctor does not need to contract the disease to make his diagnosis. Before I came across the enclosed engraving, I had no intention of sending Janna to you. But things can change. Please study it closely. It comes from a rare edition of Bredero's Low German verses.

'Oh new man of arms so able and refined / who Wise Art with strength in unity combines.'

This engraving is not simply a curiosity. This is lost learning with the power to save lives. If you are interested, there is more to be found on this subject, not least the method itself, beautifully illustrated. I sat in a deserted library in Amsterdam, turning pages with gloved hands, taking notes. It is a remarkable book. This is the science of swordsmanship. They call it a secret, the clandestine knowledge of inviolability, but let us leave those mysteries for what they are. You know my views on such matters. It is merely the science of not conceding a hit—probably far from simple, but a subject that can nonetheless be studied. Do so, Egon. Protect yourself, your country, the whole world for that matter, protect them from even more misery. The peace is no older than my daughter, no older than you were when you decided to enlist as a soldier. I hope, no, I believe beyond all doubt that ...

# 1

You might say von Bötticher was disfigured, but after a week I no longer noticed his scar. That is how quickly a person grows accustomed to outward flaws. Even the hideously deformed can be lucky in love if they find someone who, at first sight, cares nothing for symmetry. Yet most people have a peculiar tendency to fly in the face of nature and divide things into two halves, insisting one should mirror the other.

Egon von Bötticher was handsome. It was his scar that was ugly: a careless wound, inflicted by a blunt weapon in an unsteady hand. No one had warned me, so his first impression was of a startled girl. I was eighteen and dressed far too warmly when I stepped onto the platform at the end of my first journey to another country. A train trip from Maastricht to Aachen, blink and you're halfway there. My father had waved me off at the station. I can still see him standing beneath the window of my carriage looking surprisingly small and thin, columns of steam rising behind him. He gave an odd little jump when the stationmaster signalled for the brakes to be released with two blows of the hammer. Alongside us, red wagons from the mines rolled past, followed by trucks packed with lowing cattle, and in the midst of all this din my father shrank steadily into the distance, until he disappeared around the bend.

Up and leave, no questions asked. My departure was announced one evening after dinner, in a monologue that scarcely left room to breathe. The man was an old friend, had once been a good friend and was still a good maître. *Bon.* Besides, we had to face facts. We both knew I had to seize this opportunity to achieve something in sport, or would I rather go into domestic service? Well then, see it as a holiday, a few weeks of fencing in the beautiful Rhineland.

Forty kilometres separated the two railway stations, twenty years separated the two friends. On the platform at Aachen, von Bötticher was looking the other way. He knew I would come to him; that's the kind of man he was. And sure enough, I understood that the suntanned giant sporting a cream-coloured homburg had to be him. Instead of a suit to match the hat, he wore a worsted polo shirt and what I took to be sailor's trousers, the type with a wide waistband. The height of fashion. And there was I, the daughter, in a patched pinafore. He turned to face me and I backed away. The gnarled flesh of his torn cheek was still pink, though it had paled with the passing of the years. I think my shocked expression must have bored him, a reaction he had encountered all too often. His eyes drifted down to my breasts and I clasped my locket to cover what my pinafore was already doing an excellent job of concealing.

'Is that all?'

He meant my luggage. He kneaded my fencing bag to feel how many weapons it contained. I was left to carry my own suitcase. The romantic image I had cherished before our meeting was fading fast.

It was an image conjured up by a blurred snapshot from our family album. Two men, one earnest, the other out of focus. Below the photograph was a date: January 1915.

'That's me,' my father had said of the earnest man. Pointing at the other figure, little more than a smudge in an unbuttoned military overcoat and a fur hat, he said, 'That is your maître.'

My friends thought the photograph was divine. Girls my age were all too eager to sketch in that blur of a face. He was sturdy and he was gallant, that was what mattered, and he had a country estate for me to swan around on. Surely this was a Hollywood ending waiting to happen? Yet all I saw was a worn-out man without a weapon. Instead of Gary Cooper or Clark Gable gazing down from my bedroom walls, I had the Nadi brothers staring at each other. A unique photograph, one I have never seen since: Olympic heroes Aldo and Nedo, both right-handed, saluting before a bout. It's not a pose in which fencers are often photographed: facing one another in the same stance, exactly four metres apart, bodies staunchly upright, holding their blades in front of their unmasked faces. It looks as if they are sizing each other up along the steel of their weapons, but as a rule this pre-match ritual never lasts long. Not as long as it used to in the days when a duellist stared into his opponent's eyes and took one last look at life.

It was *War and Peace* that first gave Herr Egon von Bötticher a face. I had pressed him between its pages as a bookmark. When I opened the book, his features evaded me just as he had tried to evade the camera's lens, but as I read on they began to take shape. The haze of his blurred immortalization had robbed him of his pride. His fur hat was really a tricorne, golden epaulettes adorned his shoulders and a red-sheathed sabre hung at his left hip. I knew all this for certain. During my train journey I tried to read on quickly but I was distracted by a leering passenger who averted his eyes whenever I looked up. Every few sentences I would feel the heat of his gaze taking in my body through the compartment window and I read on even faster, skipping entire passages to arrive at the point where I wanted to be: the kiss between Bolkonsky and Natasha. My timing was perfect: I reached it just as we entered the tunnel. The passenger had vanished. I tucked the photograph away. I did not need a face, I would recognize my Bolkonsky among thousands. On that late summer's day in 1936, he was the most distinguished of all the men at Aachen station. But on closer inspection he turned out to be a disfigured cad who let me heave my own suitcase into the car.

'Has your father explained the purpose of your visit?' he asked.

'Yes, sir.'

Only he hadn't. I had no idea what von Bötticher was talking about. My purpose was to become a better fencer, but my father knew the maître from a dim and distant past that would not remain so for long. He was German, an aristocrat with a country estate by the name of Raeren. At these words, my mother had begun to sob and shake her head. We had expected no better of her. The parish priest had warned her about the Nazis and their ill-treatment of Catholics. My father told her not to get herself into such a state. As for me, I barely gave these things a second thought. Nazis meant nothing to me. Von Bötticher, on the other hand, was inescapable. Without braking once, he drove me out of town over dirt roads and around hairpin bends. His knuckles slammed into my leg whenever he changed gear and his knee, sticking out to the right of the steering wheel, would have been nudging mine had I not inclined my legs toward the door of the cabriolet. He did not dress like a man his age, his sandals fastened around his ankles with a cord. My father, never one to shy away from a Gallicism, would have dubbed him a *pigeon*.

'We're here.' It was the third sentence he had fired in my

direction after a drive of at least an hour. Pulling up outside the walls of Raeren, he braked so abruptly that I shot out of my seat. He slammed the car door behind him and tore up to the gate, muttering as it groaned open, then jumped back in the car, screeched into the drive, and got out again to bang the gate behind us. It occurred to me that I would not be venturing outside these walls any time soon. Among the fading chestnut trees that lined the drive, my first glimpse of the place was the old roof turret, which was used as a pigeon loft. It would be a week before I was able to sleep through their cooing and the patter of their claws. And once that week had passed, I would be kept awake by matters far more disquieting.

Opposing mirrors reflect themselves in one other, a succession of images that become ever smaller and less distinct yet never cancel each other out. Certain memories exist in this state too, for ever bound to the first impression in which an older memory is contained. At the turn of the year, I had seen a film called *The Old Dark House*. I am tempted to say I recognized Raeren from the film, though it was only a passing resemblance. Even then I knew that I would always remember Raeren as the mansion where Boris Karloff had walked the floors. In my mind's eye, its mirrors would always be cracked, its curtains flapping from open windows, the ivy around its front door stone-dead.

## 2

The front door looked like a coffin lid. I was being melodramatic, of course, but when von Bötticher left me standing there while he went back to fetch something from the car, the house seemed to radiate a loneliness that resonated with my own. Minutes passed. I stared at the black paint, the tarnished knocker and the silver nails. Then the door swung open and as if to complete the scene a deathly-pale little man appeared on the threshold. He said nothing, a daguerreotype from a time when people were still in awe of their photographic perpetuation: rooted to the spot, eyes fixed on the horizon, face drained of colour.

'Heinz! What kept you?' von Bötticher shouted from a distance. 'The gate needs oiling. Leave it any longer and I'll never get it shut. Where is Leni?'

The little man braced himself, took the suitcase from my hands and cleared his throat. 'In bed, sir. No need to worry. She's promised to be up and about by lunchtime.'

'This is Janna, the new pupil I told you about. Remember?'

'I can make a pot of tea,' said Heinz, without so much as a glance in my direction.

'Take the girl upstairs. I do not wish to be disturbed today, for once.' Then suddenly with a smile, 'Except by you two!'

He was talking to the St Bernard and another smaller

dog that had been waiting in the hall, bottoms quivering with excitement. This was something at least. Though I had never had a pet dog, there was still a reassuring familiarity about them. Lacking words, animals simply cannot be strangers. The St Bernard let me stroke it briefly before bounding into the garden to greet its master, stamping playfully on the ground with both front paws at once. I was left alone with Heinz, who had something to tell me. 'We do not have a telephone.' He thrust a pointed finger in the direction of the outside world. 'The lines run north along the main road and don't reach this side. There's already a telephone pole on every corner of the village, but the master doesn't see the use. We don't have many visitors. That's something you should know. Other than the butcher and the students, no one comes to call.'

The clock in the hall had stopped. Later I would discover that Raeren was full of clocks that no longer ticked and cupboards that contained nothing at all. It was as if everything had been put there for appearances' sake. The interior offered two contrasting moods: rustic and faded chic. Everyday life was confined to the smoky kitchen, where the beams were hung with game hooks, pots and kettles, all in frequent use, and where a rough-hewn dining table invited you to rest your elbows on its knotted surface. The grand section of the house was steeped in a silence that was amplified by the slightest movement. Even the hint of a footstep would trigger a salvo of creaks and groans from the wooden thresholds, floorboards and furniture, noises so unwelcome that these were rooms where dust hung in the air instead of smoke.

Von Bötticher strode into the hall, the dogs trailing in his wake. 'Take the girl up to the attic room and bring these two and Gustav to my study.'

'I can't get hold of Gustav, sir.'

'Try luring him with a biscuit. *Kaninchen sind verrückt danach.*'

'Rabbits are mad about them.' Was that really what he'd said? My knowledge of German came courtesy of the summers I had spent at my aunt's in Kerkrade. There we spoke of Prussians, not Germans. My aunt ran a stall that sold coffee beans in a town where the border between the two countries ran down the middle of the street. Our side was Nieuwstraat and across the road was Neustrasse. Her customers stood with their feet in Germany while their hands counted out coins in the Netherlands. There were no language barriers to be crossed. Everyone spoke the dialect of the Ripuarian Franks, whose drawling caravan of words had left deep tracks across the Rhineland in the fifth century.

I was five years old and carrying a cured ham in my apron to deliver to a Prussian who had asked for a *sjink*. 'Come straight back, you hear!' I remember the bustle of the crowd, the ham growing heavier and heavier. Two drunken miners pointed at my apron and burst out laughing. 'Bit young to have a bun in the oven ... ' I lost my way. Three hours later, they found me in a back garden on the German side of the street, ham and all. The lady of the house saw me playing there with a serious expression on my face. What else is a five-year-old to do under the circumstances? She called to me and I ran into her arms. Though she was German, she spoke the same Kerkrade slang as my aunt, in the same seemingly indignant tone. 'Hey, ma li'l angel ... and who might you be?' Since that first foray across the border I returned home from every summer holiday with a Rhineland accent, much to the horror of my mother, who set about replacing all my Germanisms with the Gallicisms of Maastricht.

*Kaninchen sind verrückt danach.* I rolled the words around my mouth as I followed Heinz upstairs to the attic. The staircase bore our weight like an old beast of burden, groaning as it took us from landing to landing. On each one he halted, put down my suitcase for a moment and then took hold of the next banister before creaking on, step by step.

'Have you been fencing long?'

'Since the Olympiad.'

Heinz turned and frowned at me. The Berlin Olympics had ended only weeks before.

'I mean since the 1928 Games. In Amsterdam.'

'Ah, I see. You should have seen our Games. The Olympiad to beat them all. There was a torch relay for the Olympic flame. They had invented a new electronic system for the fencers to tell them when a point had been scored.'

I searched for daylight on every floor, but all I saw were hallways lined with closed doors. The higher we climbed, the more ominous the atmosphere became. Not a bad smell exactly, just the stale air of unused rooms. Once this house had been built in preparation for a life, enough life to fill ten rooms, a kitchen, and a ballroom. The staircase had borne the weight of a young master of the house as he carried his bride upstairs. Children had slid down the banister. But the decades wore on, bringing evenings when someone climbed the stairs never to come down alive. A room was kept dark, a hush descended on one floor and then the next, till silence reached the bottom stair. This house had been empty for a long time; I could feel it. Sometimes a house never recovers from such a blow, a fresh coat of paint can only give it the air of a jilted lover who feels all the more disconsolate for having dolled herself up. It's better left as it is, with its cracks and smears, the greasy imprint of a hand that reached out in haste on the way from the dinner table to the ballroom, the loose handle of a slammed door. The wallpaper on the attic floor was in tatters. Had a cat been locked away up there? A child? The heat was stifling.

'Has von Bötticher lived here all his life?'

'No.' Heinz put my suitcase down in front of a small door and sorted through his bunch of keys. 'He hails from Köningsberg. After the war he moved to Frankfurt, and then he came here. But these are matters that do not concern you.'

The room was more pleasant than I had expected, sunny with a small balcony. Olive-green wallpaper, a high three-quarter bed, a small paraffin heater, and a desk with an inkpot. The sound of birds cooing was very close. Heinz opened the doors to the balcony and two pigeons made a U-turn in mid-air.

'I have other things to attend to,' he said, backing out of the room. 'There is nothing more I can do for you at present. My wife will bring you something to eat later. You'll find water at the end of the hall if you wish to freshen up.'

He clattered down the stairs, leaving me behind with the birds. I started to unpack my suitcase. The linen cupboard was lined with dust and I sacrificed a sock to clean it out. I had to fill this room with my sorry caseful of possessions and fast, or things here would never turn out for the best. I flicked away a dried-up fly that had strayed witlessly onto the bedside table and perished there. *War and Peace* took its place. I put my fencing bag in the corner, hung my coat on the hook. The letter was at the bottom of my case, sealed in a large envelope made of stiff cardboard. Nothing but the name of the addressee on the front: Herr Egon von Bötticher, a name like a clip around the ear. I stepped into the sunlight, but the cardboard was giving nothing away.

I considered it, of course I did. If I had read the letter that day, perhaps things might have been different. But I knew from experience that the discovery is never worth all the trouble. The speculative excitement buzzing around your brain as you steam open an envelope soon fizzles out when you clap eyes on its contents. A handful of statements about someone else's humdrum existence, what good are they to anyone? And then there's the ordeal of resealing the envelope, the problem of torn edges, the anxiety and the shame. I laid the letter aside.

Muffled expletives drifted up from the garden. The shadow of a man edged across the lawn with what looked to be a ball on a leash, a ball that was refusing to roll. This turned out to be Heinz, with the biggest rabbit I had ever seen. I took a closer look—yes, it really was a rabbit. Its ears were enormous, as were its feet. It seemed incapable of steady progress and settled for the odd jump, backward or sideways. Heinz's patience was clearly wearing thin and after taking a good look around, he gave the creature an almighty kick. Just as I was beginning to wonder whether anything in this house was normal, amenable or even remotely friendly, there was a knock at the door. I opened it and we both got a shock, the woman in the hall and I. No, it wasn't her—her nose was wider than my aunt's and her eyes were blue. But if she hadn't been carrying a tray laden with food, I would have happily fallen into her arms. No matter what kind of woman she would turn out to be, at that moment I decided I liked her.

'Hello dear, I'm Leni.'

She kicked the door shut behind her and put the tray down on the desk. I saw sausage rolls and dumplings sprinkled with icing sugar, but I didn't dare touch anything. Leni took a chair and sat down at the window, leaning on her sturdy knees. She heaved a deep sigh.

'So, here you are stuffed away in the attic like an old rag.'

'It's a nice room.'

'Come now, it reeks of pigeon shit. The air up here's enough to make you ill.'

'I hadn't noticed.'

'Well, you'd better tuck in before you do.'

Her whole body shook when she laughed—cheeks, breasts, belly, the flesh on her forearms exposed by her rolled-up sleeves. If she hadn't been sitting on them, her buttocks would likely have laughed along too. I started to eat.

'The master's an odd 'un, all right,' she said bluntly. 'No need to look at me like that. Like you haven't already twigged. We'd been out of work for six seasons when he bought Raeren. We'd always worked at Lambertz, the biscuit factory. When we were laid off, we hoped Philips would open a factory in these parts. Rumours had been doing the rounds for five years but Heinz said there was no point in waiting any longer. Since then we've been in service with von Bötticher. An odd 'un, and no mistake.'

She stood up and began to whisper. 'Have you seen his cheek? Taken knocks from all sides, he has. That scar is from two wounds, you know. One from the war and the other from them goings on he's involved in. Take a good look next time you see him, he's in a sorry state. Not to mention that leg of his!'

I burst out laughing and she looked at me as if she had been served a meal she hadn't ordered. 'You must admit, he's not a pretty sight.'

'I have a letter for him, from my father. Could you make sure he gets it?'

She frowned as she took hold of the envelope. 'Quite a size. What's it say?'

I shrugged. She placed the envelope back on the desk.

'Wait a bit, that's my advice. The letter your father sent a while back fairly upset him. He wasn't himself for a time. One minute he was strutting around all pleased with himself, the next he was flying into a rage over nothing. Then came the telegram announcing your arrival, and that left him in a bit of a tizz, too. I don't need to know the details. His bad temper's his own business, even if Heinzi and I are the ones who bear the brunt of it. If you want to get off on the right foot, I'd keep this to yourself for now.'

Her voice changed key in these final sentences, took a dive from high to low, and I realized it was more than just her appearance that made me feel at home with this woman. She spoke the indignant Frankish border dialect I knew so well. If anything were to happen to me at Raeren, I knew I would cling to her like a lost child. Together we stared at the strokes of my father's pen, the careless hand in which a doctor scrawls his suspicions on a letter of referral, as if illegibility might soften the blow.

# 3

My father loved to jot things down. He always had a pencil or two concealed about his person to scribble notes in the margins of the day. *Nothing but twin primes?!* on the bill from the baker. *Argumentum ad misericordiam* in the newspaper. *Flushing half a tank will suffice* on the lavatory cistern. 'Just a sec' was a pet phrase of his, often uttered as he leaped to his feet and his mood brightened. Many of my father's discoveries were preceded by the words 'Just a sec'. He would set about repairing the radio and end up reinventing the ear trumpet. Or he would find a new Bryozoa fossil on Mount Saint Peter, one that on closer inspection turned out to be half of a fossil he knew well. A practitioner of non-monotonic logic, his corrections were primarily directed at himself, cacographic messages that steadily filled the house. An addendum was scribbled on the cistern: *i.e. approx. two seconds.* After all, from the outside it was impossible to tell when half a tank had been flushed. This was not nitpicking or penny-pinching. He had simply discovered that the cistern was too large for its purpose. He would spend entire evenings writing and crossing out in chaotic piles of thin exercise books. He didn't even miss them when they suddenly vanished. 'Another set of problems laid to rest,' my mother would say as the pages lay smouldering in the hearth. One opinion on any given subject was enough to last her a lifetime. She formed them instantly, an advantage true believers have over scientists. What had those two ever seen in each another? My mother apparently took to piety after I was born. For an entire week she lay wide awake in the bed where she had given birth to me, insisting she would never have to sleep again because she was already dead. She felt no urge to suckle me and when they brought me to her she would fly into a panic, convinced her cadaverous state was contagious. Expressing her milk made her gag. 'Can't you smell it?' she would yell at the astounded maternity nurse. 'That milk has long since curdled!' Eventually my aunt sent for the priest and he prayed my mother to sleep. 'From that moment on,' said my father, 'I woke up next to a complete stranger who happened to be your mother.'

They had a dreadful marriage. Housemaids came and went, their departure always ushered in by my mother's sobbing fits. As soon as I heard her lashing out, I knew another maid was on her way. Father was no stranger to histrionics either. On more than one occasion the neighbourhood was treated to the spectacle of him marching out of the house with a huge suitcase, swinging it so demonstratively through the air that anyone could see it was empty. It was all about the grand gesture: 'Your mother and I are getting a divorce.' In the end, my father packed me off to Aachen with the very same suitcase, but the first time he stood on the doorstep with it we took a walk together and he told me about the war.

In 1914, he had interrupted his studies at the Municipal University in Amsterdam and travelled south to serve with the Red Cross in the city of his birth. He made no claims to heroism. Taking care of the wounded provided him with a unique opportunity to gain practical experience and exempted him from mobilization. But before long the front had advanced so far south that the staff of

the emergency hospitals in Maastricht soon found themselves bored to tears. Six months later my father was on
the train back to Amsterdam. He resumed his studies and
became a medical doctor, the highest possible achievement for a young man from his non-academic background.
He would have liked nothing better than to study for his
PhD, even though it involved sitting an extra state exam.
But then I came along and a doctor's house became available in the Wyck neighbourhood of Maastricht. The Spanish flu came and went, and after that traffic accidents provided him with most of his patients. In a city without
traffic lights, the number of motor vehicles was doubling
annually and everyone was making up the rules as they
went along. Competition with trams and rival bus compa-
nies was fierce, and bus drivers resorted to recklessness to
give them the edge. The horrific injuries he saw reminded
my father of his wartime experiences. As a GP his sole re-
sponsibility was the patient's long-term recovery. Mr Bonhomme came to grief under the wheels of a Studebaker
owned by the Kerckhoffs brothers and drank away his
phantom pain in the public house. My father went down
to collect him when the landlord complained of the stink.

'Daddy?'

'Mmmm ... '

'When will Mr Bonhomme's leg grow back?'

'It won't. In fact, there's every chance his other one will
drop off.'

'Jacques, please! Keep a civil tongue in your head.'

Without my mother around, I could well have become a
very strange child indeed. She preserved the peace and
quiet of the domestic routine. Not a day went by without
my father dreaming up some new adventure. Off to the
summer fair in Beek, making our own pottery in the
Preekherengang, shutting Grandma's goat up in her box-

bed, scaring the wits out of unsuspecting citizens by jumping from behind the Helpoort and shouting 'Boo!' For Christmas he gave me a little monk that peed apple juice when you pressed his head.

Sport did not interest him in the slightest. To this day I have no idea why he took me along to the Amsterdam Olympics. We stayed with an aunt—or at least I called her 'Auntie'—who looked like Clara Bow. When we went out together, she slapped a cap on her mop of black hair and slotted one cigarette after another between her painted lips. My father was the picture of contentment as he strolled down the street with a lady on either arm. At a stall he treated us to Coca-Cola, tasting it first with a sceptical frown. What was it made of? Was it suitable for the ladies? Auntie Clara Bow insisted we go to see the fencing. My father thought this a very bad idea. The matches were not even held in the stadium but in a hall out front, where later all hell would break loose when a fight erupted between the spectators after a boxing match. The mood at the fencing was boisterous, too. See, said my father, combat sports are contagious. The spectators are infected by the aggression on display, proving this is not sport at all, simply an excuse for a common scrap. Auntie Clara Bow gave him a kiss and that was enough to bundle him through the entrance. She knew a remarkable athlete would be fencing that day: Helene Mayer, *die blonde Hee* as the Germans liked to call her. She had the allure of a film star, not unlike Auntie Clara Bow herself.

When I saw Helene Mayer for the first time, I was filled with the kind of adoration that can make a young girl queasy. I was ten, she was seventeen. Helene was a demigoddess, an untamed creature on the brink of womanhood who drove every full-grown woman from the fencing piste. This was only the second time women had competed at the Olympics. Who else was I supposed to model myself on? One of those biddies in bloomers who collapsed in an exhausted heap after running all of eight hundred metres? My father was a reluctant spectator, not only of the duel but of the fever taking possession of his daughter. He tried to talk sense into me, but to no avail. Whichever way you looked at it, surely these ladies would have been better off devoting their agility to a feminine pursuit—ballet, figure-skating or gymnastics? With their beautiful faces locked in those cage-like masks they screamed like animals when they were hit. Not cries of pain, those ridiculous outfits put paid to that, but cries of fear. Remember the day when Pontius the rooster escaped and Granny had to grab him by the legs? He screeched at the top of his little lungs, thinking his hour had come, and hadn't we all felt so sorry for him? Well, that's what it means to fear for your life. Pain doesn't enter into it. It's not a game. Perched on the very edge of my seat, I wasn't listening to a word he said. The rules of the sport were a mystery to me. For the uninitiated, fencing matches are almost impossible to follow. Even the trained eye of the president falls short and he often has to rely on his judges to spot a hit. My gaze homed in on Helene Mayer, the victor. My father, as usual, only had eyes for the victim. He rambled on about the scaffold and vengeful mobs, but Helene had already drowned him out. Later she would loom large in the mesh of my mask as I prepared to lunge. No one could lunge like Helene. Every sinew, from her Achilles tendon to the tip of her weapon, conspired to conjure a lunge of at least three metres from a frame of 1 metre 78 and a blade of no more than 90 centimetres.

Before Father and I returned to Maastricht, Auntie Clara Bow braided my hair in the style of Helene. A middle parting and two pretzels over my ears, held in place by a bandeau. This kept your hair out of your face while allowing you to slip a fencing mask over your head. During her match against Olga Oelkers, Helene's braids unravelled and her hair had fallen in golden strands over her shoulders. How could such a Teutonic force of nature lose? I was slender and a head shorter than she was—not exactly advantages for a fencer—and I was a brunette into the bargain. From that moment I resolved never to wear my hair any other way. My friends, obsessed with trimming each other's pixie cuts on a monthly basis, thought I was being absurdly old-fashioned.

After my Olympic initiation, it was only a matter of time before my father gave into my moods. My reproaches were anything but loud, not a tear was shed, but for the best part of a year my anger was inescapable. I hid under the blankets with Dumas and self-baked biscuits for company. Every evening I disappeared upstairs with a baking tray, my books and my body increasing in size, the books growing fatter as the crumbs piled up between the pages. When my father finally summoned me for a chat, a small fencing jacket lay on his lap. 'For my angry little musketeer.' How typical of my doctorly father to put protective measures first and launch my fencing career with a jacket the colour of a plaster cast. He had heard of a small fencing school in the city, run by a young man called Louis. The fees were modest and beginners were allowed to hire their equipment. The maître had no official qualifications—to this day I have no idea how he came by his title—and he was having a fling with the cashier at the Palace Cinema.

I was allowed to borrow a rusty child's foil. Everyone in Louis's class fenced with rusty equipment, a good incentive: avoid being hit or end up with a reddish-brown mark on your pristine jacket, one that will never wash out. It wasn't until my sixteenth birthday that I received my first adult foil. After class, when everyone else had gone home, Louis called me in and with a flourish produced a bewitching weapon. This was the real thing! The blade looked new to me, gleaming and flexible. Louis opened his fingers to reveal a ridged leather grip.

'Take it.'

I took the foil from his grasp. My hand barely fitted around the grip, the end of which rested against the wildly pulsing artery in my wrist.

'Not too big?'

'No, it's wonderful,' I whispered.

'It will mould itself to your palm before long. The steel is still very stiff, let me bend it for you a little.'

I looked on anxiously as he drew the weapon under the sole of his shoe to curve the blade.

'That's more like it. This foil is yours if your father will do something for me. It is important that you ask him immediately. It has to be done soon and requires complete discretion. From you too, so mum's the word.'

My father frowned when I passed on the message. Of course, I immediately asked whether there was an abortion in the offing. Perhaps my maître's bit of skirt down at the Palace had a little problem that needed attending to? My father was as dismissive as he was indignant. Who on earth had been planting notions like that in my head! And whatever Louis wanted in return, there was no call to assume that I was about to become the owner of a brand-new weapon. Such decisions were not Louis's to take. Father had wanted to give me something else for my birthday, not a weapon for heaven's sake. That was when I looked at my father, the pacifist and professional healer of wounds, and explained all. I told him a foil is not made to kill. It is a weapon to practise with, a sporting invention, never once used on the battlefield. The blade bends on impact to prevent fatal stab wounds and could never be used to sever limbs; besides, the rules of foil-fencing only permit hits to the trunk of the body. I told him it used to be called the *fleuret*, its point protected by a small leather cap that was said to resemble the bud of a flower. It was the first time my father took note of anything I had to say. With this weapon, my own dear foil, I became a grown-up.

My father idolized me, his only child, but my only idol was Helene Mayer. For years I dreamed of fencing against her. On the Olympic podium in Berlin the 'strapping lass from the Rhineland' had stood solemn as a statue in her high-necked fencing jacket and white flannel trousers, the swastika like a brooch below her left shoulder and her right arm extended in front of her. One step higher stood a Hungarian, gold medal around her neck and a little potted oak in her hands. By all accounts, making do with silver did not trouble Mayer much, but oh how she wept over that tree. She had so badly wanted a memento from German soil to take back to her new home: America. Only later did I discover that she was leaving Germany as I arrived. As if we had just missed each other. Perhaps it was for the best. Von Bötticher insisted that to be a good fencer you needed only one idol: yourself.

# 4

On my first night at Raeren, the pigeons found their way into my room. I dreamed of wrinkled claws walking all over me and a fat-necked grey bird trying to peck a birthmark from my throat. Stifled by the heat, I had left the balcony doors ajar and now I was too frightened to get up and close them. The birds seemed to be everywhere, scratching about the room. A preening silhouette was perched on the chair. The flapping curtain only let in fitful streaks of moonlight and, too tired to look for the light switch, I pulled the covers up to my chin. The second I woke up in the morning, the stink of the birds hit my nostrils: there were creamy splatters on the carpet and down floated through the air when I threw off the covers. The balcony looked like a battlefield. The pigeons had strutted around in their own droppings and seemed to have lost half their plumage as they wandered in and out. What had they been after? Now the roof was eerily silent.

'A proper disgrace,' said Leni when she came to tell me breakfast was ready. 'Pigeon shit contains all kinds of germs. It can give you pneumonia, I read it in *Die Woche*. I'll ask Heinzi to fit a screen. Or maybe we could furnish a room on the next floor down.' She took the water jug from my washbasin and sloshed some of its contents over the balcony. In the end she had to fetch a scrubbing brush from the hall. Feet planted wide, she went at it, hunched and cursing. 'The filth I've had to clean up today! It's more than my job's worth. What does he think we are, muck collectors? Oh, it's a far cry from the biscuit factory.'

She was going to be a while yet, so I would have to find the kitchen on my own. Downstairs to the entrance hall, the door to the right of the mirror, all the way to the end of passage and down the steps at the end. I couldn't miss it. No need to worry, the master was in the very best of spirits. He had been out for a walk, shot a young hare and was making breakfast himself. Oh yes, and she was to let me know that he was looking forward to my company. I felt the blood rise to my cheeks. This gallant invitation had ushered Bolkonsky back on stage. I pinned up my hair, straightened my back and off I went to meet him, doing my best to sweep silently down the creaking stairs. As soon as I set foot in the kitchen my expectations were shattered. Instead of sitting at the head of a table decked with white linen, von Bötticher was standing with his back to me kneading a lump of minced meat over by the sink.

It seems to me now that I spent all my young life daydreaming. The dedication I devoted to my fantasies made this a tiring habit. There was never enough time to see them through and, picking up the thread when I next had a moment to myself, I was confronted with all manner of imperfections. Even castles in the air needed cleaning, and there was always the risk of some young wench stealing away your beloved or an old harpy ruining your picture-perfect romance with her interfering ways. Besides, what exactly did a prince do all day? It could easily take me a good hour to iron out the wrinkles. My daydreams kept me awake at night and I lived with some stories for years, layering detail upon detail, down to the trim of the sleeves of my bridal gown. Only girls daydream with such dogged determination, of that I am sure. All young souls idealize the future, but it takes a girl to idealize the present along with it.

There he stood, von Bötticher, not Bolkonsky, in a long shirt, his wide sleeves rolled up to his elbows. Without his homburg, I noticed his hair was already turning grey. He was only a few years younger than my father. How long would it take for that fact to sink in? Imagination is more stubborn than reality—ask any madman who experiences moments of clarity. An illusion will always steal back onto the scene as soon as the original is out of sight, like a lover stepping out of a wardrobe and every bit as alluring. Even though von Bötticher tarnished his ideal image time and again, I had dreamed up enough to keep me going for nights on end. He turned his good cheek toward me and nodded as if he knew what I was thinking. He did not ask me whether I had slept well. It was a matter of indifference to him.

'Where's Leni?'

'Cleaning up pigeon mess in my room.'

Von Bötticher pretended not to hear. He took white plugs of ground bacon fat from the mincer, pushed them into the stuffing and added an immoderate glug of brandy. These were unfamiliar smells. My mother spiked her stews with vinegar, as tradition dictated. Wine wasn't something to be poured into a pot but something we drank once a year. Spirits never made it past the front door. Our next-door neighbour had once slipped me a slug of bitters during a snowball fight in the street, passing it off as apple juice—his idea of a lark. That morning, the maître's kitchen must have smelled of the ingredients for a pie: bacon fat, cognac, a hunk of marbled boar meat, calf's liver, kidneys, pickled mushrooms, and the egg pastry rising under a tea towel on the windowsill. The scent of the countryside poured in through the open window: vegetables sprouting in the kitchen garden and the clover on which the cows were grazing. The same clover was in the stomach of the hare that had just been shot. It lay limp-eared on the table, ready to be hung by its hind legs, which had been bound together with twine. In a few days' time, its innards would be rinsed out and the smells released would drive every animal in the house to distraction. For now, it smelled of the sand in its fur and the grass between its toes—as did Gustav, still alive and well and hopping around under the table. That overgrown specimen didn't give a damn about anything, least of all what was going on above his head. Though well-mannered enough to deposit his droppings in a neat pile in the corner, he sank his teeth into every piece of furniture he came across, shook his head, balanced on his outsized feet and washed his ears with his front paws. It was one surprise after another. Von Bötticher gave Gustav a piece of bacon, which disappeared little by little between his grinding jaws.

'There's something you didn't know, eh? Rabbits eat anything. Even meat,' said von Bötticher. 'Just like cows chew out dead animals in search of minerals. Ever seen a cow with a dead rabbit in its mouth? They'll happily gnaw a bone or two for the sake of calcium. It's eat and be eaten in the natural world, no waste. Every last morsel gets consumed. The insects are first on the scene when an animal dies. Flies and mites can smell a hare like this one from miles away. Then birds of prey arrive and tear loose the skin, exposing the guts to foxes and badgers. But the rotting process alone will ensure that a corpse bursts open within a few days.'

He stroked the hare's fur and sniffed his hand. 'This one needs to be taken down to the cellar immediately. What on earth is keeping Leni?'

'Are you planning to eat Gustav, too?'

'Absolutely! With cowberries. Or smothered in cream, braised in Riesling and served with parsnips. Or wrapped in bacon and roasted after a night soaking in buttermilk. I'll be sure to give him the attention he deserves. Ah Leni, at last!'

Leni was barely through the door when the toe of her boot connected with Gustav's backside, to no discernible effect. 'That monster has chewed the fringes off every carpet in the house. And unless my eyes deceive me, it's produced a fresh pile of droppings. Sir, I ask you, I beg you on my aching knees: for God's sake leave those animals of yours to roam around outdoors for a week or so. It will spare me all kinds of mess. The nights are still warm enough.'

'And where would that leave me? How is a lonely man like myself to find warmth and companionship?'

Leni spread her arms wide. 'And lonely you'll remain while you continue to lock away your lady guests in the pigeon loft!'

Irked, von Bötticher tossed the dead hare into her open arms. 'Here, woman. Take this down to the cellar and quick.'

Heinz came into the kitchen and sat down to wait while von Bötticher cut thin slices of sausage. This was clearly a morning ritual. The lord of the manor boiled eggs, removed a young cheese from a bowl of water, served cream with a small basket of berries on the vine, and put a plaited loaf on the table. His manservant did not lift a finger, and when his wife returned he pulled back her chair and together they prayed in silence. Through half-closed eyes, I watched von Bötticher stare unashamedly at their knitted brows. I think he took pleasure in the fact that the first sight to greet them after their moment with God would be that mutilated mug of his. Once grace had been said, he made sure we filled our stomachs with the food from his table, as if we were stray dogs. He himself ate next to nothing. When the dishes were all but empty, he solemnly broke the silence to address a practical matter. 'Well, Janna,' he said on that first morning, 'have you brought me anything? Something from your father perhaps?'

Leni's eyes were ablaze in an instant, while her husband went on chewing steadily. He was all too familiar with the consequences of speaking out of turn. Besides, what was the harm in a letter? I put my knife down on my plate.

'An envelope, maître. I'm sorry. I wanted to give it to you straight away but you didn't want to be disturbed.'

'An envelope, of course. Yet another letter. Well, let's be having it.'

Von Bötticher dispatched me with a gesture an adult might make to a child who has been hesitantly holding up a drawing. I obeyed in a heartbeat. Back up the stairs I headed, in leaps and bounds, swinging around the pillars. I was childish, it's true. Girls today are worldly-wise, independent, but in my youth we were simply passed from one sheltering wing to another. The only condition was that we in turn should have a caring disposition; it was not a condition I met. I much preferred being taken care of, so I could continue my playful, sheltered existence. Despite the inevitable physical transformation, I had no intention of becoming woman. Not that I was a tomboy or a wild child or anything of the sort, it was more that I preferred things to stay as they were. It was an annoyance when I began to develop breasts at fifteen. Those bumps swelling under my nipples had nothing to do with me and I was seized by a curious melancholy that was a long time in passing. Helene Mayer took no extra measures to protect her breasts during her matches, and so neither would I.

With that kind of padding under your jacket you are asking to be hit square in the target area. Admitting the pos-
sibility of a hit is a compliment to your opponent and
refusing to do so made my parries stronger, especially
*quarte* and *sixte*. A hit to the chest during a fencing bout
left me sick to my stomach. I had no desire to feel those
milk glands, those maternal appendages. I would never
become a mother. Nor would Helene. It could be no coincidence that my idol bore the name of the most beautiful of
all the Greek goddesses, the protectress of young virgins,
she who had been abducted and overpowered. We were
girls of Sparta, who battled on so we would never have to
grow up, but we were passionate just the same. In my daydreams I increasingly became the object of desire. At night
my painstakingly composed allegories were thrust aside
by impatient, unbridled phantoms who left me panting
and satisfied. Phantoms I had been unable to capture, just
as they had been unable to capture me.

Fencers are often a little childish: playing at musketeers,
wearing their hair long, swigging wine from the bottle,
stamping around in their boots and pounding on table-
tops. Such antics end on the piste, where deadly seriousness is the order of the day. Even von Bötticher was playful
in his way, though his imagination was directed at animals. He taught them to behave like humans and when he
succeeded he was happy as a sandboy. The task of opening
the letter fell to Gustav. This was pure showmanship, of
course: look how clever my rabbit is and how little store I
set by this epistle from your father. His bunny nibbled
neatly along the edge with mechanical dedication, even
giving a little tug when he arrived at the corner so the
resulting sliver of envelope could be detached and
devoured. A letter opener could not have done a better job.
Von Bötticher slipped his hand between the cardboard

sides, pulled out the letter and began to read. For three full pages, I hardly dared draw breath. I stared intently at his eyes, as if my father's words would be reflected in them, but they darted from line to line and, as Leni had feared, began to smoulder furiously.

'I'll spare you the embarrassment of reading it aloud. You're his daughter and it's not my place to shatter the image a daughter is apparently supposed to have of her father. I have said enough already.' He folded the letter and stuffed it back in the envelope, which still had more to divulge.

'And what else do we have here?'

It was a yellowed sheet of paper, an illustration. I grew dizzy with curiosity but von Bötticher walked over to the sink, placed the envelope between the pages of a cookery book that was thick as a fist and slammed it shut.

'Very well. We shall see who is right,' he said scornfully. 'I expect you in the fencing hall for your first lesson in half an hour.'

The fencing hall had once been a ballroom. The parquet in the middle had been worn by a century in which dances traced circles. The floorboards, on which laced-up satin boots once followed the heavier tread of army officers, now only bore the weight of footsteps that advanced and retired, still following but never in the round. Three pistes had been drawn in black paint, delimiting the strictest of choreographies: fourteen metres long and two metres wide, two adjoining triangles pointing out from the centre toward the on-guard lines at a distance of two metres on either side; it was a further three metres to the warning line for sabreurs and épée fencers, one weapon's length beyond came the warning line for foil fencers, and then it was back another metre, and not a single pace more, to reach the end line. The net curtains billowing in front of half-open terrace doors were the sole reminder of rustling tulle ballgowns. It was warm. I tugged at the collar of my quilted jacket and caught sight of myself in the large mirror: the swordswoman. My face and my hands looked brown against the white of my suit, which my mother had given a quick soak in a dolly blue. I took up my favourite foil, pulled on my glove, and stood heels together, feet apart. Salute. At that moment, von Bötticher entered the hall. It was there, in the mirror, that I first noticed his limp.

'Salute yourself, as well you might. For now, you will be your only opponent. A formidable foe, as every fencer knows.'

'When will the other students be arriving?'

'You will have to make do with two sabre-wielding boys. Don't worry, I am planning to have them practise with the foil again. You know the type: young hotheads incapable of placing a decent riposte but all too happy to wave a big sword around. Speed and endurance, the mainstays of youth—they have nothing more to offer. They were due to arrive last week, but two days ago I received a telegram from their mother. There appears to be some kind of problem. You will have to be patient. Until then, let's see whether you are as good a fencer as your father claims.'

He came closer, dragging his leg irritably. 'My gait is not always this laboured. My leg is playing up today. Show me your weapon.'

I grasped the blade of my foil and proudly offered him the grip. One wrong word about this weapon and all would be lost. Von Bötticher kneaded the leather, stretched his arm, peered along the length of the blade, let the foil spin between thumb and forefinger, kneaded the grip again, weaved his wrist this way and that, and then nodded. 'Very well, now show me you are worthy of such a weapon. *Stellung!*'

'Unarmed?'

Before I knew what was happening, he struck me full on the chest. 'Ninny! When you hear "*Stellung*" you take up your position, understood? Or must I resort to French? *Stellung!*'

I assumed the on-guard position, my hand thrust out before me, gloved and empty.

'What do you call this?'

He tapped my left hand, which I held in mid-air behind me. 'Relax those fingers! Keep them loose. You're not hailing a carriage!'

He then turned his scrutiny to the distance between my feet and kicked the back of my heel, which perhaps deviated one per cent from the line he had in mind.

'Tsk ... *Ausfall!*'

He left me standing in the lunge position till my thigh muscles began to tremble, correcting my stance down to the last millimetre. I knew he could bark another command at me any moment. '*Stellung!*'

I shot back into position. The maître gave me my weapon and slapped his chest. 'Now, show me a splendid lunge.'

'But you are not wearing a jacket.'

He fastened a single button, a tiny shell, half a centimetre across. 'This button is your target. If I were you I'd worry about the impression your lunge makes on me, not the indentation your weapon leaves behind.'

I was almost beginning to miss Louis back in Maastricht. He may not have been a bona fide maître but at least I could count on his admiration, stamping for joy when I landed a hit. I was Louis's best pupil and he would much rather have seen me bound for an academy in Paris than the retreat of some obscure military man in Germany.

Those officer types understood nothing about women's fencing. When von Bötticher packed it in after fifteen minutes, I began to fear Louis was right. Having examined my body from the soles of my feet to the tips of my fingers, he declared it to be a reasonable apparatus, limber, enough of a basis to work from, but my ability to react, my speed, my tactical skill—in short everything that had won me prizes back in Maastricht—were of no interest to him for the moment. He had other matters to attend to, and I was left to fence against my reflection. I hoped he would look on in secret from the terrace. The curtains flapped, the door banged shut. In the mirror I took in my formidable opponent. She made me feel uncertain, and uncertainty is a fatal flaw for a fencer. There she stood, too short in stature, brandishing a weapon of which she might not even be worthy. She was not ugly, some even said she was pretty, there's no accounting for taste. I was not to my own taste. It was the Aryan race that made my heart beat faster. It was not something you could admit to ten years on, but I truly loved blond, blue-eyed young men who were hardy as cabbages in a frozen field. There had been boys who fell for my skin, the colour of young walnuts, but I brushed their attentions aside. In my daydreams I looked entirely different. It was a girl at the fencing club in Maastricht who had stated the cold, hard facts. 'You look far prettier in the mirror!' she had exclaimed, adding hastily, 'I mean ... well, you know what I mean, don't you?' The damage was done, I had been knocked off-balance for ever. What the Janna in the mirror needed was a mask, then all would be well. Masked I could face down any opponent, including that jealous cow at the club. At Raeren, the masks hung from a rack on the wall. One of them was a snug fit, though there was no one to see me. Von Bötticher's angry voice drifted up from the garden. He was giving Heinz what for, something about dead fish and a pond. I hung up the mask, lay down my weapon and slunk out of the room.

Back in the kitchen it didn't take me long to find what I was looking for. The book lay in the middle of the chopping block: *Gastrosophy. A Breviary for the Palate and the Spirit*. Many of its pages seemed to consist of coloured-in photographs. Fish dishes shaded in pastels. A roast piglet with its trotters in a helping of lentils. Crimson landscapes of meat stretched across the centre pages with a butcher's knife held in a pale hand to point the way: how to chop the backbone of a lamb, how to bone a leg of pork, how to slice the tendons from a fillet of beef. It reminded me of the illustrations that hung in my father's surgery, a dissected human body with muscles, organs and bones exposed. As a child I refused to believe there could be a skull hidden behind my face. The butcher's pale hand showed how to cleave shoulder from foreleg. The envelope had been removed from the book.

## 5

Everything stayed within the grounds at Raeren. Only the clematis scaled the wall, beyond which an occasional farmer's cart could be heard crunching along the path. By the sound of things the world outside did not have much to offer. The time might come when I would have to climb those walls in a fit of fear and panic. I wasn't ruling that out, but during those first few days there was still so much to explore. In the orchard I had seen a little ladder leaning hopefully against a tree laden with hard green apples. The garden was more work than Heinz could handle. The rose arbours and flower beds were overrun with ivy, while the kitchen garden vegetables had taken on grotesque shapes and sizes. Abundance run riot.

Before Heinz had a chance to even consider these chores, he had to spend the entire morning behind the house, where the animals were kept. At six the horses were already kicking at the stable door, while the smaller livestock squealed in their pens. From the terrace I could watch him unseen, our gardener from the biscuit factory, cursing a creature behind a knee-high wooden fence. 'Dirty little rotter. I'll rub your nose in it. Just you wait, I'll shove you right in.' Unable to get hold of whatever was running around in there, rending the air with its rusty scream, he pulled loose his pitchfork and continued mucking out. What else was he to do? His eccentric master had more time for his animals than he did for his personnel but ignored the filth his menagerie produced in much the same way as teenage girls ignore their boyfriends' pimples. Von Bötticher's animal utopia was a lie from start to finish and no one knew this better than Heinz. It was he and no one else who stood there every morning up to his ankles in all that these noble creatures spilled out upon God's green earth. 'Lord preserve us! Don't get me started ...'

The cattle up on the slopes were the only livestock he did not have to tend. They belonged to a neighbouring farmer, a taciturn man orbited by a swarm of the same flies that buzzed around his animals. When the weather was warm, the cattle lay down with their legs tucked under them. If you approached them, you could hear the sloshing and gurgling in their massive bodies as they heaved themselves up, their inner workings going full tilt. They refused to be patted but were quite happy to wrap their pliable tongues around your feet and drool half-digested grass over your shoes. From one day to the next they would vanish. This meant the farmer had herded them off through the woods to let the grass grow back. It had been that way for years, no need to waste words explaining it.

Out on the terrace I ran my circuits, four lonely mornings in a row. This was part of a schedule the maître had drawn up and hung in the entrance hall. Seven o'clock: morning training session. Eight: personal hygiene. Half past eight: breakfast. Half past nine: a walk and instruction. One free hour after lunch, followed by an afternoon training session and domestic chores after six. During the week, the pupils—whoever they might be—were expected to spend the evening in their room. Leni had taken the schedule down off the wall and brought it to my room so I could copy it into my exercise book. She had no need of schedules, she said. From the second she opened her eyes in the morning till she closed them at night there was more than enough to keep her occupied. Once the downstairs rooms had been mopped, she had exactly one hour to attend to the bedrooms before she began to get hungry and it was time for breakfast. Schedules were for bosses and other layabouts. I needn't think for a moment that Herr von Bötticher was the full shilling. An unhappy man, that's what he was. Back when he had only just moved to Raeren and they had been taken into service, he had no routine whatsoever. When the moon was full he would stay up all night only to collapse into bed during the day, sick as a dog.

'Don't you believe me?' she said. 'He spent those first few days standing up, like he was afraid of the furniture. It wasn't his, you see, it was here when he bought the place. All he brought with him was a few chests of books and weapons. Every time I looked he was on his feet, at the window, against the wall, in the garden, which was a complete jungle by the way … What you see now is all thanks to Heinzi. We're the ones who got Raeren running like a normal household. Leni, my mother always used to say, when a person has no routine he's done for. All that's left of him is a sad little heap of need and suffering. And right she was.'

Starting another circuit, I picked up the pace. The wind carried the peal of bells from a distant village. Somewhere people were being called on to button up their children's cardigans and send them out into the world. But the chiming soon stopped and left me alone with my heartbeat. All those discouraging sounds from within: blood pumping, joints creaking, lungs heaving. Saddled with a complaining body as his sole companion, every athlete feels lonely. I was about to stop when the doors to the fencing hall flew open. There stood the maître in an instructor's jacket, black leather so stiff it made a straight line of the contour of his torso. He wore it well, I'll give him that. Not like Louis, whose natural slouch made him look like an upturned beetle, arms flailing from his carapace.

'Keep running, stay on your toes. Arms stretched as high as you can. Higher. Faster. Come on. Now continue on your heels, knees up, stay relaxed.'

After every exercise he looked at his watch. Next I had to take up my weapon, make thirty step-lunges over the length of the terrace and counter every attack he threw at me. 'Clumsy! You have another fifteen minutes in which to redeem yourself.'

He tapped my behind with his foil. A frivolous act; a hit on the backside has nothing to do with fencing. For a foil fencer, the target area begins under the chin and ends in the crotch. That is all he has to work with, the body of a carelessly excavated Greek god. I shook my forearm loose, jogged on the spot, adopted the on-guard position, inclined my weapon against the ball of my thumb, fixed my eyes on the point of his foil and met his gaze. If only he had worn a mask, I am sure I could have stood my ground.

'Now do you understand why I asked you yesterday whether you could fence against yourself?' he asked, as he knocked my weapon away with a lightning-quick counter-parry. 'I know your next move before you've even decided on it.'

I didn't see the point of training in front of the mirror. As if it were possible to catch yourself off guard. A reflection corrects itself in a fraction of a second, but take the mirror away and errors creep back in like thieves under cover of darkness. I've heard fencing likened to playing chess at high speed. The outward spectacle is nothing compared to the forces at work behind the mask. Throw it off to see more clearly and you realize it's your mind and not the mesh that's obscuring your vision, speeding up your footwork or slowing it down. One moment everything is still clear: your opponent is standing there, well within range, ready to raise his weapon and step forward. But won't he get too close? How could he still land a hit at that distance? Where's the logic? It would make more sense if he ... Too late! Too much thinking. Von Bötticher insisted there was no point in trusting your eyes, in wasting time passing images to your brain. There was something stronger, something you couldn't quite put your finger on. A vague, melancholy memory of long-lost forces that growled in the pit of your stomach and rushed to your nose ... or what was left of it. In animals, smell took pride of place, but in us humans it had sunk to the bottom of the brain. That's what walking upright did for you. First see, then grab, we'd been doing it for millions of years. But what fencer had not been ambushed by euphoria as his weapon, seemingly of its own accord and without the least resistance, hit his opponent's body in less than the blink of an eye?

'A dog bites the hand that feeds him before he has a chance to regret it,' said von Bötticher. 'Just as animals smell their prey, you can sense an attack hanging in the air. The only question is: whose attack? Let emotion drive your fencing, only then will you know what speed is. Instinctive motivation works too. The sense of reward or punishment is swift as an arrow. Fear, pleasure, hunger, thirst: they all take the shortest route. Do you even *want* to hit me? Do I frighten or please you?'

I feigned an attack on his scarred cheek and then caught him full between the ribs. He staggered, quickly resumed his train of thought, limping as he advanced. 'Fine. Bravo. You were riled and you attacked. But beware. Fencing on intuition does not mean you can simply forget your tech-nique. First the patterns have to work their way under your skin.'

With both hands, he pulled on an imaginary set of reins. 'Have you ever ridden a horse?'

I nodded and shook my head at the same time. My grandmother had an old carthorse with the kind of fuzzy grey coat that makes old animals so endearing. It tolerated my legs dangling at its sides but had no intention of being spurred on by them. Few experiences were as calming as those journeys from farmyard to farmyard, borne by a mute creature that had been clopping along for far longer than I had been drawing breath.

'I'll ask Leni to lay out some riding clothes for you,' said von Bötticher. 'Breakfast is in half an hour, after that I want to see you ride. No need to be frightened. I'll give you the most docile horse and put her on the longe. You'll learn a lot from it. Everything I have told you today will fall into place. Now off you go.'

Five nights I had spent at Raeren. The maître had already dispensed with formalities and my life lay entirely in his hands. My bed was under his roof and he was the one who determined when I had to attend to my 'personal hygiene': thirty minutes before I put his food in my mouth. Obediently, I stood at the attic window with my feet in a basin. Heinz had fitted a screen and on the other side of the mesh a wood pigeon was nodding off. It opened a beady yellow eye when I poured the water. On waking up, I had gone to the washroom, filled a jug with water and left it standing in the sun. Leni was adamant I should wash downstairs with warm water from the boiler, but that made me feel uneasy. I would rather be up here being leered at by a pigeon. My moment of triumph was enough to keep me warm. A shivering heat flowed down from my navel as I thought of the tip of my foil making firm contact with von

Bötticher's jacket. An immaculately executed feint below his weapon. He had wanted to maintain appearances, feign indifference, but one half of his face had refused to cooperate.

How long does the triumph of the crippled war veteran last? Six months at most. By then his mutilation no longer inspires admiration but pity, and a surfeit of pity becomes an irritant. When I was younger, a blind Belgian used to beg on Market Square; both his legs had been amputated. He accepted money from passers-by without so much as a word and you immediately understood that, however much you gave, it would never be enough. Here was a debt that would remain unsettled. When it became clear that every contact would be rebuffed by his empty eyes and bare stumps, people began avoiding him. He became a war monument no one had asked for in a country tired of looking on from the sidelines. True, those few cents could never weigh up against the millions of guilders the Netherlands had demanded from Belgium after the war for housing its refugees, while handing Kaiser Wilhelm a castle for his trouble. But everyone was relieved when the veteran disappeared from the square. About time, said Uncle Sjefke, good riddance. The war had been over for ten years and it was about time those Belgians stopped their whining. After all, everyone in Maastricht remembered those dodgy characters with plenty of money, those so-called refugees who drove up the rents in 1914 and undercut local workers by accepting low wages to top up their government handouts. For all we knew, that blind misery guts had been one of those ungrateful sods, always complaining about the food served up by their host family, one of those drunks who out of sheer boredom ended up back at the front playing the hero. And who's to say he was a hero at all? He could just as easily have been a common smuggler who had crawled under the Wire of Death and survived the two-thousand-volt shock while his legs went up like charcoal. It wouldn't have been the first time. My mother hissed between her teeth, there were children present, but Uncle Sjefke just snorted and crossed his arms. He had said his piece. He wasn't planning to sympathize with anyone, no matter what. You had to watch out for sympathy, before you knew it people thought you owed them something.

I crouched down in the basin until my bottom touched the soft soap suds. Von Bötticher didn't frighten me. Of course, he didn't please me either, what did he take me for? I could try to pity him but pity is a worthless emotion for a fencer. Feel pity when you are ten points ahead and you can end up losing 15–10 as a result, only to have your opponent triumphantly pull the mask from his face without a trace of remorse and thank you cordially. But if pity was out, what else was there? I had to find a way out of this impasse. And now there was a riding lesson to cap it all. If half an hour of next to no personal hygiene wasn't enough to strip me of my dignity, a spell on the back of a horse tethered to the longe held firmly in his hand was sure to do the trick. To start with, that docile horse of his was anything but. It was a brownish-grey Barb, one of those arrogant desert mares. Von Bötticher had fallen for the breed's warlike reputation. 'Many a battle has been won astride a Barb horse,' he said as we walked out to the meadow. My heart sank into my hand-me-down riding boots, two sizes too big.

'The Prophet Muhammad, King Richard II and Napoleon swore by them. Napoleon was forced to give up Marengo at Waterloo. That horse was already pushing thirty, but went on to gallop for the enemy for years to come. Even in death he was pressed into service: his hoof was a tobacco box on

General Angerstein's smoking stand.'

Von Bötticher only had to point and she trotted over to him. She wasn't big, that was some consolation, but she took one sniff and turned her backside toward me.

'Loubna, be good now,' said von Bötticher in a sugary voice.

She pricked up her ears and leered at her owner with one eye. If a human being treated you that way you wouldn't stand for it, but von Bötticher had all the patience in the world. 'Come now.'

With a grand sweep of her tail, she relented at last. He laid his cheek against her head as he offered her the bit. Then he slid his fingers under the noseband to make sure it was loose enough and lowered the saddle onto her back with such circumspect precision that I began to wonder whether this young madam would deign to carry me at all. As he tightened the girth, I saw myself reflected in her eye. Embarrassed by my round, pasty face, I looked the other way.

'Isn't she a beauty?'

'I don't think she's going to let me mount her.'

'Never talk like that in the presence of a horse. You'll ruin your relationship before you've even started.'

I burst out laughing, but von Bötticher was in earnest. 'What did I tell you this morning? They understand everything. Even before your doubts become words, she has drawn her own conclusions.'

In that case it doesn't matter what I say, I thought despondently. Perhaps I should just call the whole thing off? After all, there were plenty more unspoken doubts where that one had come from.

'Around horses it's a matter of acting,' he continued. 'Play a part, pretend you're the finest horsewoman in all of Aachen, make something up.'

He could say what he liked, my imaginative powers had up and fled. The horse walked at the end of her rope and the rider stood in the sand with his legs apart. And there was I, the rag doll in the saddle, an afterthought. After four circuits I was ordered to tighten the reins and press my calves against Loubna's flanks. Needless to say, she didn't bat an eyelid. She wasn't born yesterday.

'Keep your legs still,' said von Bötticher. 'No need to spur her on. Just take her as she is.'

'It doesn't seem to be working.'

'Don't give up so easily. Focus on your posture, keep your breathing calm and steady. You are the finest horsewoman in Aachen and you're about to trot. It's your decision, and that's final.'

Nothing happened. The horse remained singularly unimpressed. Von Bötticher tried to distract us with talk of the weather. True enough, it was a sweltering day. The trees stood motionless, the birds had been left speechless and sweat trickled from beneath my helmet—much too big for me, of course, just like the rest of my riding clobber. I felt like a simple-minded child treated to a ride around the circus ring while the audience look on with forced grins on their faces.

And then came a new sound. Loubna was first to hear it. The hum of an engine beyond the gates, growing steadily louder. Von Bötticher hastily rolled up the longe, unbuckled us and off he went.

'No need to be afraid. You're doing fine.'

He was talking to the horse. He couldn't spare a word for me, not even the faintest of smiles. The hum continued. I shortened the reins, looked over my shoulder and saw von Bötticher duck under the fence with surprising suppleness. He broke into a run—well, more of a hop-skip-jump—as he headed down the drive. He pulled open the gate and in rolled a butter-yellow cabriolet. The gleam of the windscreen denied me a view of the driver. Once we had disappeared around the side of the house, I tried to spur Loubna on and she quickened her pace to an uneasy clip-clop. The sound of the engine died away and was replaced by a woman's voice, birdlike. She stood next to the car. A platinum blonde in a veil and a cherry-red coat dress. Despite her high heels, she stood on tiptoe to kiss von Bötticher. Loubna tugged sharply at the reins.

'Easy, girl,' I whispered. 'He'll be back soon. He'll always come back to you.'

We had already broken into a trot. I sat deeper in the saddle and tensed my calves. Von Bötticher said something that made the blonde laugh effusively as she circled the car. All this time two boys had been sitting inside. That'll be them, I thought: the young sabreurs, the hot-headed swashbucklers. They sat motionless in the back seat while their mother chirped and twittered, wiggled her hips, lost her veil. Von Bötticher went down on his knees. That's what veils were for, to bring men to their knees. He seemed very young all of a sudden. Why wasn't he looking at us? Loubna lengthened her back, we were almost trotting on the spot. I hardly needed to do anything and when I relaxed the rocking motion continued of its own accord. Then Heinz came out of the house to park the car and Loubna was off like a shot. An immense power unfurled beneath me and I fought for some kind of grip as I was tossed like a frail boat on a tidal wave. I looked down in horror at the horse's thrusting neck, the force that was whipping up the storm. The car's engine sprang to life. Loubna thundered across the sandy enclosure, jumped sideways and thudded to a halt with four hooves at once. I lurched backward, clinging to whatever I could lay my hands on. Straightening up my riding helmet, I hoped no one would see us as I tried to recover from our breathtaking trot, but the horse began to whinny in loud fits and starts. Strolling arm in arm down the path, von Bötticher and the blonde stopped in their tracks. He looked at me with his twisted face. 'Get off her, Janna. Take her to the pasture and wait for Heinz.'

I slid from Loubna's back and led her away through the loose sand. Heinz turned the car around. The young sabreurs were still sitting in the back seat. I took a closer look and saw they were completely identical.

**6**

The mother must have been stunningly beautiful once. Now she was less sure of her charms, though she fluttered her eyelashes as she sipped her wine and held her head like a porcelain trinket on her thin, bejewelled neck. Empty cigarette holder between her fingers, high heels abandoned in the grass, stocking feet resting on von Bötticher's lap.

'This heat just won't let up,' she said. 'Perhaps I should take something off.'

Von Bötticher, a dominant presence in his riding boots, was smoking a cigar. He peered in the direction of the percussive crescendo of baking trays, pans and slamming cupboard doors that was coming from the kitchen. The sounds of someone cooking with a vengeance.

'Why is Leni taking so long?'

'Leave that poor woman alone for once.' She stretched out in her garden chair and the skirts of her coat dress parted. She made no attempt to rearrange them. 'Or are you utterly famished?'

Von Bötticher continued to stare morosely at a point somewhere above her head. She pressed her toes against his belly. 'Is my big growly bear so very hungry?'

As if I wasn't even there. Perhaps I'd have been better off playing on the lawn like the sabreurs, who were charging around in circles with the dogs at their heels. They were solidly built for twins, but they behaved like little children. I guessed their mother must be in her forties, perhaps even a little older than von Bötticher himself.

'Egon, are you being sweet to this poor girl?' She sized me up with her bright blue eyes. I was still wearing my hand-me-down riding togs—handed down by God knows who. Not by her, I hoped. What an indignity that would be, walking around in the skin shed by that serpent. I had taken a distinct dislike to her without really understanding why. Von Bötticher went as if to remove her feet from his lap, but then sat still with his hands cupped around her ankles. She smiled. Granted, her beauty was still intact.

'Well? Are you sweet to her? You can be such a brute at times.'

I stood up. 'May I be excused? I would very much like to get changed.'

'Be quick about it,' said von Bötticher, without turning his head. 'Dinner is almost ready. If you run into Heinz, tell him to come too.'

From upstairs I could hear her chirping again. Clearly von Bötticher only turned jocular when I was out of earshot. I would not be gone for long, with all of two summer dresses to choose from. Strictly speaking, even this was an exaggeration: the gold-coloured satin option was actually a slip, meant to be worn under the other. Of course, I could always put on my fencing uniform and march downstairs to demand my afternoon training session. According to the schedule it should have started long ago, but clearly all appointments were off as soon as she showed her face, the woman who could make him laugh. Now they were laughing together. I closed the balcony doors. There was no way I could wear the slip on its own. Static made the satin cling to my thighs. In a flash I saw myself sitting down at the table as a gleaming Isis, clad in gold leaf. Open-mouthed astonishment: look how dazzling she is, our blessed virgin, how could we have been so blind? But no, on went the cotton dress over the top. Grit fell from my hair. That blasted desert mare had engulfed me in a cloud of sand. Would anyone notice if I undid my braids? I'd die if anyone thought I had been tarting myself up for someone else's benefit, if anyone were to say, 'My, haven't *you* made an effort.' This was a simple, striped summer dress, nothing special. My pinafore was too warm, my skirt was dirty— all perfectly plausible, surely? Besides, I could hardly walk around in riding gear all day. I was determined to be inconspicuous and slip lizard-like onto the terrace. No such luck. Leni was ahead of me with the tea trolley and the wheels got stuck in the gravel. She turned around and immediately began to coo, 'Pretty as a picture! Sure you won't catch a chill once the sun goes down? Hurry to the table now, our honoured guests are waiting. As for those strange boys, let their mother round them up. We're not at the fairground now, for heaven's sake. Oh look, there she goes already. On her stocking feet across the grass! Oh well, why ever not … Nothing around here surprises me any more.'

At the table, the sabreurs shoved their food into their mouths without so much as glancing at it. A toddler lets himself be fed, grinning trustingly at the world around him till he tastes what's on his tongue and his face clouds over. With these boys, even that realization failed to dawn. They only had eyes for each other. They left the asparagus untouched and fed each other devilled eggs, a sight only I appeared to find distasteful. Their mother made no comment. Von Bötticher shook water droplets from the glasses and filled them to the brim. She tipped back the bottle when he spilled some on the tablecloth.

'You're keen! Can you actually see what you're doing?' She

shot me a conspiratorial look. 'He can't, you know. That eye of his has affected his depth of vision, don't you think?'

'There is nothing wrong with my eyesight.' Von Bötticher pushed his chair away from her. 'With my eye. I wasn't hit in the eye, in case you hadn't noticed.'

Heinz came marching up to the table wearing a black-smith's apron. His master showed him the bottle.

'Don't mind if I do,' said Heinz.

'Whose hooves have you been trimming?' von Bötticher asked.

'Careful,' said the mother, 'there will be more spills if you don't watch out. Heinzi, don't you agree that Egon has trouble judging depth?'

Heinz stared at her blankly. You could almost hear the wind whistling in one ear and out the other. 'Megaira. And I treated the crack in her left back hoof.'

They raised their glasses and drank greedily. The wine brought a flush to Heinz's cheeks, and his paper mask became a face of flesh and blood. He gazed down at his half-empty glass as if it were a source of amusement, pulled up a chair and in a single motion shoved three stalks of asparagus and an egg onto his plate. Von Bötticher nodded approvingly. 'Thank you. But keep those hooves greased in future. Prevention is better than cure. Why aren't you drinking?' He was talking to me all of a sudden. Having cast a fleeting eye over my summer dress, he said firmly, 'You're allowed to drink you know. It will help you get over your fright.'

'Leave the girl be,' said the mother. 'You're always picking on her. She doesn't know whether she's coming or going.'

'Why don't *you* leave *me* be, and spare me your nonsense. Or would you like me to show you how deep my vision goes? The depth of this garden, for example. I'll knock you from one end of my estate to the other. Heinz, fetch my rapier, so I can drive this woman off my terrace. A fencer with no depth of vision, now wouldn't that be something.'

She did not react but drank with her eyebrows raised, gazing at her stocking feet in the grass. She looked fragile. It was hard to imagine she had ever been through such a difficult birth. To say nothing of what came next! One child, fair enough. A single infant you can park on one arm while holding onto your hat with the other, but two— two boys at that—must have been hard going. Suckling both at once, like an animal.

'The blacksmith told me cracked hooves have nothing to do with greasing,' said Heinz. 'But don't worry. I've carved a notch in the hoof to stop the crack spreading.'

Von Bötticher shrugged irritably. He poured me a glass of wine, passing the sabreurs over. Not that they showed any interest. They behaved as if they were still getting to know each other. I had been introduced to them briefly out in the hall — Friedrich and Siegbert—but seconds later I had been unable to tell them apart. Most twins differ in height—not these two. They wore their hair the same way and the golden lock they kept flicking out of their eyes struck me as their mother's idea. When Siegbert asked if he could go to the toilet, Friedrich leaped up too, but his mother reined him in: 'Stay here Fritz.' Without his brother, Friedrich barely knew what to do with himself. He sat out those few minutes looking like he might choke. Such was his plight, it pained me to look at him and he didn't eat a thing until Siegbert returned. Together they were at their most beautiful, no doubt about it. Both had their mother's blue eyes and flawless skin, both had a hint of golden down along the jawbone. There were differences, but even these seemed calculated. Siegbert had a mole on his left cheek, Friedrich on his right. Friedrich had the same smile as

Siegbert, but it began at the opposite corner of his mouth. Siegbert revealed a chipped top tooth when he laughed, while one of Friedrich's bottom teeth had taken a knock. They moved with chronometric precision. Their pale hands crumpled their napkins simultaneously. They even chewed in synch. If Friedrich wanted water, Siegbert had already picked up the carafe before a word was spoken. They were well aware of their beauty, sitting bolt upright at the table in their red waistcoats, two kings of hearts pulled from identical packs.

Leni brought in the second course, her voice ringing with reproach. Her oblivious husband hadn't even cleared the table. What a useless creature he was, while in Leni he had a real woman with a plentiful supply of everything a man could need. He was halfway through his second glass and already reaching for the bottle.

'Top up my glass while you're at it,' said the mother.

'How are things with your husband?' Heinz inquired.

Leni hurriedly began serving up helpings of meat. 'There's more in the kitchen if this isn't enough. The butcher always gives us more than we order. That swindler knows I can't just send him away once he's here at the gate. Might as well pick our pockets and be done with it.'

'Your husband was a first-rate sportsman,' said Heinz, dodging his wife's behind. 'Far and away the best long jumper at the club! No one else came close. You know what he should be doing with his talents?'

'Do tell,' said the mother, icily.

'*Kraft durch Freude!* Now there's an organization that can use people like him. Excursions, activities for the working man. Sport in the open air, and then it's back to serving the fatherland with renewed energy!' He slammed a triumphant fist down on his blacksmith's apron. In the silence that fell, he quickly drained his glass and continued his rant.

'We cannot allow ourselves to be overtaken. Negroes winning medals at our Olympiad: it should never have been allowed to happen. What did your husband make of that?'

'I have no idea. I didn't ask.'

'We missed the boat, me and my Leni. KdF didn't exist when we were younger, all we had to join was the union. Oh, I would have loved to go on a trip like that, even if it was only to the cabaret. Matthias Schmidt tells me the whole club is off to the Baltic coast next month. Imagine! And for free! They don't have to pay a pfennig!'

Leni huffed. 'Matthias Schmidt is always shooting his mouth off about something. Raeren beats the Baltic coast any day. Am I right, sir?'

Von Bötticher's face was drawn as he chewed his meat. I sensed his anger brewing. Two pale-brown moths fluttered in front of his face, heralding the approaching dusk. Anyone else would have swatted them aside, but because von Bötticher let them be—perhaps this was a mating flight—they seemed to give him the gravitas of a man of nature. Next to him, Heinz looked more threadbare than ever. But the sickly biscuit baker, condemned to the natural world in spite of himself, was busy taking all kinds of liberties with the lady at his master's table. She went to light a cigarette and he provided the flame. He must have thought they had something in common, an urban brand of *savoir-vivre* or something of the kind. There was no stopping him.

'Be sure to pass my recommendation on to your husband. About the KdF. Tell him Heinrich Kraus urges him to do so. I know his heart is in the right place. He's not one for jumping on bandwagons. He was a member of the Party from its earliest beginnings. I can ask around if you like, find out from my old chums who he should get in touch with.'

No one said a word. Not even when the twins left the table and darted off toward the field, like a couple of colts let loose.

'Why, I made a similar recommendation to you. Remember, sir? Fencing lessons for the working classes. Raeren would be ideal. Bags of room for *Kraft durch Freude*.'

'*Freude*,' von Bötticher muttered. 'Joy has nothing to do with fencing. Fencing is an art, a world away from seeing who can jump furthest in a sandpit. How can I explain in terms you might understand? It is the difference between my Megaira and a carthorse.'

'Oh, I would have loved to go on a trip like that. If only to the cabaret.'

'Free time controlled by the state can hardly be called free time.'

'You and your imperialist cronies don't want the workers to have anything, you old *Stahlhelm* rogue.'

The word crackled in the air. I had no idea what it meant, but Leni leaped out of her chair, grabbed the first thing she could lay her hands on—the carving fork—and waved it in Heinz's face. 'Sir, you must forgive him. You know he can't hold his drink. Just look at the old mongrel, all bark and no bite. He'll never interfere in your affairs, sir. You know that don't you? Heaven forbid.'

Von Bötticher let out a deep sigh. 'It's fine, Leni. His Communist prattle is fascinating in its way. *Stahlhelm* rogue? Interesting choice of words. Lest you forget, Heinz, we fought for this fatherland of yours.'

'As did we all,' said Heinz. 'And I am anything but a Communist.'

'Communist, socialist ... what exactly did you do during the war? I don't believe I've ever asked you. Wait, let me refresh your glass. This, in case you hadn't noticed, is an outstanding Riesling from the Rheingau. A great German wine, with more than a hint of National Socialism, after all I am sharing it with you, my worker.'

Leni was still wielding the carving fork. She did not look at her husband: he had become someone to be spoken about, not spoken to, a point she was eager for their master to grasp. 'No more drink for him. Does him no good at all. See for yourself, he's no use to anyone.'

'Surely a real man can handle a glass of wine? Even the ladies are drinking it! Come, Heinz, enlighten me. How did you spend the years between fourteen and eighteen?'

'Twenty-fifth reserve corps, Lodz. Until I wound up in the field hospital.'

Out on the grass, the twins were spinning around like mad, hanging from each other's arms. It was a game I knew from the school playground. As the paving stones whirled beneath your feet, you clung to your partner's wrists for dear life—by that stage slowing down was no easy matter. It was best to close your eyes, and give in to the blur of terror and delight. The twins had long since surrendered to centrifugal force. They were perfectly in balance, so what had they to fear?

'Take a leaf out of our book,' said von Bötticher. 'We find joy in the close companionship of a select company. Why invite the masses in? What is there left to enjoy if everyone is doing the same? The new politics is focused on the neutral. The faceless masses.'

'Look who's talking,' giggled the mother. 'Faceless, indeed.'

'The anonymous multitudes. Who wants to devote their energies to them? We are all prepared to help our fellow man, provided we are free to decide which fellow we help. Where's the good in depriving people of their natural instinct to love their neighbour?'

'Matthias says factory strikes are a thing of the past,' said

Heinz. 'They've fixed everything up. Life's getting better, brighter. Showers, bigger windows. *That* is what the Führer has done for the worker. Oh, if only I could ... '

Von Bötticher dashed his glass to the ground. 'Then go, man! Don't let me hold you back. I gave you work when you were out on the street, when that union of yours could do nothing for you. And now I have to put up with this? Run on back to your stinking city, perhaps they'll have a job for you now.'

This was the last straw for Heinz. He rose melodramatically to his feet, untied his apron and tossed it aside. He must have had an entirely different image of himself, the image of the worker on the posters, gazing off into the distance, sun rising behind his broad shoulders. He was drunk, his eyes were watery, and the veins were pulsing beneath the thin skin of his forehead. 'No sooner said!' he roared. 'I am not your property. Come Leni, our work here is done.'

Leni ran off and Heinz tottered along behind her, putting an end to any pretence of manliness by bending down to pick up the carving fork she had dropped in the gravel.

'Well, this is turning out to be quite an evening,' said the mother. She sat on the chair with her knees drawn up in front of her, the red coat dress draped around her shoulders. Cleopatra. Hadn't she given birth to twins after a fling with Mark Antony, a married man, and wooed him a second time four years later? Another persistent piece of skirt. Perhaps there's not much mothering to be done when your children always have each other to fall back on. The mother sat with her back to her children, she had no desire to see that bizarre little dance of theirs. They danced in the pink glow of sunset without music and without an audience, just as birds and native tribesmen have no need of such things. They spun around each other, tumbled across the grass, walked on their hands with their belly buttons showing. Sometimes they seemed to merge into one, like a disappearing trick with mirrors. Just watching them made me dizzy. Gingerly, I put my empty glass back down on the table, having held onto it all this time for fear it might be refilled. The house echoed with wailing and the slamming of doors. Von Bötticher looked around under his chair and found nothing. He gave a tragic smile, the only kind in his repertoire. By this time I had realized that some of his facial nerves must have been severed and looking stern was the expression that came most readily to him. Heinz, an alarming shade of puce, re-emerged from the house with his wife trailing wearily behind him. They looked like sailors after a stormy voyage. 'Sir! Sir!' The words could be heard from afar. It was a pitiful display. 'I spoke out of turn. Please accept my apologies. I only wanted to offer a word of advice. It's none of my business ... not my place ... I wouldn't dare! I'm a humble gardener, sir, in every way your subordinate, no question about it.'

'Apology accepted,' said von Bötticher, pointing to the apron lying on the grass. 'You are not worthy of a duel. From tomorrow you will grease Megaira's hooves every day, do you understand?'

'Listen to Egon,' the mother slurred. She uncoiled from her garden chair and flopped onto his lap, burying her nose in the spot where her toes had been. She was not a natural blonde. Dark hair curled in the nape of her neck like tree roots on a riverbank. 'Listen to my sweet hussar. Look at me, my hussar sweetheart, at this little horsey of yours. Saddle her up, ride her all you want. See how well I've been broken in, *mein lieber Leibhusar!*'

'Janna! Come here,' hissed Leni. 'A nice young girl like you shouldn't have to witness such goings on.' She had her hands full with Heinz, who was determined to remain

standing. Routinely, she dodged a slap, like a mother staying clear of her infant's clawing little mitts, before dipping
under his shoulder, parking him against her hip and dragging him off to their den behind the kitchen. Poor thing,
before she could crawl into bed beside him she had a least
two hours' work ahead of her.

Up in my room, the first thing I did was look out of the
window and, sure enough, there they were still out in the
field, the sabreur brothers. They were taking a stroll,
talking earnestly, arms around each other's shoulders.
Alone at last. The adults had all gone inside, the front door
had been locked with a bang, a glass had shattered on the
paving stones, there had been the sound of crying or
laughter, and insistent whispering that had carried all the
way up to the attic, but no one had paid the twins any heed.
They did not seem to mind in the slightest. They had ignored me completely. I was growing accustomed to such
treatment from the maître, and the attentions of their
mother left me cold, but these boys were my fellow students. We were almost the same age.

A few hours later I woke with a start. The hard, metallic
light of the moon was shining through the curtains. I got
out of bed to push them aside and was just in time to see
the cabriolet driving off. Leni, in her dressing gown, closed
the gate and trudged back toward the house. I was about to
turn away and crawl back between the sheets when I saw
them lying there. Was I dreaming or had the grass around
their bodies grown taller? They lay beside each other, looking so inert in the nickel-grey light that it was easy to take
them for dead.

# 7

Raeren made a spy of me. Closed curtains, strange letters, muffled exchanges—I was drawn to them like a thief to a safe. Hunting for clues is a glorious game, sweeter than the discovery itself. This was more than just the whim of a naughty girl. On the fourth morning I woke to the realization that I was being excluded. I was an unwelcome guest. There was plenty to see within Raeren's walls, yet none of it was intended for my eyes. Some voyeurs revel in exclusive viewing rights, seeking out images even their victim cannot see, observing them when they are asleep or alone in a mirrorless room. Others persuade themselves they are sharing something with the person they are spying on, convinced their victim wants to be watched because he has neglected to slide the key into the keyhole. I was the angry voyeur, in search of evidence. While the rest of Raeren slept, only I saw the twins playing at musketeers in the fencing hall. The doors to the terrace had been flung open and the flapping net curtains provided alternate glimpses of the two halves of a fencing bout. From the fragments tossed in my direction, I concluded that the sabreurs were more beautiful than the Nadi brothers and identical as two drops of blood. They fenced without masks or tunics. Their night on the grassy field had left no trace on their faces, even their bare chests were immaculate. Cause for concern, or then again perhaps not, since the best fencers are battle-scarred. I never thought my bruises ugly, as long as they were outside the target area. Once I paraded around for a week showing off a dramatic bruise on my upper arm till a girl I knew told me I would catch cold in that sleeveless blouse of mine. But the sabreurs' bodies were pure and waxen, as if they had been moulded especially for this demonstration. Suddenly they went in for the attack, swinging wildly. This was swordsmanship at its crudest. The parquet creaked under the thud of their footsteps. A chandelier took a hit and shed a candle. This could not end well. Their blades scraped through the air, the clang of steel against steel was far too frequent. That is not how it should be done, a good fencing match has moments of stillness, and the one who breaks them has to strike in a headlong rush, like a spider homing in on its prey. Without stillness, a duel descends into a blind scuffle that ends in slaughter. How long can a spectator look on before becoming an accessory? Yet there was something odd about this scene, something that stopped me from intervening. Every thrust was met with a riposte; the twins never once hit each other, though there were enough opportunities for the taking. In the end, one of the sabreurs swivelled his torso 90 degrees and his attacker tumbled across the piste with a loud cry. The two of them erupted into laughter. It was a routine they had learned off by heart. Pure theatrics. I cleared my throat. They were not surprised to see me—they even took a bow.

'What did you think?' asked the brother who had taken a dive. 'Mama taught us. The full act involves a chair. That's Siegbert's speciality. He leaps onto the seat and then onto the back, so the chair tips over, and then he jumps clear—do you want us to show you?'

'Is your mother a fencer too?'

'She's an actress. But now she's gone. And the maître is

ill. We went to fetch him. His door was open but when we stood at the foot of his bed he rose up like the Golem. You know, from the film? In slow motion, with his arms stretched out in front of him. Scared us half to death.' His eyes grew wide as he took hold of a chair and lifted it above his head. 'Der Golemmm!'

I burst out laughing, but his brother remained deadly serious. 'I wasn't scared, Friedrich,' he said. 'Speak for yourself.'

For the first time I became aware of a genuine difference between the two. It was how they spoke. When Siegbert said something, his face froze into an icy mask. It aged him somehow, whereas even Friedrich's nose joined in when he chattered. 'Come on, Siegbert, show her your trick.'

'Not on your life. Before you know it I'll have broken a chair and the Golem will be after us. Let's put our kit back on and do some fencing. I'm sure Janna can keep score.'

It wouldn't have surprised me to learn that Siegbert had taken the lead when they were born as well. He had exerted himself during their bout, his chest was still heaving as he laced up his waistband. Sweat trickled down into the hollow of his back.

'Come here, Fritz, I'll help you into your jacket.'

They fell silent and became identical again. Siegbert's fingers glided over Friedrich's back from button to button. He blew his brother's hair aside to fasten the collar, then grabbed him by the neck and turned him around to face me: 'Isn't my little brother astonishingly handsome?'

When they had been excluding me, I had been unable to take my eyes off the sabreurs. But now I looked away in the hope that they might abandon this show of childish affectation.

'Fritz is better-looking,' said Siegbert. 'Everybody says so.'

Friedrich pulled himself away. 'That's a lie! Siegbert is

bigger than I am. And stronger.'

'Am not.'

'Are so.'

They chased after each other, panting like schoolgirls. But when they skidded to a halt, Siegbert dragged his brother over to the mirror and thrust him in front of it. 'See for yourself, Fritz. Look how beautiful you are.'

'Let go of me,' squeaked Friedrich. 'Please, dear Sieg. Don't be so cruel.'

'Tell him, Janna,' Siegbert insisted.

My cheeks were flushed with shame. 'Leave me out of it!' I blurted. 'We came here to fence. Now put on your masks!'

Remarkably, they obeyed. Everything went according to the rulebook. I knew the rules that governed sabre-fencing, all the same it was a terribly fast-moving sport to preside on your own. Yet they never questioned my authority. As I expected, they were evenly matched, hopping back and forth across the piste like Punch and Judy. After Friedrich's first thrust on target, Siegbert equalized with a slash to the shoulder. Four hits for each brother followed until Siegbert suddenly lowered his sabre.

'Wait!' He held a finger up to his mask. 'Quiet, I can hear something!'

We pricked up our ears. All I could hear was a songbird showing off in the branches of the lime tree. The sabreurs stood stock-still with their masks covering their faces, expressions hidden from view. Perhaps they were laughing silently, chuckling away to themselves as they looked at me. Before I could ask them anything, Siegbert raised his finger again. I wasn't even sure it was Siegbert. Perhaps they had switched places when I wasn't looking. The other brother brandished his sabre as if expecting an attack. I still couldn't hear anything out of the ordinary. A curtain flapped against the wall, a downstairs door slammed. The bird had shut up at last. When I turned around, the sabreur was standing with his back to the window, wielding his sabre.

'The Golem!' he blared, and they both fell about laughing. Siegbert pulled the mask from his face. 'We had you worried there for a minute.'

'Yes, we had you worried there,' said Friedrich. 'Admit it.'

'Nonsense,' I said. 'I've never even heard of that film.'

'Never heard of *Der Golem*?'

I shook my head. I wasn't about to tell them I had only been to the cinema three times in my entire life.

'The Golem is a monster made of clay,' said Friedrich. 'He was created by a rabbi who wanted to protect his people. He comes to life when you carve a star on his chest. But then everything gets out of control and he smashes everything up and ... '

'You're not telling it right,' Siegbert interrupted. 'We have to make it dark in here otherwise it won't be scary enough.' He started unfastening a heavy curtain. Thick strands of dust drifted to the floor, but the red material was not enough to keep out the morning sun. Siegbert beckoned us closer. 'It all takes place in Prague, a long, long time ago ... ' Footsteps could be heard in the hallway. His eyes opened wide, but his pupils stayed small. It's a look I have seen in vicious dogs, blind as frozen water. 'Hear that? We've raised the Golem from the dead. I always knew this place was haunted. Listen!'

The clock said half past seven. It must be Leni coming to fetch the cleaning buckets from the cellar. But I was more interested in what Siegbert had to say. In those days we were all obsessed with spiritualism. My friends back home quivered themselves into a state of ecstasy in the back rooms of their parents' homes. I was amazed at the efficiency with which they clipped letters from newspapers, fashioned a cross from two pieces of wood and directed questions at the silent void. Inevitably a parental row would break out at the decisive moment, clearly audible through the thin walls. You could cut the tension with a knife in most Limburg households during the Great Depression, but that wasn't the kind of tension we were after. At Raeren, I had been hoping for the real thing. The twins had known the house for some time and during their last stay they had slept in the attic room and been visited by a horde of—demons, Friedrich thought, wandering spirits, according to Siegbert. Whatever form they took, there was something ghostly afoot and here we were to soak it all up.

'I'm sleeping in the attic room,' I said. 'Can't say I've noticed anything.'

'I'd watch out if I were you,' said Friedrich. 'They *will* come, of that you can be sure. Who they are, we do not know, but there's a host of them. If you listen closely, you can hear them talking. Hushed voices, almost like rustling. Just thinking about it gives me the willies!'

'Come on, let's go up there,' said Siegbert. 'Then you'll see how haunted this place is.'

So while the adults were trying to shake off the night with cold water and plans for the day ahead, we egged each other on in childish whispers and stormed upstairs on our occult adventure, oblivious to the glaring common sense of the morning outside.

'Wait, let me go first!' said Siegbert, when we arrived at the door to my room. As he reached for the handle, it turned all by itself and the next moment we were blinded by a flood of light. There, in the middle of the room, a silhouette in a cloud of dust stood rooted to the spot. The twins bolted down the stairs.

'Pair of rascals,' Leni muttered, pulling my pillow from

the pillowcase. 'You'd never believe they're old enough for military service.'

I only half heard what she said, as I tried to conceal my unease. The balcony doors were open. She had bent the wire screen to one side and scrubbed the tiles.

'No class this morning, then?'

'We were left to our own devices. They said the maître is sick.'

'Who? The boys? Don't take their word for anything, Janna. Not an ounce of sense between them. The maître has been up and about for an hour. Fresh as a trout in a stream.' She stepped out onto the balcony and pointed into the distance. 'See for yourself!'

A horseman was galloping over the hill. The reins held loosely in his hand were the only sign that this floating trinity of rider, horse and the flock of white clouds above them were ever parted. Who breathed life into whom? Was it the young god who took possession of the horse that danced along beneath him, or was it the other way around? The rider, with his long legs and supple movements, bore little resemblance to the maître I knew.

'I can't help but worry, Janna.' Leni's hair smelled of last night's dinner. I took a step back and she eyed me anxiously. 'Heinzi's loose tongue has made the master suspicious. According to Heinzi, the twins should've been sent off to the army long ago, but that mother of theirs has no intention of losing her poor little mites to the Wehrmacht. She's no patriot, that's for sure. Why the master lets himself get roped into these schemes of hers is beyond me. I do not trust that woman. But the worst of it is Heinzi's rant has given the master a reason not to trust *us* any more. I'm not even sure he'll allow us to stay.'

All at once the strain showed on her face, transforming her into another woman. I wasn't exactly feeling comfortable either. If Leni had been up here in my room all this time, who had been responsible for the ghostly footsteps we'd heard in the fencing hall?

'Heinzi says times have changed,' she sniffed. 'He says the tables are turned and the master will be lucky if he's allowed to stay here.'

Von Bötticher trotted back in through the gates of Raeren. The mighty cavalier. *Mein lieber Leibhusar.* Snooping around this house of his, I had come across a magazine with a photograph of the Kaiser's daughter wearing a hussar uniform. A boyish girl sporting a richly embroidered jacket, a faint smile on her tender face. On her head she wore a hat as top-heavy as an anvil, with a skull and crossbones glinting among the black fur. What had von Bötticher looked like during the war? He must have made a deep impression on the Walloons — those insects under their rocks, as Uncle Sjefke liked to call them. From behind their blanked-out windows, Belgian snipers had picked off the German invaders in all their finery, just as the Aztecs had fired their arrows at the conquistador horsemen. Had the roles been reversed in Liège now, too? Had the hussars with their skull and crossbones and their sharpened broadswords become the savages, while the native tribes had pulled their triggers with exemplary finesse?

'Herr Egon von Bötticher is one of the old guard all right,' said Leni. 'But Heinzi should never have called him an old *Stahlhelm* rogue. He's not a rogue and he's certainly not old. Men like him don't age. They've cheated death too often. Once you've had a close shave like that, they say each day is brand-new for the rest of your life, like being a child again.'

She stuffed the dirty bedclothes into a pillowcase. I was so under the spell of the hussar that I didn't lift a finger to help her. His coal-black mare walked as if she were proud to be under his control, though her elegant neck alone contained enough power to kill her rider.

'A majestic animal, isn't she?' said Leni. 'I've known her since she was a foal. When the master first came to live here, they were inseparable. During the day he saddled her up and rode her, at night he slept in the stable. As if he was scared someone would steal her. And with good reason—if Heinzi's to be believed, she must have cost him a fortune.'

She made to leave the room, but halfway to the door she reconsidered. 'You didn't hear it from me, mind, but they say he lost a horse during the war. A very special animal, a gift from his father, some say. In any case, they had a bond the likes of us can't fathom. But the horse abandoned him, ran off while he lay dying. They say it drove him insane. Mad with betrayal. Imagine, the horse from his childhood, his only playmate ... And if there's one sure thing it's that the man had a wretched childhood: the only child of a despotic father and a mother who died in childbirth. And then that dreadful creature runs off, never to return! But you hear all kinds of stories. Others say the horse was stolen out from under him, or the poor thing was injured and he had to put it out of its misery. He spent a good long time in hospital back in Eastern Prussia and, take it from me, it wasn't just his leg they were treating. One thing I can tell you: the way he hung around the stables here wasn't natural. Fifteen years after the war, this was, but there were times when me and my husband would look at each other ... I once heard him howl like a wolf. I wanted Heinzi to go and check on him but he refused. No way, he said, it's none of our business. He's not from these parts and a man on the run will never let down his guard. He's buried his secrets and he's trying to forget where he dug the hole. The twins' mother is the only one who knew him before the war, but she keeps *stumm* as well. Don't think I haven't tried to ask.'

She slung the bundle of bedclothes over her shoulder and her tone turned almost threatening. 'Not a word, mind. I've told you too much already. He's a queer fish and no mistake, but life here at Raeren isn't so bad. He's a man of his word. You'll find clean sheets in the chest in the hallway.'

And off she went. Von Bötticher was now trotting close enough to see me wave from the balcony. He looked briefly in my direction but did not wave back. As if I were air, an apparition that haunts the place till everyone's sick of the sight. I was about to throw myself on the bare mattress in a fit of self-pity and cast myself as a tragic heroine in a new daydream, when two voices called me in unison.

'Janna! Come quick, please ... Oh, the horror! You won't believe your eyes!'

I was downstairs like a shot, though I had heard the smothered giggles in their distress call. I regretted it instantly, feeling little better than a mangy dog, elated by every pat on the head. They called me again, summoning me out into the garden.

'The spooks are everywhere, Janna. There's no holding them back!'

The front door was ajar. The shock at what I saw was only momentary. A shapeless form was moving about in front of the house without getting anywhere. There it stood, four trotters sticking out from under a sheet and two circles drawn in charcoal staring blindly into the distance. Siegbert tried to spur his phantom into action but it held its ground, rubbed its snout with a foreleg and let out a grunt. The excitement only began when a fury came charging out with a voice like thunder. She tried to pull the tablecloth from the animal but, with one leg tangled, it fell onto its side, presenting its teats like a dozen fondant fancies. The twins emitted loud squeals of disgust. Leni turned out to be more nimble than any of us expected.

Friedrich took the first blow, while Siegbert milled his arms around in an attempt to counter her attack.

'Keep your hands off my brother, woman!'

'A woman! Well spotted!' Leni screeched. 'With any luck you'll hook one of your own sometime. Unless you end up wedded to that brother of yours first!'

Siegbert and Friedrich shared a complacent look of approval.

'Only the devil himself could be so vain,' said Leni, shocked. 'Healthy young men should know better with a pretty young lady in their midst.'

Siegbert looked from me to the sow. 'Who exactly do you mean, Leni?'

I had never been in love, not with someone of flesh and blood. I saw no problem in that. When night fell, it was just as easy for me to conjure up a Siegbert from my own desires. One who courted me instead of his own likeness. Knowing the sound of his breath, I could easily feel him pant against my throat. And now I had seen his sweat, I could let it drip from his chest to mine. My fingertips became his lips and I kissed them. My palm was his cheek. But up in my attic room no ghosts came out to haunt me. They must have looked on jealously from their hiding places as my own imaginary phantoms brought me to a climax.

**8**

'Tonight is the Mensur.'

In the bleariness of waking I saw Bolkonsky, or another lover from my slumbers, shoved aside in the blink of an eye by a man as stubborn as reality itself. Arms outstretched, he appeared to be bracing himself in the doorway. Perhaps he had been standing there a while.

'I didn't know the Dutch went in for siestas, too.'

It was Saturday afternoon; I had only intended to take a little catnap. My skirt had ridden up my thighs. I grabbed for the sheet but I was lying on top of it with my shoes still on. What time was it? What had I been doing and what had he seen?

'The Mensur begins in an hour. Do you know what that is?'

Oh yes, I knew. A friend of Maître Louis's had studied in Stuttgart and returned with a red scar on his forehead. A *Schmiss* he called it, a badge of honour. Louis thought this was childish. Swearing allegiance in blood was something for little boys in the school playground. And what serious fencer would make a song and dance of having been hit square in the face? His friend had replied with a conceited smile that tucked his scar away among the creases on his brow. We sporting types would never understand. Fencing with a foil, now that was childish! A coward's game with a toy for a weapon. The aim of the Mensur was to conquer oneself. If you were incapable of that, why even try to defeat anyone else? He was right. I didn't understand it at all.

'You have my permission to attend,' von Bötticher said. 'It could well be your last opportunity. Who's to say? Men in high places have deemed the Mensur old-fashioned and are out to put an end to it.'

He stretched his stiff leg and stepped into the room. A brazen move under any other circumstances, but this was his house and I was within his walls, like the chair on which he was leaning. He bent forward to inspect my possessions laid out on the dressing table. My brush, strands of my hair caught between its bristles. My worn nail file, my thumb-marked mirror, my hollowed-out jar of lip balm. *War and Peace*. Since arriving here I hadn't opened it once, and if he were to open it now, he would see himself. His hazy reflection from a distant past. But he left it closed, resting his hand on the book as if he knew what was inside and wanted to keep it there.

'Old-fashioned,' he mumbled. 'Everything has to be erased, brought into line with a new system, as if we were already dead and buried. But I resist. The more they warn me to keep my head down, the harder I hit back.'

I had no idea who 'they' were, but I approved of his tone. It was the voice of an intractable cavalier who strode through your bedroom with the muck still clinging to the soles of his boots. I pulled the sheet over me.

'As I said, you have permission to attend,' he said, 'a rare exception. I am leaving the twins out of it. Don't say a word to them. Heinz is taking them down to the village. The fair has arrived. Or would you rather go with them?'

He looked at me in the dressing-table mirror. Under the sheet I clamped my legs together and fought to control my nerves. Here I was in bed, albeit fully dressed, while the master of the house let me in on a secret that was a far greater thrill than any fairground attraction.

'No,' I said hastily. 'I would rather see the Mensur.'

'Good. You won't be fencing, so wear something pretty. Perhaps you can help Leni. She will be catering for twenty guests on her own.'

Half an hour later I was downstairs in an apron. We had waved off Heinz and the sabreurs, which became a drawn-out process when Heinz stopped the car at the gate to deliver a couple of well-aimed slaps in the direction of the back seat. 'Good for him,' Leni had muttered, as if she knew what the twins had done to deserve their hiding. Then she began to make haste. The plan was to serve liver loaf accompanied by apple, potato and bacon hash, with apple pie for desert. A pig's head had been bobbing about in a pot of simmering water, grinning blindly till the flesh fell from its bones. She forced the meat through a mincer. Gagging, I walked over to the window. I saw nothing except the red glow of my fingers held up against the sunlight, but I could smell trouble brewing: an instinctive, sickening warning that no sense but smell can provide. When I lowered my hands, I saw three DKWs crawling up the drive like matt-black beetles. It took a while for the doors to swing open and the eleven occupants to emerge, clad in the same hermetic black as their vehicles. They were wearing caps and sashes, and one boy was waving the national flag. *Carnevale* was the word that shot through my head. *The renunciation of meat.* Every year on Ash Wednesday, the parish priest back home began his sermon by asking us if we had swallowed down every last bit of fat, consumed every scrap of meat that might lead us into temptation during our Lenten fast. His bloated parishioners were usually too hung-over to respond. The priest would then knead together a nauseating sermon from the flesh corrupted here on earth, its weakness and temptations, the living flesh of the lepers, and the Son made flesh. He pounded away at this concoction for a good hour till the belches echoed through the church. The stink was nigh on unbearable by the time he relented and we all lined up to receive the Corpus Christi.

'Let the carnival begin,' nodded Leni, as if she had read my thoughts. 'These little lads know the way. They don't need me to show them.'

Sure enough, the students entered of their own accord. They stood whispering for a while by the front door before making their way to the fencing hall. Leni examined her cook's knife and decided it needed no sharpening. (Knives are blunt in a house without men, my mother used to say, so often that my father eventually refused to run anything but his own table knife over the grindstone, with the destructive compulsion of a dog gnawing at a bone.) Leni cut up the suet, while I peeled the apples for the mash. Bees had flown in from the honeysuckle bushes and were buzzing around above the table. Fear turns you deaf before it makes you blind. The buzzing became so all-encompassing that I failed to notice the other guests arriving: eight young men and a grey otter of a man with a walking stick. The young men all wore the same caps as the first group, but sashes of a different colour. The Otter raised his stick in the air and shouted, 'Herr von Bötticher!' I did not see their greeting; the maître must have been standing in the doorway. Leni counted time, guests and ingredients. 'Nineteen hungry boys and two old bellies to fill. Let's get the hard stuff sorted first.'

Why, I don't know, but she dispatched me to do the serving. Off I went, carrying a tray heavy with schnapps and *Schmalz*. Shuffling tentatively toward the fencing hall, advancing step by halting step toward my first love.

I strenuously deny the suggestion that it was a uniform I fell in love with. Girls of my generation were immune to the cliché of a man being desirable simply because the cut of his uniform lends his body an air of resolve. We claimed those uniforms as our own, the first to wear jackets that were modelled on an officer's coat. Our blouses featured epaulettes, and over them we wore trench coats and a beret to top things off. Besides, in those days almost every man you saw on the street sported a uniform. Even the chap who came to collect our leftovers wore a striped apron and matching cap. In a fencing hall packed with tailored male bodies admiring their own sashes and insignia in the mirrors, there was only one I wanted. Admittedly, he was kitted out in a fashion that would have kindled a fire in any woman's loins, my prudish mother's included. It was a while before I saw him. Waitresses who are wet behind the ears keep their eyes glued to the tray instead of looking up at their guests. It was up to them to help themselves. I saw immaculate student hands take hold of the jug as if it were a kitten, heard their mumbled words but only glanced up when I was sure there was no danger of toppling glasses. There were beautiful young men among them. Earnest faces, most of them marked: a casual scratch on the cheek or a line across the forehead. Nothing serious. As if a higher power had checked them off one by one. Some were without a sash. One, in a doctor's coat, seemed to me too young to be a doctor. Another, in black skirts, looked as if he had been sat on: a stumpy little man with bulging eyes. I recognized the duellists immediately from an illustration in my collection, supplied by my aunt, who clipped pictures and articles on fencing from German magazines and kept them for me. *Der Herr Paukant.* It showed a man trussed up like a chicken and holding a rapier. Neither the cryptic word 'Paukant' or the oldish-sounding 'Herr' seemed to suit these students, who refused their drinks with barely a murmur, yet wore the same padded sleeves and leather strapping around the carotid artery as the man in the illustration. Once the steel goggles were put in place, only a small, pale target area would be left unprotected, like a patch of empty canvas on an unfinished portrait. For now their skin was still intact. The stumpy little man raised a reproving finger: no alcohol for the duellists, and although they were permitted to eat, their stomachs were too full of nerves. This was plain to everyone, though they tried to hide the fear in their as yet unmasked eyes. It was time for me to move on, but when I turned around I was felled. Twenty men witnessed the theft of a young girl's heart. It had taken next to no effort on the part of the culprit; his victim was already wearing the glum and foolish expression that comes over us when we greet an unspoken love.

It was not only his jet-black jacket with its white braiding, or his kersey pelisse adorned with silver ribbon. My breath caught in my throat for a second at the sight of the polished skull and crossbones pinned to his fur hat. Memento mori. He wore death on his forehead just as desert tribesmen wear their shroud as a turban. His eyes dealt the decisive blow. Perhaps I had not looked into them deeply enough before, distracted as I had been by his scar, which now seemed little more than an exuberant variation of the check marks on the students' faces. Those eyes were both fathomless and clear. Perhaps they only looked that way when he wore his uniform, heedful of death below the black border of rabbit fur. In any event, there I stood with my tray as he raised a glass without filling it.

'Brothers in arms!' he cried. The room fell silent. 'As I said, we have no choice but to improvise. We will see to it that the Comment is observed with the requisite rigour, but as you well know, recent political developments have made their impact felt. I see no need to waste words on such matters. Suffice to say, the *Consenior* of Ebura is unable to be with us today, and I am most honoured that they have sent their Senior, Professor Reich, here to Raeren. He will also fulfil the role of physician for the duellists.'

The Otter nodded his assent. He reminded me of my father, whose hair was not yet grey but who could not have been much younger than this professor. I was struck by the sudden fear that he might be able to read my thoughts with the same ease. He stood there amicably, as my father would have done, while the hussar—a *Consenior*, and below him in rank at the Mensur—continued his address. The tunic von Bötticher was wearing did not suit him at all, and it was then I knew for certain that my feelings had nothing to do with the uniform and everything to do with the man who fitted it like a sabre fits its sheath.

'On our side, junior doctor Herr Wolf will fulfil the role of physician. Since there are only two duellists we have decided on a match of fifteen rounds, four strokes in each. As you have all been able to read in the Comment, both low and high strokes are admissible. We trust in the judgement of the Arbiter. *Hoch bitte!*'

Loud applause. The Arbiter was not a divine entity but the stumpy, bug-eyed little man I had noticed earlier. He marched into the centre of the room as if haste was suddenly of the essence. The duellists were lined up a weapon's length apart and the seconds, trussed up identically to their protégés, took position in their shadows. They too were armed. All four weapons were dipped in methylated spirits. Lastly, steel goggles were placed over the duellists' eyes, offering protection but doing nothing to improve their sight. Perhaps sight was far less essential at such close range. The greater the distance, the coarser the wound.

Hits at closer range usually result in wounds to the head, which are only to be admired many years later when the duellist grows old and his hairline recedes. I knew from my father that scars on the head usually heal well, as the skull keeps the skin taut. But stitching a tear at the corner of the mouth requires the patience of angels. Too much flesh on the needle and the face is forced into a grimace for ever. How tragic to partake in so serious a ritual only to go through life with the face of a clown.

I am sure I was not the only spectator to compare the Mensur to a cockfight. The palaver. Grown men crouching, fussing over two creatures that had no choice but to draw blood from each other. These two young men had been reduced to cheeks, chin and head. They would bleed all right, though they would not bleed to death. The leather strapping around their necks was tugged tighter. The battle could begin.

'Young lady, do you have any *Schmalz* on white bread?'

The Otter pointed at the tray on which only two forlorn pieces of rye bread remained. I understood what a fool I had been to serve the students first, for now at the decisive moment the professor left me no choice but to return to the kitchen. Before leaving the room, I stole another glance at the maître. I had not been mistaken. A part of me regretted that fact. I was overcome by a sense of gloom, as if at a parting. I was saying goodbye to my dreams, like a child on his first day at school who realizes he is now condemned to the daily grind of life. My mother once told me that as a crestfallen six-year-old I had picked up my red school satchel and sighed, 'Oh, if only I hadn't grown up.'

Leni saw what had happened. She shot me an inquiring look and wiped her armpits with the back of her hand. 'Are you all right, girl? You're as red as a robin. Sit down a moment. I should have warned you about all that nonsense.'

'I feel fine,' I mumbled, 'they haven't started yet. They want *Schmalz* on white bread.'

She wasn't listening, but was leaning over a basin murmuring frightful spells to herself. 'Half as much fat as meat, twice as much fat as blood, half as much blood as fat.'

As if proof were needed that the stink had found its way into the open air, the dogs began to whine. There was worse to come. Apart from the meat from the pig's head, half a litre of blood had to be mixed in, along with suet and half a kilo of buckwheat flour. Once it was all in, Leni began to bash the ominous concoction into submission using her full body weight. She stood pounding away by the sink until everything turned red: the stuffing, her face and the haze clouding my field of vision. In the meantime, I did my best to spread *Schmalz* on the slices of bread.

'Go back to the hall,' Leni said. 'Get back in there and watch the circus. Not that it's worth the trouble. Where I'm from men let fly if their pride has been injured. Insult my wife? Take that, scumbag!' She lifted a bloody fist from the basin. 'A good, honest fist fight in the middle of the street. Their sort fight in secret, so the hoi polloi don't know what they're up to. And they're supposed to be an example to us all? Heaven preserve us! They think it's a disgrace if a man pulls his head away while he's being carved up with a sword. Back to the Dark Ages! The sooner the Führer closes that circus down, the better.'

Could the ritual in the fencing hall really be called a circus? A circus loves an audience, though I can't say I've ever felt much affection beneath the big top. Affliction is closer to the mark, like pulling up a chair at a family dinner where old feuds are being fought out behind the polite façade. An old clown hiding his sour-faced grievances under a mask of greasepaint and taking out his frustration night after night on the girl from the flying trapeze, that brand of misery. But all smiles when the spotlights come on, grinning for that cursed audience. The duelling circus of offence and satisfaction had no need of prying eyes. In the olden days when quick-tempered men were ready to cross their elaborately decorated swords at the drop of a hat, the Mensur retreated to fencing pistes deep in the forest. No one needed to see how pride was earned on pain of death. It was nobody's concern that the battle against loss of face was fought with open visor and weapon drawn. There were no winners or losers, since honour was at stake, and the dead might earn it just as soon as the living, perhaps even sooner. No hard feelings. The friends in the fencing hall would both be leaving it alive. They had the good fortune to be duelling one century after people had decided that the true enemy was not the man facing you but the spinelessness lurking within. To conquer the snivelling cur inside you, it was enough to be marked for life.

The fencing hall had been locked from the inside. I rattled the handle and the Otter eased open the door just far enough to grab his bread and lock me out again. But I was in luck: someone had obligingly pulled back the curtains and the terrace windows afforded me a splendid view of the duel. There was even a garden chair ready and waiting. The warriors were halfway through their match. Blood was already streaming down one duellist's face but the bout continued. This was not a fight. The cramped movements initiated from wrist and elbow were dictated by the short distance, not born of hatred or fury. Spontaneous emotions were to be kept under tight rein. The Comment regulated victory over the self down to the very last detail. Mensur—more than the distance measured, the word spoke of a measured approach to the human passions.

'Halt!'

A hit. The Arbiter stepped in to inspect the duellists. To my surprise he concluded there was no cause for alarm. 'Not deep enough,' he said, examining the head wound. The weapons were disinfected and 'Fence!' they were off again, thrust after thrust, stroke after stroke, until the final round. It all went quiet. The circle became a scrum. Even standing on tiptoe I could see nothing. Then my name was called.

'She's a doctor's daughter,' I heard von Bötticher say. 'She is not afraid of blood.'

He was waiting for me in the hallway. I wondered if he might notice. Would he realize he had just become someone's first love? Not that it would have made any difference, it's hardly a role you can turn down. Schoolteachers know this better than anyone, especially the pretty ones. For some that immortalization is a reason to become a teacher. But von Bötticher looked at me as sceptically and as wearily as he had at Aachen station.

'I need you,' he said. 'Our junior doctor is suffering from an unsteady hand and it occurred to me that you must have helped your father stitch people up.'

I knew where to look when my father asked for his surgical instruments, but it was mainly my mother who helped him with his patients. She had a natural calming influence. I did not: the last thing the sick and ailing need is a flustered teenager hovering around them. The young doctor not only had an unsteady hand, he was out for the count. Someone volunteered the information that he had started drinking as soon as they had reached Aachen. His patient was slumped next to him, a bloody grin plastered across his face. The others were slapping him on the back. He was now one of them: a real man. They lowered their eyes as I approached. A female was being admitted to the rites of the tribe. They might need me, but I was not part of the scheme of things.

'No need to be afraid,' von Bötticher said to the boy. 'Her father is a doctor.'

'I don't know if I can … ' I stammered. 'Where's the other doctor?'

He was too busy attending to the duellist from his own side. Von Bötticher pulled me roughly to my knees in front of the casualty. Still the boy refused to look at me. I found some cotton wool and alcohol in the doctor's bag and carefully dabbed his forehead.

'You are a hero, Hugo,' said von Bötticher. 'Well done.' He was sitting so close to me that the fur of his hat touched my face. The blood rose to my cheeks. The young man's face was sweet but dirty. Perhaps all the showers at his student lodgings had been occupied and he hadn't even had the chance to wash for his initiation. His forehead kept bleeding, a cut above his left eyebrow was gaping like a nestling's beak.

'You see, a woman's hand works wonders!'

It was the Otter, thank God. He crouched down and took hold of the wad of cotton wool I was pressing against the wound.

'Herr Paukant, you look so at ease lying there I feel sure you need no anaesthesia.'

The boy shook his head briefly and drops of blood fell from his thick hair: there was another wound. I hunted around in the bag for more cotton wool, but the Arbiter stopped me. He was chewing on something. It turned out to be indignation.

'Gentlemen, would you like to tell me what she is doing here? This contravenes the rules of the Comment.'

'Calm yourself,' muttered the Otter, threading the needle. 'The girl was not present at the Mensur itself.'

'She is assisting the doctor,' said von Bötticher to the little man. 'Her father is a doctor in Maastricht. She is a guest here at Raeren, come to work on her fencing tech-nique.'

'Don't you fence with potatoes in Holland?' asked a tall young man. 'I'm sure I heard that somewhere. They attach four potatoes to your body; one to your head, one to your belly, and one on either side, and you have to slice them down the middle in a single motion. Like William Tell, only with a sabre. Sounds like a jolly good wheeze to me.'

Everyone laughed, except for the injured duellist. He gazed up at the ceiling, impassive as an angel, as the shell of his ear filled with blood.

'Be sure not to sew him up too neatly, Herr Reich,' von Bötticher asked. 'Without a mark, the lad will have fought for nothing. Of course, you doctors do not understand such things. In your world everything has to heal, as if experience counts for nothing. As if life cannot be allowed to leave a trace. These days we even have doctors to wipe the psychological slate clean. You set about us like zealous housewives; inside and out, nothing escapes your fervour for scrubbing everything clean.'

The Otter looked over his shoulder in amusement while his hands kept on working. The duellist wiped the sweat from his upper lip. Before a decent moustache had grown there, the mark on his forehead would have faded from red to pink.

'Right then,' said the Otter at last, 'that should heal nicely. Herr von Bötticher, where's the music? We seldom have a lady present at the Mensur. I am in the mood for a dance.'

'No music,' said von Bötticher. 'And the girl has to help prepare the meal. This very minute.'

To my astonishment, a mouth-watering aroma had filled the kitchen. Leni's spells had conjured up two darkly mag-nificent meat loaves. She prodded the crust to see if they were ready to slice. Pie in the oven first, then the bacon could be added to the apple and potato mash, and—giddy-up—with a slap on the behind I was dispatched to the hall, bearing the terrine. As I walked in, the students crowded around the table.

'If I may be so bold?'

Behind me stood the tall young man who had made the quip about fencing with potatoes. He had an engaging face, one of the few in the room. Perhaps he only looked friendlier than the others because his skin healed well. Whether it was to his liking or not, his wound had closed to become a vague irregularity below his left cheekbone.

'After dinner, I would be delighted to fence against you,' he said. 'Not with a real weapon. Just a foil.'

He pointed at the two antique thrusting swords on the wall, their rusty blades still razor-sharp by the look of them.

'They are not foils but *Parisers*,' the Otter interrupted. 'Dangerous enough to get you killed. They may only leave a small scar, but they can puncture a lung with ease. Strictly forbidden these days, such weapons.'

'I don't mind telling you,' the student suddenly whispered in my ear, 'that what you have seen today is not how it's supposed to be. The Mensur has had the life squeezed out of it. We used to get through twenty matches on a day like this, but times have changed. If it wasn't for Herr Egon von Bötticher putting Raeren at our disposal, we would have no place to hold even these duels. A sorry state of affairs.'

We were summoned to the table. Von Bötticher at the head, the Otter at the other end. He insisted I sit next to him, gallantly pulling out my chair and intent on unfolding my napkin, till the tall student beat him to it.

'And then they insist that we usher in the rabble,' he

whispered. 'In the name of comradeship. Our fellow Germans. Between you and me, all that leaves me cold.'

'The rabble?' inquired the Otter.

'A jumped-up bunch of plebs.'

'As long as they are hardworking students, I see no harm in it.'

'You don't understand,' said the young student, his voice clouded with emotion. 'Distinctions have to be made.'

'The student corps has to move with the times.'

'Doctor Reich,' the young man shook his head as if trying hard to swallow something, 'that a man of your stature should leap to their defence ... honestly!'

The Otter emphatically tucked his napkin into his collar and examined the handle of his knife. No politics before dinner. The young man got the message. For minutes on end they stared at the door, until Leni wheeled in the trolley and began serving with gusto. There was no time for a speech. Von Bötticher raised a glass to this distinguished fraternity, still very much alive as long as its members were sitting at his table, whatever anyone said. To the Mensur! The students pounced on the food as if the smell was unleashing the emotions that had been reined in by the strict rules and the length of a sword. The tall student saw it too. 'Like animals in flight, tugging at a clump of grass before the wolf sinks its fangs into their heels,' he said. 'The plebs are hammering at the door, so eat, drink, and be merry.'

A strange atmosphere set in. A couple of students laughed loudly and incessantly, while others wiped away their tears on their cuffs and no one thought to ask what the matter was. Two fat young men started to quarrel and the table shook with the pounding of their fists, someone burst into song in a wailing falsetto and had a hand clapped to his open mouth. Von Bötticher oversaw the proceedings with a paternal smile. He had often witnessed this animalistic frenzy in the aftermath of a duel. He only had to raise a glass to restore quiet.

'Today you have shown how a man defends his honour and the fatherland. These days all anyone can talk about is tanks, but a true soldier does not encase himself in steel. He meets his enemy head-on. As the Kaiser said: it is up to the sword to decide. My young brothers, let us raise a toast. To the Kaiser. To honour, liberty, and the fatherland.'

Some brought their glasses to their lips in agreement but others, the Arbiter among them, began to mutter agitatedly under their breath. Von Bötticher shot them a questioning look.

'With your permission, I will not drink to the Kaiser,' said the Arbiter.

'That is your own concern,' said von Bötticher icily. 'I will not have my appetite ruined by men who lack a sense of history.'

'Doesn't he live in *your* homeland? The Kaiser?' the tall student asked, too loud for my liking. All eyes were on me, including von Bötticher's. He looked forbidding.

'That's right. In her homeland. The land of her father. A nation of cowards.'

It was an unexpected attack. What the hell was I still doing here? An uninvited guest, a hapless doctor's assistant, a girl who fences potatoes. I was about to get up, but the Otter placed his hand on my shoulder.

'No need to be upset. He means nothing by it,' he murmured. 'Tell me, your father, a doctor from Maastricht ... wasn't he the Dutchman who nursed Egon during the war? He came from Maastricht, unless I am mistaken. I've heard one or two things in passing, but never from the horse's mouth. As far as he's concerned it's a closed book.'

He looked at me expectantly, the inquisitive professor. If

he had remained a general practitioner, his curiosity would have cooled long ago. GPs are fed life stories on a daily basis, till they are fit to burst. Some write them down, others lose interest in experiences and immerse themselves in facts, like my father. I decided the Otter had every right to know. Von Bötticher would live to regret his attack. My ripostes were harsh.

'They knew each other in the war. I have a photograph.'

'A photograph of what?'

'I can show you. I've brought it with me. It's upstairs.'

A few minutes later I was standing in my room, an offended young woman clutching the weapon that would bring her satisfaction. My own dear father, still so young. Beside him, the hat with the skull and crossbones was unmistakable but the other man's face would always be lost in a blur. It would have to do. The moment for hesitation had passed. I rushed down the stairs in leaps and bounds, swinging around the pillars once again. Before I reached the fencing hall I slowed my pace and entered as the very model of restraint. The Otter had cleared his plate with endearing dedication, only a thin smear of gravy remained. I placed the photograph next to it.

'That's my father. And that's Herr von Bötticher.'

The Otter wiped his hands thoroughly before picking up the photograph. 'Ah! My word! January 1915. The man's a hussar and no mistake. But his face is out of focus. Herr von Bötticher! Is that you?'

My heart pounded in the back of my throat. The photograph was passed down the table from hand to hand. Von Bötticher had just put a forkful of food in his mouth when he laid eyes on the picture.

'Is it you, Herr von Bötticher? During the war?'

Everyone stopped eating, knives clinked on plates. The students on either side of von Bötticher peered over his shoulder. His hat, the only clear resemblance between him and the man in the photograph, had been laid aside for dinner. I watched his anger grow. His chewing slowed, like a machine grinding to a halt.

'That is not me.'

'But it is clearly a hussar,' the Otter persisted. 'And that other chap is the girl's father. It is dated 1915.'

'That,' von Bötticher repeated, 'is not me.'

# 9

Who was Egon von Bötticher? He was even less clear-cut in real life than in the photograph. By the age of eighteen, every girl knows that the real can never match the imaginary for sharpness of focus. Whoever came up with the notion that thoughts run free? They don't. They trot meekly along the path laid out for them while the imagination conveniently sweeps aside all the incidentals that make the real world so bewildering. It's a path on which you seldom encounter a stranger; most of the passers-by are people you have met already. They may look a little different—even figments of the imagination tend to age—but they remain comfortingly recognizable.

I knew all this, yet somehow I had hoped the riddle of the photograph would be easily solved. The picture wasn't even all that blurred. The photographer's hand had been steady, the brick wall in the background was plainly visible. My father was crystal-clear in all his earnestness, braving the long exposure time for the sake of an immortalization by which he set great store. It hadn't helped that he had thrown his arm around his companion's shoulder. The hussar had flinched. When a duellist in the Mensur pulls back his head to dodge the weapon, he is sentenced to as many duels as it takes to restore his honour. Under those circumstances, one scar is not enough. The hussar had been startled, had feared the clarity of the print as a novice fears the point of the sword. But why? Why was that moment to be avoided? Von Bötticher had already tossed the photograph away. My father had landed face-down in the middle of the table. My father the coward — that is what he had meant. The land of my father was a nation of cowards, the land from which I came. And here I was at the opposite end of the table siding with the Otter, another bandage merchant out to obliterate life's traces.

Both men lit a cigar. Between them sat two rows of students, saddled with a date from the distant past. January 1915. Some of them hadn't even been born then. They left as Leni and I were doing the washing-up. We looked out of the window and saw von Bötticher shaking the Otter by the hand, the duellists holding their bandaged heads at a cautious angle, like eggshell trophies. The Otter pulled the car door shut and the engines fired up simultaneously. *Carnevale*. Leni had the same thought. That was that, she said, the circus was moving on. But in the same moment, two headlights appeared at the gate. Heinz and the boys had returned early from the fair. Leni got herself into a flap, wailing that it had all gone horribly wrong. I was about to reassure her that the meal had been delicious, but what she meant was that the twins on the back seat would be gazing longingly at the Mensur caravan, which had come to a standstill, engines throbbing, until the exit was free. With the table linen still tucked under her arm, Leni ran to the front door and began to shout that Heinz was as dumb as an ox to come back so early. Heinz reversed his car to one side and the DKWs began to move. With any luck the sabreurs might not have realized what they had missed out on. Leni unfurled the tablecloth like a flag of truce and something fell to the ground. She saw it too. Let it lie there, I thought. Let them sort it out between them, those two men from 1915. But Leni managed to retrieve the photograph.

'It's the master with some fellow or other,' she said when she returned to the kitchen. She laid the photograph on the table and gave me an inquiring look.

'That fellow is my father,' I said as breezily as I could. 'I'm not sure about the other man. Von Bötticher says it's not him.'

'In that case, your father is a fine figure of a man. And von Bötticher can say what he likes but that's him all right. His build, his posture. No doubt about it, that's the master. A long time ago, of course.'

All at once my eyes filled up and, with my hands in the dishwater, there was nothing I could do to stop the tears. I did not indulge my own tears as many women do, I would rather have swallowed them. But for some reason I couldn't. Leni seized her chance and began to comfort me with a hand that felt like red-hot iron. Witch of a woman. Look into my eyes, she kept repeating, and those words were the only thing that kept me from fainting.

'You can't hide a thing from me,' she said. 'I understand. He has a way about him. But don't let yourself get carried away. For as long as you live, you'll be thankful I warned you.'

That night I dreamed of Helene Mayer. She was standing on the Olympic podium. I was sitting on the grandstand, my father on one side and von Bötticher on the other. Look, von Bötticher said, she's burning. We nodded as flames shot out of Mayer's laurel-crowned head. She's the Olympic torch, he said. No, my father answered, she's the Blessed Virgin. And he made a sign of the Cross, my father of all people! Mayer grew as the flames rose higher until she became a giant goddess who merely had to bow to reach into the crowd and touch me with a hand of red-hot iron.

It was still dark when I woke. The curtain was flapping in

the open window as if the house were sailing away at high tide. Anyone who has always fallen asleep to the regular pulse of the city is bound to be jolted awake by the noises of a night in the country. When people fade into the background, all other sounds are amplified: gusts of wind, raindrops, a branch brushing against the shutters. I got up to close the window. As if things weren't melancholy enough, an owl hooted close by. I looked down at my hand on the windowsill; in the moonlight it could have been the hand of a dead girl. Everything was different, belonged to someone else. It would be better to say goodbye to Raeren, to leave behind its murky feelings and apparitions—if only they *had* been ghosts, at least then they would have disappeared when you turned on the light. I would take the train back to my old self, to the girl who hadn't yet fallen in love. Since my father had waved me off, everything had changed, my father included. All at once he had become a coward. I had to go back. As far as I was concerned, even Louis's fencing class was better than the hall downstairs, where blood still stained the piste.

Morning offers wiser counsel than the night, or so my father liked to say. Taking decisions in the dark was certainly foolish, but I was afraid of going back to sleep. Even my dreams had become strangers to me. Don't let yourself get carried away, Leni had said. I slipped back into bed but continued to peer into the darkness until a pair of birds began twittering. When their chatter ended an hour later, it was time for the morning training session.

In the fencing hall, the twins were standing opposite the maître, one as angry as the other. The maître was taking it all in his stride. It was only when Siegbert took one of the antique *Parisers* down off the wall that he intervened.

'Put that back. It's very sharp.'

'Well, if it isn't the little witch herself,' Friedrich called.

'Tell me, Janna, was it a splendid party last night?'

The maître slipped me a conspiratorial wink. I needn't worry about anything the boys had to say. He seemed full of life, as if his rancour had left Raeren along with the Mensur, though I couldn't imagine he had forgiven me for the scene with the photograph. He had no desire to heal old wounds, he had said so himself. More than once I had seen him run his fingers over the reminder on his own cheek, as if to make sure it was still there. He would continue to cling to his ill will, like a dog tears at its own skin. That was not something I could change. I only wanted to know what wrong my father had done him. I shared in my father's blame. It was etched on von Bötticher's face, a fact no wink could alter.

'Janna was helping Leni. She did not see the Mensur,' he said. 'Your time will come. For now I have other plans. If you would both listen for a moment ... '

With some difficulty he managed to return the *Pariser* to its old place between the nails on the wall. He took a coin from his pocket and tried to scrape off some of the rust. The twins stood waiting, their anger tempered by curiosity, but the maître went on scraping and only mumbled something about sandpaper.

'Right,' he said at last, 'this is the plan. The two of you will become the best team I have ever taught. You will train with the girl. No shame in that, she is not without merit. Your strength will come from your resemblance. Imagine ... '

He picked up a foil and stood in front of the mirror, poised to attack. As I had expected, his stance was perfect. All of the power in his tensed body was channelled into his elegant left hand, held effortlessly in mid-air as if his right held no weapon at all. Between the tip of his foil and the mirror there was no more than a breath, just enough to suggest that his reflection was an opponent of flesh and blood. A fraction closer and the illusion would have been shattered.

'Two identical sabreurs, but trained differently. Your opponent becomes rattled: which one is he facing? He tries to respond exactly as he responded to your likeness, but the two of you fence differently every time. This unsettles him. Is this the sabreur who repeatedly braves his attacks, parrying nimbly, or is it the other, the one who always seems to be on the retreat ... '—without altering his stance he backed off at lightning speed—' ... only to lunge forward and make good his position? Racked by doubt, he concedes a hit.'

It struck me as an absurd plan. Didn't all fencers look pretty much alike when they were suited and masked? Besides, the names were announced before every match and opponents on both sides were changed at the same time. Nevertheless the twins were delighted.

'Like Zorro!' Friedrich cried. 'No one knows Zorro's true identity either!'

Von Bötticher frowned. He had no idea what the boy was talking about.

'What? You haven't heard of *The Mark of Zorro*? It's a film. Zorro always wears a mask and leaves behind a sign with his sword: Z for Zorro.'

'You're not telling it right,' Siegbert piped up, but von Bötticher tossed him the foil, which he caught with disdain.

'Yes, we are starting with the foil,' said von Bötticher. 'Show us what it is to be one man in two bodies. Janna, take up your weapon. This promises to be quite an experience.'

We saluted one another and took up our positions. I noticed that my opponent was restless. By the time we had donned our masks, I had forgotten whether it was Siegbert or Friedrich. The other twin was standing behind me, a turn of the head would have been enough to tell me who was who, but I wasn't about to let them think I was the least bit worried. Von Bötticher's whole resemblance theory was about to be exposed for the nonsense it was. The first hit would not be long in coming. Handed to me on a plate. My opponent was unable to hold his weapon still. He squeezed and shook the handle as if he were wielding a cutlass. The maître corrected his grip and whispered in his ear—had the boy never fenced with a foil? This was going to be fun. I could open with a direct attack. No nonsense: get in first and go straight for the target. Too much expectant footwork can sometimes leave you paralysed. If he parried, it would be crude and I could sail in under his weapon. The low thrust was one of my strengths. Throw in the odd Helene-Mayer-style extended attack and he wouldn't have a leg to stand on. The maître was still whispering instructions. Brusquely, I pulled off my mask.

'Maître, we have already saluted. I await your permission.'

'Patience,' said the maître. 'This is an exercise, not a match. We change when one of you scores five hits. Ready? Fence!'

It worked. The dolt parried my direct attack too late: 1–0. I strolled casually back to my place. The maître betrayed no emotion, merely giving the sign for us to continue. This time my opponent danced up and down the piste, the typical footwork of a nervous young sabreur, much ado about nothing: 2–0 with a thrust under his weapon.

'Come on, Fritz!' a voice behind me shouted. So it was Fritz. Well, Fritz my boy, take that: 3–0, an immaculate advance-lunge. I scored my fourth with a thrust after an envelopment: our weapons interlocked, I parried and hit.

Fritz began to dance again, like a boxer on the balls of his feet. This was getting on my nerves. I thought I was fencing beautifully, far better than he was, a fact the maître was choosing to ignore. I took a hit to the breastbone. The pain jolted every joint in my body. No apology from Fritz, who kept on dancing though the call to fence had not yet been given. In his haste to switch the twins and implement that idiotic plan of his, the maître said nothing.

'Fence!'

A stab to my upper leg: no score. And still he danced. The blood pulsed in my temples. I had to regain my composure, expel my anger along with my breath, or see my advantage evaporate. It had happened to me often enough: defeat by indignation.

'Fence!'

Parry, riposte to his midriff: 5–1. I crouched down to massage my collarbone while Friedrich handed his weapon to Siegbert. The maître began whispering again. From his gestures I surmised that he was advising the boy to keep his thrusts low. He pointed at my torso with his outstretched hand. As if making a sign of the Cross, he halved then quartered me. Just like the pale hand with the butcher's knife in his cookery book: this is how we separate shoulder from foreleg. Of course, his foil could do no such thing, and there were no points to be had from touching my limbs. Did the maître only see me as a target area or could he tell that under my jacket my breasts were unprotected and bathed in sweat? Siegbert was a better fencer than his brother. I chased away the thought that I might be better off falling in love with him, but too late: 5–2. Ready? Apparently not. Von Bötticher had yet more whispering to do. Once again his hand extended toward my body. I stretched and my skin pulled tight over my breastbone, where a sizeable bruise was forming.

'Fence!'

I can only attempt to describe what happened next. I was barely conscious throughout. I saw my weapon cross his, but as a spectator, in the mirror. I had no part in it. I heard the repeated clash of metal striking metal, muffled by the blood singing in my ears. The girl I was watching stopped attacking. Her opponent fenced well, and she resigned herself to his hits. Hard between the ribs. Tidy work. No needless pitter-patter up and down the piste. She stumbled backward, was she tired? A glancing blow to her arm, no score. Fence! The girl kept her distance, good, but now she was almost at the rear limit. Another hit, one she could easily have parried. Resume positions. Ready, fence! Again? What was the point? She was no longer in it. 5–5. Of course. What else could you expect? There was nothing more for me to see. A red haze appeared before my eyes.

When I opened them again, I saw the braided wire I had been staring up at all week. It straggled across the chalky ceiling of my bedroom and disappeared behind a seam of wallpaper, sprouting into a wall lamp whose oval wooden fitting made it look like a photo frame. In the seconds between waking and realization, the simple decoration etched into the milky glass revealed a different image every time. Now it was a little girl in a straw hat, holding a hand that reached down to her shoulder. The Prussian woman from Herzogenrath who had found me in her back garden knew who I belonged to. She had offered me her hand and taken me across the street into the Netherlands. My aunt had been beside herself with worry. I can still see her hunched and desperate, tears streaming down her cheeks, a neighbour tugging at either arm as she wailed, 'Oh where's ma little mite! This'll be the death of me!'

All I had to do was rein in my thoughts to make the little girl in the straw hat disappear. There were more pressing matters to consider: someone had laid me here on my bed. I sat up to peel off my fencing gear. Burning pain, as if my chest were being gouged by a sharp fingernail. No mark yet, though my thigh was blotched red where the blood had already begun to collect. Whoever it was had filled the basin with water. The steam disappeared as I carried it into the sunlight over by the balcony. The temperature was just right. The pigeons had returned from goodness knows where; judging by the skittering up in the attic, they had plenty to tell one another. Only one was sitting on the balcony, peering out from the vivid depths of an eye designed to brave mile after mile of lashing wind and glaring sun. I soaped my thighs and asked him where he had been. He did not fly away when, dripping with suds, I bent back the wire screen and stepped onto the balcony. His feathers brushed my ankle. I saw the maître leaving the estate. Even from this distance the awkward fury in his gait was plain to see. He passed through the gate and turned left. I stepped forward to see where he was heading, but as I cooled my tired body against the stone balustrade, he disappeared from view. Without stopping to dry myself I pulled on my dress, stuffed my feet into my shoes and set off after him. A direct attack, I still had that in me. What did he want from me? Was he ever going to teach me or was I merely a pincushion for the twins? Was he the one who had carried me upstairs after my fainting fit?

Outside I started running. Shamelessly, with no thought for saving my strength, the way children run. I used to try to imitate the long, loping strides of a gazelle, opening and closing my fists, pulling myself up through the air. But coming to the edge of the woods where von Bötticher had vanished, I had to slow down. From the road there was only one way in, a soft, undulating path scattered with mouldering pine needles. I was not fond of the woods.

Back at home, woodland walks were never undertaken for the sake of enjoyment, but to tamp down family quarrels. My father would take the lead, Mother would dawdle and I would follow in silence, as if sneaking through a house where I was not welcome. Now, too, the woods seemed inhospitable. Mould and rot beneath my feet, while the trees towering above me creaked unnervingly and plagued me with falling twigs. The branches were so densely knit that the sun only broke through sporadically, like a search-light. The songbirds of Raeren were nowhere to be heard, only the blighted rattle of a woodpecker. This was not nature in all its glory but a tumbledown ruin; even the path petered out. My only choice was to retrace my steps or plough on downhill through the trees. No one had passed this way in a long while. With every rustling step I sank into piles of dried leaves, grinding them to dust. The smell they gave off was more aromatic than unpleasant. Eventually I reached a hollow path, a dark gully where water might once have flowed and where trees now forced their roots through the black soil. Up ahead the path rose steeply to a thicket, while the woods behind me had changed beyond recognition. I was lost. I decided to follow the upward path but the bedding grew deeper and I felt like I was sinking even though I was climbing. I could not run. The tree roots were slick and I had to balance like a tight-rope walker. A twig bored into my foot, a side shoot from a branch that snaked low over the ground. I carefully pulled myself free, snapping off the twig. All I had to do was plant it in the soil and it would continue to grow. Trees carry their duplicates within them, populating entire forests with endless copies of themselves. Even the smallest twig is a miniature of the tree from which it grows. Another reason why a loner like me had no business being here. As I clambered on, the blood on my foot clotted. Soil clung to it—the wound would have to be disinfected. The banks on either side of me began to fall away. And then I saw him, sitting on a toppled tree, his back to me. As he sat there, upright yet relaxed, braces strapped over his shoulders and a linen shirt stretched across his broad back, he seemed far less out of place than I. He even caught a little sunlight. If nothing else happened, if I never declared my love for him, I would still belong with him. The branch is still part of the tree, though the tree wants no part of the branch. I wanted to speak, but he turned and saw me there and I was silent.

## 10

He pointed to a footpath behind him. Neatly laid out, easily passable, perfect for those less inclined to claw their way through the woods on their hands and knees. With all the dignity I could muster, I tried to clamber out of my gully, but he insisted on pulling me out.

'You're feeling better, I see,' he said. 'I don't understand what got into you. You weren't fencing badly to start with ... '

'I don't believe in your theory,' I interrupted him. 'About identical fencers. I don't think it will work.'

'And yet you lost. You know why?'

I had no desire to find out. My body was glowing with pain and fatigue, and the blood on my foot had congealed under a muddy crust.

'Because you rose above it,' said von Bötticher. 'Never stop taking part. When a fencer becomes a spectator, he loses the appetite for victory. And then he is lost.'

'The twins aren't identical,' I said stubbornly. 'One fences better than the other. Besides, the names are called at matches. So you always know who you're up against.'

One crow swooped to attack another in mid-air. Flapping awkwardly, they kept themselves airborne. Few things are as vulnerable as the body of a bird, yet they appeared to have no sense of their own fragility. A wing is easily broken ... and then? The long wait for death. A wounded bird stops eating, not out of self-pity but because it has ceased to function. In death, animals do not look back at life. Von Bötticher seemed to feel at home in the forest, where death was not swept out of sight but lay there on the ground for others to feed on.

'Have you seen the twins fence each other?' he asked. 'It's fascinating to watch. They are evenly matched because they each know exactly what the other will do. Don't we all want to be a twin? To have the certainty of someone to share this life with? Knowing there is at least one person on this earth who will never betray you, simply because you are evenly matched?'

A barrage of questions went off in my head. Some I had already formulated for myself, simple inquiries, a few words at most. But standing there eye to eye with him—he dressed for the occasion and at one with himself, and I a filthy and bewildered swamp creature—I realized all my questions seemed ridiculous. Except one. I asked him if he knew Helene Mayer. His whole body froze and I sensed a narrowing of the eyes, the kind of change you might see in the evening sky before a thunderstorm.

'*Die blonde Hee*. Yes, I know her. Why do you ask? In fact, I knew her father very well indeed. Dr Ludwig Mayer, a physician in Offenbach. He was a fencer himself. Not a good one, of course. Doctors seldom make good fencers. They do not see the point in scoring a hit.'

'But they father good fencers,' I ventured.

His eyes narrowed to slits. 'Didn't Jacques object when you took up fencing?'

My father's name, coming from his mouth for the first time. So, once they had been on first-name terms, names that still meant something to both of them. Now was the time to follow through with my questions. But von Bötticher ignored my gaze. With the point of his shoe, he flipped the cap off a mushroom that, on closer inspection, turned out to be inedible. The tenderness with which he tried to place the cap back on the stem threw me off balance.

'Yes, my father was against it,' I mumbled. 'But I managed to persuade him that fencing is harmless.'

'Harmless? Why should everything be harmless? Even harm has its purpose. This mushroom has been harmed, but at least now its spores have been spread. Helene enjoyed inflicting harm on an opponent during a fencing match. She always shouted "Yes!" before she attacked. She knew announcing her intentions wasn't smart but she claimed she simply couldn't help it.'

'Did you train her?'

'No, she trained with Gazzera, the Italian. I was *Consenior* for the university in Frankfurt at the time. Her father used to help me patch up the duellists now and then. A fine physician and a gentle, humorous man. Fortunately he died in time.'

He waved a dismissive hand when he saw my puzzled expression.

'I mean that he did not have to endure the idiotic times in which we are living. Two years after his death, the fencing club expelled his daughter. Imagine! The German champion stripped of her honorary membership.'

'Why?'

'Ludwig was a Jew. Helene is the daughter of a Jewish father and a German mother. A *Mischling*, a "half-breed". So there you have it. The International Olympic Committee insisted that Hitler have at least one Jew represent Germany in 1936, so Helene had to put in an appearance. The other two medallists were also Jewish, by the way: the Hungarian who won and the Austrian who took bronze. But Hitler would rather damn the entire sport of fencing than admit he was wrong. They will find out soon enough that National Socialism is a pointless experiment, that it's insane to defy differences for the sake of uniformity and symmetry.'

He paced in circles, looking for something to his liking. Eventually his eyes lit upon an acorn. He held it between thumb and forefinger, before burying it in the ground a few metres from the mother oak.

'Oddly enough, their drive toward sameness would have pleased old Mayer. He believed everyone could achieve sporting success if you applied the right dose of training to the body. Like adding a chemical to a test tube.'

The laugh that burst from him sounded forced, as if, feeling buoyed by the company of trees and animals, he would still like them all to agree with him.

'Isn't every living creature incomparable? The little tree that grows from this acorn will differ from the common oak over there. The only word I have to describe how and why is "passion". The passion to grow and to die if need be. Only death makes us feel alive.'

He gave a satisfied nod as he savoured his last words. I wondered if he really thought that acorn would germinate. According to my father, only one in a hundred ever became a tree. I told von Bötticher about the miniature oak given to the Hungarian fencer, the souvenir Helene Mayer had wanted so badly but only gold medallists got to take home with them. Even if home was a house on the other side of the ocean and belonged to Jesse Owens. It was hard to imagine a better souvenir. Not a curiosity on the mantelpiece but a living thing that becomes one with the land, a precious memory that does not gather dust but takes root in a ripening consciousness.

'Oak simply means tree in Old German,' said von Bötticher. 'If you want to know where a people come from, look at their names for trees. Familiar trees have simple names as fundamental to the language as yes and no. Names that tell you these are the trees we grew up with. Yet the horse chestnut thrives here too. In the heart of Europe, we have lived for centuries among all kinds of woodland giants, a coherence that goes beyond the identical. Unlike Russia, where unyielding forests of conifers tolerate a stray birch at most. Have you ever seen the oldest oak in Germany? The Raveneik. It stands not far from the Dutch border. A trunk so broad and hollow that, during one manoeuvre, Friedrich Wilhelm IV hid thirty-six infantrymen in there. Complete with all their gear.'

We dawdled back along the footpath together, warming ourselves in scattered patches of afternoon sun. The tension building between us was almost audible. Perhaps there were insects able to pick up the vibrations in the air that separated our hands. We did not touch. I held my breath, scared to look up, as if I were carrying a bowl that was full to the brim.

'I only ever come here with Megaira,' he said at last, clearing his throat. 'Look, these are her hoofprints. No other riders take this path. Very few people come here at all. I seldom see another soul.'

'It sounds very lonely.'

'In nature, a man is never lonely,' he said harshly. 'Out here so many animals live solitary lives. Trees stand alone, streams lead nowhere. On it goes, day after day, and no one thinks it tragic. It's only in the city that a man is compelled to meet others or be branded lonely.'

We did not say another word. I looked down bashfully at my trudging feet, searching for something to say, something to bring us closer together again, but nothing presented itself. Until we came to a cornfield. I had never seen such a sight. In those days we did not grow corn in Holland.

It was green maize most likely, animal fodder, yet the top-heavy corn cobs looked like precious objects balanced on top of their stalks, each one wrapped in its own sheath of leaves. I chose a sizeable specimen and peeled it. I stripped away the fibrous net until it was a knot along the shaft. In all its gleaming, upright glory I presented it to von Bötticher. Did he realize at that moment that I, an eighteen-year-old girl, honestly had no idea what I was doing? He took the thing from me looking mildly embarrassed. He was still holding it as we approached the gates of Raeren.

'Sir?'

He turned around.

'What exactly did my father, Jacques … Did Jacques hurt you?'

He stared down at the corn cob. Most of nature's trophies lose their value once you bring them home. They keep company with the shells that looked so much prettier on the beach you took them from, a nod to your own gullibility in believing you could ever take such beauty with you. He tossed the cob over his shoulder.

'Hurt me? Pain is something your father wants no part of,' he said as he strode off. 'He only works with anaesthetic. He creeps up on his patients while they sleep, and if they are not asleep, he will soon see to it. And once they have been knocked out, the great disappearing trick can begin. Suffering healed, atonement smoothed over, honour hemmed in. All that remains is a neat line of stitching, intended to fade with memory. Only memories cannot be stitched up. They surface of their own accord.'

'Then why am I even here?' I screamed after him. 'Why did you let me come?'

I did not receive an answer. Two masked idiots came storming out of the house, sabres flashing, blaring gibberish that was supposed to pass for French. Von Bötticher stood there as if nailed to the ground. He was not used to people getting in his way. Leni stood in the doorway, shaking her head. She had been unable to stop the twins from raiding the dressing-up box. Costumes had been scattered from one end of the hall to the other, she complained, and it had taken her a good half-hour to fold and tidy them away. Perhaps it would be better to lock up part of the house from now on. Nothing was safe with those two brats around.

'The costumes were made to be played with,' von Bötticher mumbled. 'After all, the days of masked balls at Raeren are long gone. I need a drink, Leni. A glass of brandy.'

Friedrich was the first to raise his mask. He tugged at the tassels of his dressing gown, which he had donned for want of a cape. It suited him. The richly embroidered fabric came from a time when young men were still proud of a gilded complexion like his. The pupils of his ice-blue eyes had shrunk to pinheads, yet he made no attempt to shield them from the sun. He was, I realized once again, disturbingly beautiful. Since Siegbert only made the same impression when he was silent, they would inevitably grow apart where beauty was concerned. As the years passed, Siegbert's harsh expressions would leave their mark on his face, while Friedrich remained as they had both once been. They would no longer be equals, yet by force of habit one would continue to see the other as his mirror image, and so they would remain oblivious to the difference.

'You hit the deck and the maître picked you up like a feather,' said Siegbert. 'Your whole body went completely limp, you still had your mask on. By rights, I should have been the one to carry you off. I beat you after all.'

'What do you think of our costumes?' Friedrich asked. 'There were girls' clothes in the chest, too. Take a look, it's at the end of the hall, opposite the maître's room.'

Truth be told, I had no desire to stoop to their childish games. In Siegbert's eyes especially I was determined to keep my dignity. Carry me off, indeed! Who did he think he was?

'Aw, come on, Janna. Don't be a spoilsport. One for all! All for one!'

Curiosity won out and I relented. I had never entered that part of the house. It had never occurred to me to pass through the door to the quarters where our host hid himself away with two dogs and a rabbit, yet it wasn't even locked. It opened to reveal a sunny hallway, with large windows that were seldom cleaned. The parquet was cracked, but a pleasant smell hung in the air, as in a museum where dust piles up among bone-dry artefacts too fragile to be cleaned. The maître was sitting in the garden with his back to the house, brandy glass in hand. I recalled what he had said about only being lonely in the eyes of others. My eyes were on him but he was oblivious to my presence, and it was up to me to decide whether he was lonely as he sat there nursing his empty glass. The dressing-up chest reeked of roses. Someone had put chunks of soap in among the clothes and the smell was there for good. Under the doublets and hose of the musketeer outfits I discovered a red taffeta gown, clearly too big for me, a hideous hat with a veil and lastly a white crinoline, collapsed like a lampshade. There was a matching corset. I crouched down behind the open lid and unbuttoned my dress. Lonely or not, the maître was still sitting with his back to me, while behind me was the door to his room. Forbidden territory. Or was it? I could hardly get undressed here in the hall, where the twins might storm in at any moment. Besides, von Bötticher had not been bothered by them nosing around among his things, nor had he protested when Friedrich sent me off to look for the chest.

Memories surface of their own accord. And now they lay in wait behind that door. Easing down the handle, I felt as if something was letting me in.

His room turned out to be no bigger than mine, but it was furnished with touching dedication. Many of the curios on display were animal-related: a stuffed squirrel in top hat and tails, smoking a pipe; an aquarium clock with two fish to tell the time; a wooden pelican with a globe in its beak. Under the window, a high three-quarter bed stood at an angle, on it a single pillow and an expensive bedspread that struck me as too flamboyant for a man's bed. I draped my dress over a chair and took a look around. On the wall was a painting of a horse's head in three-quarter view, with the mood of an official portrait. The books on the shelves were stacked one on top of the other. Next to the desk stood a small copper stove with a little kettle, but the cup and saucer on the desk had not been used. I sat down on the cool leather seat to thread the laces into the corset. The material encased my body gently, starting just under my breasts. Only a lace frill covered my nipples—simply leaning forward would be enough to cause a scandal. I would have to be reined in tight. Could I ask Leni to lace me up? And then walk into the garden as if I had stepped out of a Delacroix painting? But the girl in the mirror looked more like a gypsy, her skin dark against the immaculate cotton. Her feet were those of a tramp. As I turned around, I knocked a framed photograph from the chest of drawers. A respectable young man, dead most likely. An unremarkable snapshot of someone who had not lived long enough to merit a decent portrait. This was the immortalization his loved ones would have to make do with. There had been no time to fill albums with moments when he might well have shown emotion. There was only this empty gaze, a likeness to shed tears over. The back of the photograph proved me right. *Thomas, † 1916.*

I slid open the top drawer. Clutter. Folded newspapers, pencil shavings, a small shaving mirror. An album full of group photographs from the Mensur. *Frankfurt, 1922, 1923. Bonn, 1924, 1925.* Mustachioed duellists, all sporting caps and striking the same courageous pose. Blood brothers. To open the bottom drawer, I had to press its contents down with my finger. I was in a hurry. Just as an animal can never rest till it has marked out its own turf, any sensible person on foreign ground is aware he might be discovered at any moment. A box containing a military decoration— of no interest. A frayed piece of card, scribbled full of Latin. A photograph of four gents playing chess al fresco— no date. A green envelope with Poste Restante on the front ... And an envelope I recognized, bearing a doctor's scrawl. Formally addressed, though they had been on first-name terms. I forgot to breathe as I pulled the yellowed document from the envelope, the page von Bötticher had slammed between the pages of a cookery book before I could lay eyes on it. It was an engraving, eighteenth-century, perhaps even older. Geometrical. A man drawn within the circumference of a large circle, half his body dissected to the bone. A smaller circle next to it showed an illustration of his skeleton in profile, with footprints drawn along intersecting lines. There were Latin terms that I was unable to decipher. The geometrical drawings were framed by scenes of smaller figures in the most unnatural fencing poses. Disappointed, I folded open the accompanying letter. Legible by my father's standards, he had done his best to get his message across.

Could it be true that the ground where war has raged can only bring forth conflict? Janna was conceived at the site of the battle, an admission that leaves me somewhat shamefaced. Was this an act of desecration on my part? If so, it was not my intention. By then peace had returned to the land. The wounds had healed, the scars were gone, the grass had grown back thick and lush. The weather was mild and the air smelled fresh. The scent of life carrying on regardless.

What was this? I felt my heart pounding beneath my breastbone. Even with a younger version of my father in mind—a fine figure of a man, Leni had said—this was not a scene I had any desire to dwell on. Not like that, not there, and certainly not with my mother. My eyes raced through the rest of the letter.

I sat in a deserted library in Amsterdam, turning pages with gloved hands, taking notes. It is a remarkable book. This is the science of swordsmanship. [...] It is simply the science of not conceding a hit—probably far from simple, but a subject that can nonetheless be studied. Do so, Egon. Protect yourself, your country, the whole world for that matter, protect them from even more misery. The peace is no older than my daughter, no older than you were when you decided to enlist as a soldier. I hope, no, I believe beyond all doubt that ...

A door slammed—the front door probably. I rifled hastily through the contents of the drawer. At the bottom lay a whole packet of letters from my father addressed to von Bötticher. Rough edges revealed that the envelopes had been ripped open. These letters had angered him, but he had kept them nonetheless.

I hope, no, I believe beyond all doubt that Janna will remind you of what you were like before you took to wearing the skull and crossbones, before you elevated wounding others to a way of life. You do not have to wound

in order not to be wounded. Maître Girard Thibault knew
that as far back as 1630.

I did not need to read on. The know-it-all tone of these sentences set my teeth on edge. Had I been dispatched to Raeren to prove a point? Was my father using me to show that he was right yet again, the kind of dogmatism that could only be endured in silence, by clinging fervently to a deity as my mother did? My time was up, but I resolved to come back later and work out who was right. Before I left, I took a quick look inside the Poste Restante envelope. It contained five smaller envelopes, all addressed to my father. Sealed but never sent, written with a flourish. There was a postage stamp on the last envelope but no postmark, a picture of a woman with a lion at her feet and the words *Kingdom of the Netherlands, Internment Camps.* I tucked the letter into the hem of my crinoline and closed the drawer. Now I had to be careful not to faint again. I could feel it coming on. It was a pleasant sensation when my field of vision filled with red, a curtain pulled across a sunlit window. To stay on my feet I had to stay calm, breathe through my nose and fix my eyes on a spot in the garden till the rushing in my ears subsided and first sounds, then images broke through again. But I could not breathe. Strong hands pulled my corset tight. In a red haze I saw them push my breasts up out of the soft fabric. I was about to go under but he planted intense, commanding kisses on my neck, on my shoulders, till a feverish tide threw me ashore. It was exactly as I had always imagined it would be. Exactly.

# Part Two

Dear Jacques,

My patience is wearing thin.

A year has passed since I was wounded. When I look at my
ravaged face in the mirror I feel no regret and the burning
that gnaws at my leg leaves me all but unmoved. The real
pain runs deeper. You stitched up my skin as best you could,
but to disinfect this wound more rigorous cuts were needed.
Every day, humiliation clenches to a fist and strikes blow
after blow below the belt. I am not her only victim, this
cursed place is full of them. Young men torn from the front
when the war had barely begun. All hope of an honourable
life is lost to them, unless someone is quick to put an end to
this wastefulness. There are deserters here too, but they
chose this fate. Sharing my days with them behind the same
barbed wire is torture, even if they are housed in separate
barracks. If I could wrap my hands around one of their
throats, I swear I would never let go. I would squeeze till I
saw his life trickle away, till the terror in his eyes gave way to
resignation and the understanding that this is the gaze with
which he will be buried. You doctors close the eyelids of the
dead before rigor mortis sets in. But what lies beneath? The
look in our eyes as we greet death differs from one man to
another.

Last week a number of deserters took a beating. I was not
involved, I was out working the land. They bumped into our
boys on their way back from the prick parade, a matter on

which I have a thing or two to say. Your colleagues are pigs. Other than the officers, it is unlikely that any of us have had relations with a woman, yet every week we are forced to line up with our trousers around our knees. This month, the physician delegated this duty to an elderly assistant, a grey, sickly man who disgusts us all, crouching watery-eyed in front of our private parts. It is almost as much of a humiliation as being stripped of our weapons. But I digress; a fight broke out between our men and the deserters. There were no fatalities, but the Dutch were barely able to control the situation. What a placid people you are! You treat us as if we were on a school trip. The only Dutchman for whom I have any respect is the sentry, a man who served in the Dutch East Indies. We smoke the occasional cigarette together out by the gate. His job is to keep away any curious locals. The war is little more than a circus to those gawping villagers, and we the animals housed in a hastily knocked-together habitat. Our keepers have compiled a library of German books for us and organize excursions to the beach. What larks!

This week's supervisory duties are being carried out by my chum, a corporal from the 9th field artillery regiment. It is an assignment we both loathe. The southerners in particular are unwilling to accept our authority. They are so coarse and vulgar, I do not consider them capable of a decent duel. They kill time playing football and korfball. Unfortunately we are not permitted to fence. One of the officers, a well-known sabreur who knew my father in Schwerin and holds him in high esteem, likes to invite me into the officers' barracks. When I see the portrait of the Kaiser hanging there above the mantle, I lower my eyes. If he knew what an empty and idle life his officers lead here while his soldiers are dying at the front, I believe he would have them gunned down on the spot. They are out on the town almost every evening and bring women back to barracks with them. I am certain General von der

Marwitz would never debase himself in such a way. I wonder how he is faring in his campaign against the Russians?

Speaking of women, did you notice the postage stamp on the envelope? We are allowed to send two letters a month and for this purpose we have been issued with internment stamps. A brand to make the humiliation complete when we write to our sweethearts back home. The woman on the stamp is supposed to represent the Dutch Maiden, a symbol of the Batavian Republic. The Netherlands appears to be proud of protecting its maidenhood in this war. But why then is she holding a spear? I have my doubts as to whether I should use this stamp when I write to Julia. I have spared her the details of my detention, as I do not want her to think less of me. She will wait for me, of that I am sure, but she does not need to know of the injustice that keeps me here.

Today, as I lay down in the field to rest, a wasp buzzed by just above my face, followed by a bluebottle, and then from another direction a bumblebee droned over on its heavy engine. I fancied that they had deliberately chosen a route through my airspace. I wish there were more animals here. In foreign parts, where people repel you with their peculiar ways, an animal can often be a beacon. Your landlord might be a toothless, unwashed idiot, a filthy piece of work, yet his dog is still just a dog, sensible and reasonable. As we advanced into Belgium we came across a rough-haired sheepdog standing guard outside a village with such dignity that I pulled my horse up short and almost doffed my hat to him. What a contrast to the boorish people we found there, who set about scratching themselves as soon as you spoke a word to them!

I find communicating with people an increasingly onerous task. Even when a conversation seems to be at its most recip-rocal, one disengages from the other to assess the exchange from a distance and to draw his own furtive conclusions.

You can find them everywhere, Jacques, people who, as you refill their glass and have so much more to share, suddenly look at their watch and tell you they have to go. Busy hatching other plans as they look you in the eye.

I do not believe you, Jacques, and this tale you want me to swallow. I do not believe I was conscious when you carted me off to the hospital. Why do I remember nothing of that journey? All I remember is waking up in hospital and you continuing to observe me in spite of everything. Why couldn't you have simply let me go? For fear of reprimand? In your letter you write that you stand by your decision yet here I am, surrounded by prisoners of war and deserters, for God's sake! You sat there taking notes, gawping at me like the villagers here. You write that if you witnessed a murder you would always try to prevent it. You insist that you have protected me from bloodshed by removing me from the conflict. But what about the blood of my brothers? They are dropping like flies day after day and I have been unable to help them, while the front is already out of reach of your ambulances.

In the fields of Belgium I lost my honour, my duty, and my horse. Since honour and duty mean nothing to you, I ask you once again: find my horse. You already have a description. She is my only hope of recovery.

I am waiting,
Egon

# 1

I took the envelope from the windowsill. The flap curled where it had been steamed open. To reseal it without any telltale signs, I would have to handle it with care. Not yet though; perhaps I would feel like reading the letter again in the morning. I turned off the oil heater. This night was colder than the last but a moon the colour of melted butter hung low in the sky. I pressed my hand to my mons pubis. Time and again the same pulsing sensation surged upward, only stopping when I crossed my legs. I felt no pain; it was his heat that had shocked me. Gripping the laces of my corset in one hand, he had held me still, tugging down my skirt with the other. At first I was only aware of his groin pressing against me and then, almost casually, his erection. I had never expected it to be so hard. I was too surprised to feel pain, surprised at how he was able to feel his way into me. He pulled my hips toward him as if easing into a saddle. My surprise continued as I thought of Loubna, the desert mare who also obeyed this man yet moved him to tenderness, too. I wanted to turn and kiss him, the way I thought things should be. He thought otherwise and held me down with his right arm. His strong arm, his fencing arm. As he pushed deeper inside me, I saw his fist open and carefully cup my breast.

He did not want me to move him to tenderness. It struck me again as we lay side by side on the bed. He searched irritably for a cigarette, matches, exhaled smoke, avoided my gaze. For a moment he laid a hand on my stomach, but then raised it to his lips again to continue smoking. I gawped at him. His right thigh was covered in scar tissue. He was muscular, but chunks had been sliced out of his shoulder. The thought that I had held this big, wounded man inside me made me feel euphoric. I had felt the force within him when he lost his self-control. He fell asleep without warning. Sleep makes contented children of most of us, but he looked deeply unhappy.

It was dark by the time I left his room. As I picked up the skirt from the floor, I made sure the letter was still tucked in the hem. Outside, the linen was still on the table but the other occupants of the house had made themselves scarce. I felt sure they had discussed me in detail, no cliché left unturned: I had become the sheath for von Bötticher's sabre. After all, some sheaths are lined with red velvet that does not tear, closing tight once the blade has been removed. At Raeren, nothing went unnoticed. In this cold house sensitive information drifted through the slits under doors, along the polished wall panels, over the cracks in the windowpanes until someone took note with the words 'I saw that coming.'

If they had bumped into me that evening, as I ran in panic up the stairs with my clothes pressed in a wad against my thighs, a nod and a wink would have sufficed. Yet at that moment my only concern was the letter. It had to reach my room intact, so that I could steam it open carefully, soak up its words. He had not said a single one to me all evening.

It took a while before the water in the basin was hot enough. When the flap of the envelope came unstuck, the pulsing sensation began again. His words on the paper were black as fresh ink. I was the first to read them, though

I had not been born when they were written. The prick parade. The loutish southerners. I needed more from the Poste Restante envelope. Not the letters that had been torn open so violently, written by my father in the blind conviction they would be read, but the four sealed envelopes that after twenty years of waiting would reveal their contents to my eyes only.

In the moon's amber light, the postage stamp was difficult to make out. *Internment Camps.* Yes, the Maiden had a spear in her hand. There was something masculine about her, with her solid torso and a Phrygian cap on her head. The symbol of liberty—who were they kidding? More like the cap King Midas wore to conceal his donkey ears.

I first understood that I had been born in the twilight hours of a world war when I stayed with my aunt in Kerkrade in the twenties. Back then, the border with Germany ran a few feet from the doorsteps of Nieuwstraat. A series of holes in the middle of the road was all that marked the divide. When I stepped in one, my aunt told me they had once held fence posts. She recalled how the Dutch had looked on helplessly as the Germans across the street had disappeared behind the chicken wire of their war, how even their windows had been sealed to prevent them escaping. Those days were over now, she assured me, yet one half of the street was still worse off than the other. The German shops were empty. Why didn't the Prussians all come and live with us, I asked. My aunt replied that if they did, things would end up being just as bad here as they were there. The shortages on the other side gave rise to all kinds of shady dealings. Some days the street was teeming with people. Fortune seekers came from all corners of the Dutch hinterland—bawling farmers with wheelbarrows piled high, westerners with big ideas who opened tobacconist shops—and meanwhile the Prussians came pouring over the horizon with their empty carts. In these lawless times, Nieuwstraat became a shopping strip. The mayor complained in vain to the government and the customs officer sat smoking in the same guardhouse from where he had gunned down a deserter only a few years previously. Three months later the street was empty again. When the Reichsmark went into freefall, the vendors followed their customers eastward, hoping to cash in on the ensuing chaos. My aunt did not follow them. She stayed at her stall and flogged her wares to weary stragglers: coffee beans, butter, little flasks of Bols and torpedo-shaped cigars sold individually. Did she feel like Egon had felt in the camp? Surrounded by gawpers who were free to turn on their heels at any moment and carry on with their civilian lives while he was trapped in a fenced-off patch of war? To Egon my father was no better than those gawpers, looking on while his charge had been unconscious. The prick parade. I could guess the implications. That watery-eyed old medic had seen more than me in any case. Egon von Bötticher had lain beside me wearing breeches that gave nothing away.

I licked the glue on the flap, still sticky enough for me to reseal the envelope. Reading the letter twice had not been enough to take it all in. My father had cared for Egon when he had been wounded. The patient saw no sense in his treatment, yet this alone could not justify his rage. He had accused my father of creeping up on his patients in their sleep, of stitching up their honour with needle and thread. I found it hard to believe that, as a young medic, Jacques had possessed the authority to have Egon sent away to an internment camp. But even so, what had Egon wanted instead? Would he rather have ended up like the Belgian beggar on Market Square, a legless body on a little cart, top-heavy with military insignia? There was clearly a score to be settled here. Perhaps Leni could shed some light on things. After all, she knew that his horse had deserted him, an animal he had loved, his only chance of recovery. And more to the point, who was Julia?

I picked up my foil and looked for a target area in the darkness of my room. Fencing clears the mind. When the point of your weapon hits its mark, there can be no doubt about the rights or wrongs of your decision, even if it only came to you along the way, like a walker altering his path to skirt a shower. I chose a spot that irritated me, two mismatched strips of wallpaper. Julia. I wanted to slash her very name to shreds. Satisfaction was a foreign concept to the Dutch according to Egon von Bötticher; if only he had seen me that night. I gauged the distance to the wall and launched my attack. The weapon bounced out of my hand, my grip had been wrong. Just a sec, my father would have said. All at once I pictured him sitting at his desk, pen poised above a pile of writing paper, waiting for the words that might convince his friend of his good intentions. *You do not have to wound in order not to be wounded.* As a rule, my father expressed himself clearly; in his exercise books crammed with logical inferences there was no room for woolly language. I was more than willing to convince myself that Egon and I had no need for words because we shared a passion, and in passion one gesture is enough. But when he had lain next to me on his bed without saying a word, I had felt cold. All expression had ebbed from his face until it became a portrait from long ago, like the young man in the photograph.

The first death in my life had been three years before. Sitting next to me on the bus from Maastricht to Kerkrade, hands clamped around the steel corners of my suitcase, my father had nodded at the dreary view and sighed, 'Border towns, what good are they to anyone? Places where everyone's in a hurry, as if no one can be bothered to stay. Vaals, Eijsden, Kerkrade: provisional settlements on roads leading elsewhere, surrounded by land that was once a battlefield. Soil made fertile by the blood that was spilled there.' At that moment the driver slammed on the brakes. I flew forward and felt a sharp pain in my temple. The woman in front of me lost her hat, my father the suitcase, and then everything went quiet. We had hit something. In a minute that would be spun into a lifelong memory, no one spoke a word. There was none of the screaming or yelling you see in films. If anything the life went out of us, everyone sensing that out there in the middle of the road another life had ended. My father stood up at the same time as the driver. I saw the victim lying a short distance from the bonnet, a thick-set man in an expensive casual suit, his walking stick still within reach. I pictured him contemplating his wardrobe after his morning ablutions and deciding to slip that particular suit over his freshly washed body. And now there it lay.

Egon was wrong. My father was not a placid Dutchman. The calm with which he rose to his feet after observing the victim's motionless chest was the powerlessness of a doctor between the wars, as yet unaware of mouth-to-mouth resuscitation and yet fully aware of the antiquated nature of the methods at his disposal—hot ash and whipping. His face betrayed professional irritation at the very least. That evening, while the rest of the passengers were clapping one hand to their mouth before recounting the spectacle with a quivering grin, my father would be brooding in his study well into the night, pen in hand. In some fencing matches there comes a tipping point, when the hero of the opening bouts turns out to be a hothead who recklessly throws away his advantage. The downfall begins. The spectators look on as he concedes hit after hit, observe his vain appeals to the referee, watch his parries grow clumsier. He kicks, he stamps, and when he finally throws off his mask, everyone can see his jaw trembling while his opponent, who has barely broken a sweat, adds insult to injury with a crushing end-of-match handshake. I peered at the wallpaper. Here. Now. Hit. And another. Night vanished and morning came. I had not slept. The pigeons had stayed awake too, and a cow down in the valley had stood there bellowing for half an hour at the top of its lungs, breathless and desperate to find the herd. An animal calls for help with complete abandon and shamelessly admits it has made a mistake. It will never hatch its own furtive plans while looking a fellow creature in the eye.

## 2

Fencers have a love-hate relationship with the mask. It protects their eyes but obstructs their vision. It conceals their insecurities, but obscures the look in their opponent's eyes, a look that can kill. At least once, every fencer has felt his grip slacken in the final seconds of an attack, having spied a taunting little smile behind the fine mesh opposite him. Perhaps I imagined it, but out of nowhere I thought I saw that same smile appear on Leni's face. She had come into my room to change the bedclothes and must surely have seen the letter on the windowsill. The look in her eyes told me that any words she uttered would obliterate my little adventure, like a bucket of water dousing a campfire first thing in the morning. She was all too eager to tell me a thing or two: she had seen it all before, enough hands had made a grab at that sad old backside of hers through the years. I had no desire to hear—to the accompaniment of pillows being stuffed into pillowcases—that men only had one thing on their minds and that there was no difference between Egon and the bag of bones she lay next to night after night. As for the letter, she would claim triumphantly that it confirmed the rumours. And as for the war—she had lived through it and I had not. She would laugh and dismiss me as a child who had made up a story, before carrying off the dirty laundry for a good airing as she did every day.

The question of what I was doing at Raeren had become as superfluous as many other things within those walls. In the kitchen garden, flowers sprouted from vegetables that would never be eaten. Heinz continued to fire off soundly reasoned diatribes at the pig. His wife rearranged Biedermeier chairs that no one dared sit on. Who on earth had put them there, and why? Raeren was not a place for asking questions; one look at your host was enough to tell you that the answers would be a long time coming. I continued to address him as Herr von Bötticher, my maître. He continued to instruct me in fencing. The morning after that evening, I stood waiting for him in the darkened fencing hall. The night had come and gone, leaving an unyielding blanket of cloud behind. That was fine with me. Lurking in the shadows gives you the chance to weigh up your options, and this was the kind of weather that has people rubbing their eyes in endless indecision. Then in he marched with his usual syncopated step. He slammed on the lights and gave me a look of genuine indifference. Turning around, I came face to face with a worn-out shadow of myself in the mirror: a night owl, and a shamefaced one at that. It would be at least a week before I looked in a mirror and saw myself again. In the meantime, the maître took note of my fencing position. There was nothing erotic in his scrutiny. The inspection of my foot, my hand, my other foot, my other hand, was a ritual, the kind hunters repeat with their rifle, knowing full well the barrel will not be at fault if the hare escapes the bullet. It wasn't long before I began to rebel, to ignore his instructions, starting with his idiotic schedule. I had hoped something might break, even if it was only one of those Biedermeier chairs. I longed for someone's patience to run out. But no one said a word. No one took me to task for missing breakfast or turning up late for lessons. Sometimes I waited out on the terrace listening to the stamping and screeching of the sabre-fencing, only strolling in when the maître lost his temper with the twins, hoping he would turn his anger on me too. On other days, I left early and called on Heinz to saddle up Loubna. The horse was the only one who listened. It's endearing how five hundred kilos' worth of animal will listen. She bore my weight with head bowed and ears rounded. Sometimes, when I leaned forward to slap the horseflies away from her flanks, she would look me straight in the eye. It is astounding how animals make eye contact with humans. How they understand that for us odd creatures it's all about the eyes rather than the position of the ears or the nose, that it's best to exchange a look of understanding with these beings whose eyes are set so close together in their immobile faces that their gaze spans no more than 140 degrees. Our friendship did not go unnoticed. The maître walked past and stuck up his thumb. If I was making too much of an effort, he would correct me. If I slid over the saddle as we galloped, he would shout 'Tilt your hips!' and I would think back wistfully to how he had pulled me toward him.

I was primed to riposte any question with one of my own. There were riddles aplenty to draw from. Unfortunately no one was tempted to enter into such an exchange. Not even Leni, and for that reason alone she could forget any help from me when it came to making the bed. I sat back and fixed my eyes on her bulging apron, which held the keys to a door that would remain locked for the rest of the month. Every day I tried the handle, but to no avail. There was no opportunity to exchange the letter. One rainy evening the students returned, but without the inquisitive old physician who had shared my appetite for answers. He had been replaced by a silent, balding man who appeared at the gate on foot and left the same way, having knocked back a glass of water held in a bloodied hand. Eventually I resigned myself to the silence of Raeren and the absence of daydreams, which sulked in a far-off corner now they had been out-bluffed by real life.

Summer was over. On a day much shorter than the day gone by, I told the twins a fairy tale. Lying between them in the long grass, I made my opening gambit: 'I know something about the Golem that you don't know.'

They looked funny from this low angle. The sun had done its work and, now that their faces were directly above mine, I found myself counting their freckles. Siegbert had more than Friedrich. I wanted to sink my teeth into their soft, round marzipan cheeks.

'Tell us!'

'He has an even bigger scar on his leg. It runs from here ... '—I pulled up my skirt and saw their eyes widen—' ... to here. Like the track of a cartwheel. And a lump has been carved out of his shoulder ... '

'The star!' shouted Friedrich. 'It's just like the film. Golem has a star carved out of his chest!'

Siegbert gave him a shove, his eyes fixed on my naked thighs. The wind began to stir. The ominous bellowing sounded again, off in the distance. Perhaps it wasn't a cow at all, but the horn of a ship that was adrift. Heinz had warned us. In this season, with this weather, anything was possible. You shouldn't be surprised to see pale figures in nightgowns hovering by the wall or long-dead aristocrats climbing the stairs ahead of you. Heinz was proud of these encounters of his, which the rest of us were somehow spared. The only spirit we saw was the ghost of a cow. If we hung around on the terrace long enough in the evening, even the maître could point her out. She never appeared all at once. First there was a stamping sound, followed by the smacking of lips. Then, one by one, white patches would materialize until eventually her entire body floated into view. When we approached her, she dissolved into the darkness again with the mixture of curiosity and timidity all cows seem to share. After a while we no longer took the trouble to get up from the table when she came to call. Friedrich was the only one who kept up the search, feeling his way innocently through the shadows, just as he now urged me to continue my story with his hand on my left breast.

'Yes, it was shaped like a star,' I continued. 'About this big. Carved out with shrapnel. When I pressed on it, I couldn't pull myself away from him. The Golem has been inside ever since. Inside me. Do you understand?'

Siegbert's jaw dropped in amazement. Not at what I had said, but at his brother's hand, which had slipped inside my blouse like a trout into a fishing net. Cautiously, he began to take care of the other side. As they explored my body in tandem, I felt how awkward my newly acquired adulthood really was. I was older than them by a year at most, but I was no longer the free-spirited girl with the foil. My stomach knotted at the thought that something had come to an end. I was certain Helene Mayer would never have succumbed to a man who turned his face away from hers, whose lips were sealed to everything that is important in love. I swallowed and took a good look. It was true. I was receiving my first kiss from a two-headed angel with blood-red lips.

'And what happened next?' they whispered hurriedly, eager to hear the rest of the story.

'He fell into a deep, deep sleep. Let's hope he doesn't wake up for a long time. Not for another thousand years.'

I saw the film years later: *Der Golem, wie er in die Welt kam*. In an unheated cinema in the middle of winter, I shivered in my seat at the tale of how Golem came into the world. I was the entire audience. By that time no one cared a fig for silent films, especially not if the film was German. Gil, the man who ran the cinema, was Jewish. A few years previously he had returned from the dead to an empty house. Everyone knew. It was a story that led people to shun him. They wanted nothing to do with the legend of Rabbi Löw and the Golem either.

'Don't worry, it's not about the war,' Gil reassured me as I bought my ticket. 'It's set in the Prague ghetto in the sixteenth century. It's even got a happy ending. There's no sound, though. Just so you know.'

I stared at the images in the icy silence. They were lit from above as if shot at a time when there was still a window in the darkness above the ghetto. The rabbi hunched over his incantations, then raised his hands to heaven, stared at the stars and dimmed the light. Other scenes were frayed black around the edges, as if they had been shot from under a hand or through a tube. In the distance, a knight was thrown from a tower. Sudden death. With no ominous music to warn me, I got the fright of my life. Gil, sitting in the seat next to mine, found this endearing. According to him, the days when cinemagoers were content with the role of voyeur had gone. People no longer wanted to be silent onlookers, he said. Now they would only pay to see films with songs they could sing or dances they could imitate. And then there was the latest craze from America, stereoscopy, which had audiences squealing and squirming in their seats as a locomotive hurtled toward them. The same people who, a few years earlier, would have been thankful for a drab existence were now handing over their hard-earned cash for the illusion of being in harm's way.

'You see, not every film needs sound,' he whispered. 'After all, Golem never speaks. It's in the Talmud. The legend goes that the rabbi puts words written on parchment in his mouth to make him do his bidding.'

The on-screen Golem did not resemble von Bötticher in the slightest. The part of the monster was played by the director, a tubby buffoon with a drooping mouth. The only thing they had in common was their reluctance to speak. Even during my time at Raeren, I knew I had to put words in von Bötticher's mouth. As long as he remained silent, I could make of him whatever I wanted. But the twins were adamant that I should leave Golem and his sinister intentions well alone. Let him sleep, never to wake again.

'If I want to sleep,' said Siegbert, 'all I have to do is cradle Fritz, and my eyelids start to droop. I hush him, talk gently to him and when I see him nodding off, I fall asleep too.'

As they demonstrated this, they actually dozed off, their hair like warm beeswax against my breasts, their angel hands intertwined in my lap. It was only when I heard the regular breathing of sleep that I dared to breathe freely myself. I gulped at the air, taking in the approaching storm. Plumes of cloud whirled in the purple sky, lining up like soldiers. The light that hung in the air pulled everything into the sharpest focus: the weathered cornice on Raeren's roof, the pores on the twins' goose-pimpled skin, the grain of the blade of grass between my teeth. The storm rose, abated and rose again. The grass shrank back. Rustling and sniffing. Something without footsteps was approaching. A hairy little devil. I sat up and saw the small dog that belonged to the maître. He was holding something in his mouth. Alarmed, he let it drop: it was a dead mole. Its black coat, closed eyes and folded paws made the lifeless creature look more like a priest at prayer than anything. The twins rubbed the sleep from their eyes and shooed the dog away. He remained standing at a distance to see what we planned to do with his catch.

'Let's bury it,' said Siegbert. 'Otherwise it'll stink.'

We straightened up our clothing and Siegbert disappeared among the grass to find a stick we could use to dig a hole.

'It'll be easier once the rain starts,' he shouted. 'We can make him a hole he would have dug for himself.'

'A hole he would have dug for himself,' Friedrich repeated. 'How will we manage that?'

He rolled his eyes and ran his hand through his hair. Then we started to giggle. We were still children. I was grateful to them for protecting our innocence, for saving all three of us.

'You truly are musketeers,' I said. 'One for all, all for one.'

Friedrich gave a little bow. 'At your service, milady.'

We sat there and stared at the sky until Siegbert returned with a length of old iron. We did nothing to help him as he stepped through the grass, counting his paces.

'Otherwise we'll never be able to find the grave again,' he interrupted himself.

'Sigi has always been good at geometry,' said Friedrich. 'Pacing out distances, measuring, comparing and contrasting. He wants to be a surveyor and lug a theodolite around with him. Making sure everything on the surface of the planet is just as it should be. I don't understand a thing about it, but then why should I?'

His brother slammed the blunt iron into the dry soil. With every blow, strands of blond hair fell in front of his face. He wiped his nose on his wrist once or twice. 'A strapping young lad,' my father would have called him with a hint of disdain. He distrusted young men who always felt the need to roll up their sleeves and leap into action for the sake of some trivial scheme. Standing between the twins, I was reminded of the de Witt brothers, remembered for their brutal deaths, strung up by the mob at the end of Holland's Golden Age. Yet one had been a courageous seafarer and the other not only a statesman, but also a geometrist, no less! I was about to share my musings with Friedrich, but he beat me to it: 'You think my brother's a real man, don't you?'

He gave me a searching look. I had trouble finding my words.

'Not at all. I mean, no not really. You're both ... '

Something felt strange. I hoped it was the sky, so suddenly overcast that it had transformed us into silhouettes, or the dark cawing of the crows that had already discovered the mole's grave. But no, it was the twins. As we made our way back to the house, they kept an awkward distance from each other. They walked on either side of me and said nothing, or else interrupted each other by making a point of talking specifically to me. Uneasy, I quickened my pace until a salvo of startling noises dissolved the tension. From the direction of the terrace, already looming behind the chestnut trees, there came a gunshot, followed by a woman's scream, the sound of an engine stalling and a man's voice distorted beyond recognition, struggling to be heard above the wind. 'Julia!'

The twins began to run, shouting for their mother. I lingered by the young chestnut trees, there was no way I was going to follow them. Julia, the mother: through the leaves I saw her contours. She was standing halfway down the drive in a raven-black dress, thin as gossamer, one hand on the door of her car. The sky was now so dark it had leeched all colour from the land. The grass was grey, the trees black, and behind them was the house, white as bleached bone. On the terrace stood its owner, a gun floating on his forefinger, the barrel trained on the only thing that was moving at that moment: a hare in the throes of death. It leaped convulsively into the air, like water in a fountain, one metre at most from the woman. She stood motionless as Egon raised the sight to his eye once again and fired a shot that stopped the hare and set everything else in motion. The heavens opened. The woman bent forward, tugged her wet dress free of her body and walked toward the terrace at a waltzing trot, holding her bag over her head. The twins leaped forward and clung to her. The wind kept their words out of earshot, but I could read them without much trouble, white flickering on black:

'Stay away, Mother! Now you have seen what Golem is capable of!'
'Oh my darlings, you know he never misses his target. Now quickly, let us shelter from the rain!'

3

Schöner Gigolo, armer Gigolo,
denke nicht mehr an die Zeiten,
wo du als Husar,
goldverschnürt sogar,
konntest durch die Straßen reiten.

Egon had his palms pressed to his ears. Chances were he
could not even hear the lyrics, entreating a hussar-turned-
gigolo to forget his glorious past. Julia had placed a gramophone on the table after dinner. The records were hers. She
had brought them with her because 'that man over there'
needed cheering up. But 'that man' was staring out of the
window, where the rain continued to fall and where smells
rose from the soil that were dearer to him than the perfume she wore. His urge was to leave, to stride through the
fields, as I had often seen him do when it was wet, stooping
to hold things up to his nose, bringing them home and
hanging them on beams to dry, where the aroma they
released changed with every passing week. That afternoon
I had found him in front of the kitchen fire, chewing on
tough little mushrooms that hung from the ceiling. He let
me taste one. They had not quite become the shrivelled
black phantoms you can use to brew a perverse-smelling
stock; they were still damp, reminiscent of soft earth,
mouldering tree bark and ram's fleece. Those were his

smells, while Julia intoxicated us with a décolleté gleaming with greasy alcohol. L'Heure Bleue. An old-fashioned perfume, dreamed up on the eve of the First World War, as the sun went down and the air turned blue. Her dress *was* strictly à la mode, an expensive creation of thin crêpe that lay like water on her body. She knew all eyes were on her as she strolled across the floor, kicking the black fabric before her and spreading her arms so the sleeves flowed from her shoulders. She cranked up the gramophone and the drawling voice of Richard Tauber took another run-up at his song:

Uniform passée, Mädchen sagt Adieu,
schöne Welt, du gingst in Fransen.
Wenn das Herz dir auch bricht,
mach ein lachendes Gesicht!
Man zahlt, und du mußt tanzen.

'Do you hear, Egon,' she shouted above the string section. 'Even though it breaks your heart, it's time you danced, hussar! I've paid my money!'

To my amazement, he got to his feet. She seemed to grow taller as he took her hand and she placed the other lightly on his shoulder, his arm in the small of her back. Suddenly her coquettish smile vanished. She stared straight into his eyes and saw what he had once seen—herself, sometime, somewhere, with him—before drifting off into endless replays of her past. Leni, who had reluctantly joined us at the table, had the same pensive gaze. And even Heinz, a linen napkin between his black fingers, was lost in memories that gave him the earnest expression he had worn when he returned home long ago, the face that had made a woman want him. Only the twins remained unchanged. They did not appear to have a past. They were animals in

the here and now, preoccupied with each other and a handful of perfunctory activities. Their shared habits were beginning to get on my nerves. I was not much older than
they were, but I at least knew something of the past. And
not just from films. I knew more than anyone here could
suspect and I had much more to find out. All those things
that were dead and gone for the grown-ups, hollowed to a
dry crust by their wistful scraping, were lying in wait for
me, fresh and fragrant. Words that Egon had written when
he was my age had been kept warm, well conserved in
sealed paper. The only thing standing between them and
me was a door.

Egon took a few steps, let himself be carried along. His
feet moved left and right on the parquet as she stepped
backward. This was not dancing. This was how you descend
a staircase in the dark, never quite knowing if the next
step is the last. The music ended and the needle scratched
mercilessly at the label. The couple stood still, their eyes
no longer meeting, like a pair of teenagers who have no
idea what happens when the dancing stops. For Egon and
Julia there was nothing more in store. They were saddled
with an uneasy history on which the last word had yet to
be spoken. Silence was best.

'Sigi, pick out something cheerful,' Julia said at last,
walking over to the window. Siegbert, the beautiful young
buck, jumped to his feet. He had not let his mother out of
his sight for a second since her arrival at Raeren. The
empress whose poise remained intact beneath the wrath
of a thunderstorm, who merely had to wave a limp hand at
her luggage—a case of records, a hat box and another
peculiarly shaped item—for her boys to lug them inside
for her. Her boys: a category that encompassed every man
in the world. Such women exist, capable of turning the
men around them, even the old and the wealthy, into

sheepish boys. They needn't be beautiful. They pick up on signs that no one else notices, just as no one sees the handiwork of the driver, only how well his horses run. The sons of such women do their bidding from an early age, while their daughters revile them. A feeling caught me unawares: I missed my mother. I had never thought of her that way before, as a carefree beauty at the age of eighteen, posing for an expensive photographer because my grandfather knew that such a prize had to be documented with no time to lose (after all, my grandmother's charms had faded after only five years of marriage). My mother had wanted no part of it, unlike Julia, who would have been at her wits' end without a mirror, as every powdered millimetre of her face attested. The signs Julia picked up on were a mystery to my mother. She saw no point in scanning her surroundings with the gaze of a young girl until her eyes met those of an agitated male. Her brow was heavy with notions of sin. I missed her, pure and simple. Her calm and sombre presence at the kitchen table. The contentment with which she absorbed real life into her Bible verses, akin to the way she removed the veins from a tough cabbage. Did I resemble my mother? Less and less. Yet although I had never been blessed with her equanimity, at least I held on to a sense of wonder that kept me young. For all their beauty, this was one quality the twins had not inherited from their mother. They only wondered at each other, at themselves. They both had Julia's blue eyes and, since few people look beyond a passing glance, most people thought they were made in her image. But a squareness had crept into their faces, in the set of the jaw, the line of the nose. I knew those features and made the comparison in a heartbeat. He was sitting there opposite me after all, lost in thought. No, it was impossible, heaven forbid! Their noses looked the same, but otherwise there was no resemblance to speak of. I glanced down and saw there were eighteen, yes, precisely eighteen peas left on my plate. Heinz cleared his throat and risked another hiding from his wife: 'Tell me, Frau von Mirbach, how are things with your husband?'

The maître had done Leni no favours by inviting her and her husband to join us at the table. Perhaps it was no coincidence that he only dined with his servants when Julia came to call. Perhaps he felt the need for spectators, a pair of talkative townsfolk to spread the rumour that something was brewing between their master and another man's wife, thereby dispensing with the formality of throwing down a gauntlet. The provocation would circulate on the tongues of the hoi polloi, all of whom would instantly take a side: not the side of world-weary von Bötticher in his woodland retreat, that much was clear. Heinz persisted.

'What did Herr von Mirbach have to say? You remember, *Kraft durch Freude*. What did he think of the idea? It must have appealed to him, as a man of the people.'

Julia did not reply. She was still standing at the window with her back to us. Heinz turned his attention to the twins. 'Boys, that father of yours is a fine sportsman.'

'Last month he came first in the discus,' said Siegbert, flicking through the gramophone records.

'I mentioned it to Matthias only last week,' Heinz continued. 'He agreed it was a good idea. "We have plenty to thank Herr von Mirbach for." Those were his exact words.'

My curiosity about von Mirbach had been aroused: the man Julia had chosen in the end. If she was the Julia referred to in the letter, Egon must have missed the boat where she was concerned. I could think of no other reason for her choice than the twins. The pair of tender young aristocrats who had touched me that morning. How much of the father was here in his sons? Was he twice the man

Egon was? Had he made love to one half of her body first and then the other?

'Things are going well and they can only get better,' Heinz went on. 'No strikes for two years! Not one! While the countries around us are making a right mess of things. Take Belgium ... '

'Belgium is not a country,' said Egon. Heinz sprang up from his chair and, there it was again, his fist on the table. 'Never a truer word! They can't even form a government! And not a day goes by without a strike. It's time the Belgians gave us our land back, don't you think? If they're incapable of governing it. Our beautiful land!'

He pointed a trembling finger at the window. 'Moresnet! Eupen! The last thing that gang of smugglers wants is a real leader. But it won't be long now. Four years at most.'

Egon pulled a sceptical face.

'The Four Year Plan, sir. The Führer's pledge, announced a month ago. Four years, he said, to restore our country. Army, economy, peace, and prosperity.'

'My husband says two years will be enough,' replied Julia. 'He reckons we'll be the richest country in Europe within two years at this rate.'

Egon plucked a walnut from his mouth. 'Why the hurry? Four years will fly by. You of all people should know that, Frau von Mirbach. Four years ...? A little patience never hurt anyone.'

When Julia slunk closer, Egon looked up with the surprised air of someone who has just retrieved something important from the tangle of his memory. L'Heure Bleue. Scent ambushes you with your own recollections and there's nothing you can do about it.

'"*Ich hab' kein Auto, ich hab' kein Rittergut!*"' Siegbert read aloud. 'That sounds like a jolly tune.'

'No,' said Julia, pushing him aside. '"*Lieber kleiner Eintänzer.*"'

I want to hear the song about the man who dances alone.
Here, put it on.'

'But you wanted something cheerful, Mama.'

A raised eyebrow was sufficient. Siegbert took the record
from her hands and nudged the needle onto the Bakelite.
The melody blared through the room with a heartrending
crackle.

Lieber kleiner Eintänzer
Sei doch heute mein Tänzer
Denn es passt doch kein Tänzer
So gut wie du.

'Vulgar little ditty,' Egon remarked. He shot me a penetrat-
ing look, one I had come to know. He was well on his way to
being drunk. '*Eintänzer.* I'm sure our Janna has no idea why
a man might hang around a dance hall on his own.'

'Leave the girl be,' Julia snapped, as she let her younger
son take her hand. Leni cleared the table with much clatter-
ing of dishes. Heinz sat where he was, empty glass in fist,
as if made of stone. It was time for me to bow out for the
evening, but my eyes were drawn to the dancers. Friedrich
knew the tango. He paraded his mother the length of the
table for our inspection. The sheen of her shapely rump,
her white-stockinged hooves, which brushed his as they
passed. She dipped her face into his shadow, a subtle sub-
terfuge that enabled her to pass for a girl his age. She was a
pure-bred filly, no doubt about it. I was not the only one
consumed by jealousy. At the back of the hall, Siegbert
stood with his arms clamped around him, as if he were
feeling the cold.

Wundervoll und flott tanzt du
Wie ein junger Gott tanzt du

Lieber kleiner Eintänzer
Tanz nur mit mir.

Egon turned back to me, seemingly unimpressed. 'Or do you already know? Why some men dance with one partner after another?'

I threw my napkin on the table, walked out of the fencing hall and down the stairs. In the hallway, I stopped in my tracks. Here I was yet again, face to face with the door. For seven nights I had stood with my nose so close to the wood that the mere thought left a bitter, resinous taste in my mouth. I dreamed of it too, the way people taste and dream their obsessions. In my sleep I saw the door rip open along the grain, allowing me to step effortlessly into the hallway behind. But now the brass handle maintained a solid silence. There was no point in even trying it. I could recognize a locked room from afar, just as you can tell the difference between a corpse and someone who is sleeping. My pocket contained a pilfered letter, now little more than a rag. If Egon ever laid hands on it, he would pick up my scent, smell my sweaty, desperate attempts to get through to him. If I tore it up, part of Julia would be erased from history. Not that her presence there was writ large: a handful of letters, perhaps a photograph, memories left unspoken. For now I had bigger fish to fry, like tracking down the apron Leni had taken off before she joined us for dinner. As long as the fools of Raeren were dancing, I could search undisturbed.

Lieber kleiner Eintänzer
Sei doch heute mein Tänzer
Denn es passt doch kein Tänzer
Solch Kavalier.

In the dark of the stairwell, the music was distorted into a tinny caterwaul. I crouched down and peered through the keyhole into the sealed-off hallway, where moonlight was flooding in through the windows. Before dinner I had peeped into his room from the garden. The door had been ajar, but I had no way of reaching it. I had stalked angrily around to the other side to see if I could climb in through his bedroom window, but it was closed and set high in the wall, like the blade of a guillotine. At dinner, Julia had brought up the subject of Mary Queen of Scots.

'When Mary Stuart was beheaded, the axe became wedged in the bone,' she said, twisting the joint of a chicken leg. 'The executioner had wanted to slice through her neck in a single blow but was foiled by a nub of cartilage. Most unpleasant.'

'And no doubt you know that her lips kept moving for a full fifteen minutes after her head was severed,' Egon remarked. 'Women talk too much.'

'Do we, now?' she countered, winking at me. 'Not all of us, it seems. This girl here has barely spoken a word. Or is that because she is not yet a woman?'

She ran her fingers down her neck as she spoke, fingertips slick with chicken grease. Egon grinned broadly. I nearly went for her then, picturing my hands clenched around her bird-like throat.

Upstairs, the song of the *Eintänzer* came to an end and a burst of laughter rang out. Someone mentioned my name and I scurried into the kitchen. It was cold and dark there. In the moonlight I made out the chopping block and on it the remains of the chickens that had been grabbed by the scruff of the neck at the last minute to feed the unexpected guest who had arrived so late in the day—the cook and the chickens had been indignant. Leni had stood there thinking, jangling the keys in her apron pocket, then went to fetch the birds. She had broken their necks, plucked them two fistfuls at a time, stuffed crushed nuts under the skin of the breast, rubbed them with salt and butter and slid them into the oven. An hour would do it. While the storm lashed against the windows, two pasty carcasses turned into golden, roasted fowl that enticed everyone into the kitchen. It had been cosy there. We stoked the fire. Leni dragged her master away from the food, but not before he had managed to tear off a wing and egged on Heinz to do the same. Even before we carried the chickens to the dining table, one had been half demolished. It was one of those moments when everything might have turned out for the best: seven people, one and a half birds, raised hands and clinking glasses, giggling on the stairs. No one spoke of the future and everyone kept quiet about the past. We wanted to eat, and our awkward stumbling on the stairs was that of children, all the same age. But when the maître lit the chandeliers in the fencing hall, the mood changed. The light glinted fiercely on the newly polished floor and was scattered across the walls. As soon as we caught sight of ourselves in the mirror, our backs straightened.

'I've forgotten the potatoes,' Leni had said, backing out of the hall. Heinz was still out in the passage. He never entered the fencing hall, the domain of the Mensur. At most he understood that it was a matter of the utmost precision, so precise that three pairs of eyes were not enough to ensure compliance with the rules. His battles were fought in the garden, where it was no good measuring anything. He had no control over what ran rampant out there, the whys or the wherefores, and cursed Mother Nature for always being one step ahead. Yet the fencing hall filled him with awe. The only order he had ever belonged to was the brotherhood of the conveyor belt, and he still went out of his way to stroll down to the factory on a weekly basis.

'I expect you both to keep us company at dinner,' Egon had said. 'There's enough for everyone. Take a seat, Heinz.'

Heinz had stepped onto the parquet as if his large shoes might sink into it. He grasped the chair his master offered him and sat down gingerly.

'As a girl I used to play with the children from the village too,' said Julia out of nowhere. She appeared to be addressing herself in the mirror. 'We would dress our shabby little playmates up as soldiers. Mama had uniforms made in their size. Greyish-green tunics, cockades of different countries on their little caps. They looked so sweet. My brother and I were on horseback and they would march along behind us. When the war broke out, little Lydia did the same, only Mama updated the uniforms. The dear girl wore a spiked helmet and exactly the same cartridge bag you were kitted out with when you went to war, Egon, my officer cadet! Oh, it was such fun.'

My ears had pricked up like a dog's as Leni slowly untied her apron and the keys clanked together. She didn't have it on when she returned with the oven dish and yet now there was no trace of it in the kitchen. It was very dark. All I had to see by was a sliver of moonlight and the flames licking the edges of a block of wood in the hearth. *Gastrosophy*. The book lay open, next to the sink. Leni had cooked from it. Did plucking and stuffing chickens, smearing them with butter and pulling off their legs and wings really count as *gastrosophy*? The book was open at the pictures of the boned cow, the strict hand pointing out how the job should be done. My father had befriended a local butcher, a serious man for whom work was not a joking matter. Unlike my father and the other doctors who came to call. For Leo, levity was out of the question. The very thought of air pockets in the pig gut he used for his sausages was enough to keep him awake at night. He would have said he was passionate about his work, but what animal carves up its prey with so much deliberation as we humans? Doesn't the real passion reside in all those creatures that slaughter each other whole, in a rage, eyes red with raw emotion?

I slammed the book shut. Perhaps Leni had hung up her apron in the little side room, through a low door beside the sink and up some steps. I knew it was where she spent much of her time and that there was a lantern for me to light, but I had never been beyond the first steps, where she hung the onions. It smelled of herbs and on the wall was a shelf lined with preserving jars. A book was splayed open on top of them, one of Baroness von Eschstruth's romantic novels. At the top of the steps I stumbled across a basket of potatoes, the ones on top shapeless and grey as a huddle of drunkards. My eyes gradually grew accustomed to the dim light. I saw a large trunk full of books, all of them damp and warped, a mirror that was missing whole sections of silver, a bag containing rusted sabres, and a stuffed hare with a panicked expression and a hole in its back. I was about to turn around when I spotted a thin figure in the corner. When your heart is pounding so loudly that you can no longer hear yourself breathe, perhaps it is best to keep going. I remembered walking to my grandmother's house over a dark and hollow road, refusing to investigate the shuffling noises I heard and the pale contours I saw out of the corner of my eye. But curiosity is more tenacious than fear. I spent months searching for that apparition at the side of the road and never saw it again. Now I raised the lantern higher. The shape was nothing more than a coat rack with one item hanging from it: Egon's hat with its skull and crossbones. From upstairs laughter rang out again, closer this time. By the sound of things, they were leaving the fencing hall. The twins shouted my name. 'It's only for a week,' I heard Julia say. 'Leave the girl be.'

The fur smelled pleasant and felt soft against my brow. When I lifted the mirror, I recognized her immediately: the daughter of the last Kaiser, the photograph from the magazine. The same slightly arrogant face, not in the least bit shy, between glinting skull and braided collar. Her regal hand gloved and resting on her hip. Dressing up, playing at soldiers, the game that had so amused Julia as a child. Aristocratic ladies who, out of peevishness, boredom or pique, poked fun at the wars waged by their menfolk. I took off the hat and, inspecting the inside, I discovered a faded stain on the ribbon that ran along the seam—blood perhaps? Was it blood they longed for, these women who had waved their men off to war? Was that why they dressed up in clothes made to kill or to die in? Was it the same fascination that made me want to fence just once with the razor-sharp *Parisers* that hung in the fencing hall—to know what it's like to hold death in your hand? I snuffed out the lantern and left the side room. Everyone seemed to have gone outside, except for Leni who was stacking dishes at the sink. She did not even notice when I crept past her out of the kitchen. Perhaps the hat made me invisible. The sound of Julia's car died away and Egon came back into the house. He leaned against the front door for a moment as if trying to regain his balance. Eventually his smile answered mine.

'Memento mori,' I said, pointing at my forehead. 'Remember death.'

He nodded and unlocked the door that led to his quarters. The hallway was wider than I remembered. He walked ahead of me at a slow pace. I looked at his hair, grey in the moonlight, and I thought of all this man had been through and smiled at the idea that I was now part of it. Whether he wanted it or not, I too was part of his experiences, even if I had not lived through the war that ruled his life. Suddenly he stood still.

'It is not death we are mindful of, but the dead. The skull reminds us of the fallen, those who died for us and whose death we must avenge. We are prepared to fight until death comes to deliver us. We do not fear him, he is a distinguished general. Only soldiers who never doubt his decisions are inviolable.'

The sex was hard. He did not take the trouble to shut out the moonlight or to turn down the bedspread. He danced alone, needed no partner. He thrust my bottom in the air and held it there till he collapsed on top of me with a sob. I didn't dare move.

'Little girl.'

His voice was gentle and hoarse. I lay there listening intently for more, but nothing else came. He interlaced his fingers with mine and soon I heard him sleeping. I squirmed out from under him, put on my clothes and pulled open the drawer. One by one, I exposed my father's letters to the light from the window. It struck me that his handwriting had not changed through the years, though his first letters were those of a very young man. As if he had always been convinced of the accuracy of his emphatic punctuation and economical capitals, both already present in his first letter from March 1915:

In the middle of February, our Red Cross in Vlissingen assisted at an exchange of British and German prisoners of war. I have heard that another such exchange has been planned for June, but in all likelihood only the critically injured will be eligible. I will do my best!

I thought of the photograph that had been taken three months before this letter. If I were to wake him now, would Egon still deny he was that blurred hussar? My father was unrecognizably earnest, both in that photograph and in his letters.

Believe me, I understand your fury. But I accept no blame. There is no point in accusing a doctor of indifference merely for obeying the Hippocratic oath. At Calvariënberg I did not—as you put it—'keep a cowardly eye on you'. I meticulously observed the workings of your body, a duty of care I have toward every patient who cannot speak. The fact that I continued to observe you thereafter was simply a way to keep you in Maastricht. Who knows where they might have sent you otherwise! You know as well as I do that only the permanently invalid were being repatriated.

Among the envelopes was a postcard without a stamp. The picture showed a sultry lady on a camel. Here his tone was more cheerful:

The sentry, who promised me he would deliver this postcard to you, told me you have been taken from Bergen and are being held elsewhere. He did not know where, or was not permitted to say … However, I was given a tour of the camp and it seemed to me most comfortable. A top-notch country residence, my ungrateful friend. Seriously, I challenge you to visit my digs in Amsterdam sometime—a good deal smaller, and dirtier come to that!

Egon rolled over on the bed and his mouth fell open. It was strange to see him looking so relaxed, crumpled and carefree. As if he might wake up any moment for a chat. On my guard, I began to read the last of the letters I held in my hand. My father had filled the page to overflowing and I was unable to read everything:


10 AUGUST 1916


Dear Egon,

I have been through a frightful ordeal. I am no longer sure of anything and understand now just how naïve I have been. I have considered leaving the medical profession. What I have seen was horrific but fascinating. Too much certainty throws dust in your eyes, convictions gather dust. I no longer have a single one to my name.

The Red Cross asked me to assist at another exchange between German and British casualties ... we in Maastricht had been ordered to treat them ... so that the poor souls could eventually be housed at Hook of Holland, in a warehouse belonging to the Holland America Line. A German hospital train came from Aachen with dozens of seriously injured and mentally disturbed Brits on board. They were horribly mutilated. Some bright spark had tried to save space by putting two legless bodies in a single bed, one at either end. A wounded officer who had lost three limbs insisted on wearing a glove on his one remaining hand because he felt it was more dignified ... he reminded me of you, Egon. You should think yourself lucky that you have been spared the trenches.

I believe this war has closed the book on civilization for ever. The mentally ill were a loathsome spectacle, a wagon full of them. They raged like demons. No living creature could utter such screams. It must be a defect of the cerebral cortex that knocks their system so far off-balance that it continuously fires off emotions at random, like an artillery unit gone berserk. It has occurred to me to consult Brodmann's map, but I have yet to reach any conclusions.

However, it was their cynicism that hit me the hardest. Until now, I was used to treating patients who had respect for their own body, who faced their illness with frightened tears but who had faith in recovery. There was a British orderly on the train, severely burnt, covered in bandages. He told me about a chum of his who had stepped on a landmine. The boy kept on screaming, 'I've lost my leg, I've lost my leg!' till everyone got sick of him. 'Give over!' one of the men shouted back, pointing at the torn-off limb, boot still attached, 'You haven't lost it. Look, it's over there!' They all laughed, the victim included.

These are the times in which we live, when a human being holds all of creation in contempt, even his own body, simply because it has ceased to function. It won't be long before the old-fashioned apparatus of hinged bones, pumping blood and beating heart will be supplanted by modern technology. What is the use in becoming a doctor? Answer me that, Egon.

For a moment I thought he was staring at me, but it was only the moonlight dancing across his eyelids. His face looked wooden. I stuffed my father's missives back in the drawer and removed a letter from the Poste Restante envelope. Before leaving the room, I stopped to look at him one more time. Deep creases at either side of his sleeping mouth had turned him into a ventriloquist's dummy. Not the most attractive sight.

Out in the hallway, I realized I had forgotten to return the rag of a letter I had been carrying around all this time. The one I had steamed open and read to death even though my stomach churned every time I saw her name. What was

I to do? In the end, the answer could not have been simpler. The kitchen was deserted, but someone had put a new block on the fire. First I tossed the envelope into the flames, then the letter. The paper crumpled instantly. I won't deny that I enjoyed watching the words burn away to ash. Some flew up with a desperate whisper, others lay still as they were scorched to blackness. I could swear I saw her name shrivel among the flames, like a moth above a candle.

JANUARY 1917

Dear Jacques,

I am for ever lost. When did I arrive here? I no longer remember. Before winter came, that much is certain. The waterways
had not yet frozen over and the tall trees along the river-
banks were rustling as I was marched across the drawbridge
between four officers, like a common criminal. Four pairs of
steely eyes staring out from under the rims of their helmets
failed to note that I had pulled the sabre from the scabbard of
the bearded man in front of me. You know how nimble my
fingers can be. I couldn't help but smile at the theatricality of
it all: those stuffed-shirt officers against the backdrop of a
seventeenth-century fort with its bastions and powder
houses ... I was half expecting the Duke of Luxembourg to
lay siege to the place. But when the gate closed behind me
everything went quiet, for ever quiet. The trees are bare and
do not rustle, and a cold mirror has settled over the Rhine.
They are shitting themselves for fear I might escape again.
Absconding from Bergen was child's play, even if they did
recapture me in the end. Here I already have two failed
attempts to my name. Their gunmen drove us back over the
ice like ducks and locked us away deeper in the cells. Do you
have any idea how thick the doors are here? They have posted
one of their little scarecrows outside my cell to keep guard.
He sets my teeth on edge. At night the air resounds with his
snoring. I would take great pleasure in strangling him,
crushing that larynx of his with two fingers. Last year, so

they tell me, the mood was very different around here. The atmosphere was friendly and the officers were barely under any surveillance at all. They say a lieutenant from Braunschweig escaped in a trunk stolen from the depot commander's room. Imagine! The commander is a typical Dutchman who has never had to get his uniform dirty. Their clothes smell of starch and copper polish, the threads from the seamstress's workshop are still attached and if there's a stain you can be sure it's from the food they shove down their gullets from morning till night. It's one big puppet show, with a bolted gate for a curtain.

Christian, a chum of mine from Koblenz, keeps saying, 'We'll get the better of them yet.' He is a fanatical hazard player, shrugging off risks with every toss of the dice in the conviction that he will be able to rake in a profit one of these days. But I do not know if I can bear any more humiliation. To be dragged inside once again, to hear the doors close behind me and the sickening scrape of the bolt ... no, I think I would go mad. I grow more malicious by the day. How well I understand Edmond Dantès! Revenge is the best way to fill a life lived in such emptiness. In the cell, where the day has no beginning and no end, I keep my mind clear with thoughts of retribution. In escaping from Bergen I was merely fulfilling an obligation to my fatherland. The only Dutchman to whom I feel any obligation is the farmer I worked for. A good man. He appreciated our help, and the food his wife served us was lovingly prepared. Our situation made little sense to him. He did not understand why I was not allowed to return to the war, even less why I would want to, but he is the kind of man who absolves himself of the obligation to understand everything. A true farmer, one who does not marvel at life beginning or ending around him. I remember a calf being born on his land, it must have been a week before my departure. The mother kept on grazing as if nothing was the matter, while the farmer pointed at the water sac hanging out of her, said 'Little 'un on the way,' and then carried on working. When I came back an hour later, the calf was standing there with four hooves on the ground gazing wide-eyed at the world. The farmer was still hard at work and the cow was steadily chewing the cud. Only the calf and I were surprised at this new life.

When I made my escape, I could feel the farmer's eyes on my back as I ran. I left him behind in a field with two hundred bales of straw to be loaded onto the wagon. He knew exactly what I was planning to do as soon as I stuck my pitchfork in the ground. His eyes pierced my back just as my eyes pierced the air before they fell shut on that fateful August day in 1914. This is what I still remember: I am lying in the sand, cold blood streaming over my scorched face. I sit up and watch them go, but they do not look back at me. They go on, in all directions, some without a horse, others hanging half out of the saddle. The half-dead and the dead, silent, screaming, shuddering. A bewildering, macabre spectacle, cooked up by an enemy who cares nothing for rules. Our horses galloped straight into wires stretched by the Belgians and ripped themselves to shreds, before falling prey to the constant rattle of the machine guns. Through clouds of dust I saw them fall, our strong and faithful mounts, their screams so deafening no one recognized them as the sound a horse might make. My last memory was of her, Fidèle. She stood unharmed in the vanguard, a short distance beyond the burning farmhouse from which we came under fire. I could only make out her motionless contours, but I knew for certain it was her. No other horse can stand so proud. In truth, I only ever knew her as a silhouette: dark as night, always ahead of the sun. She was a Trakehner, bred to keep going. They say this battle offers final proof that the cavalry is a thing of the past, that we are lost in the face of rapid fire and heavy artillery. If that is the case, the blame lies not with Fidèle but with me, the rider in the sand.

I know too well what it is to look on while others advance and to flee while others look on. These are things I will have to live with. And what about you, Jacques? You lied and you continue to lie, this we both know. I am here, you are there and you will only speak once the war is over. You are learning how to heal wounds, but I am here to tell you that those wounds will open up again. I will claim my right of attack. A new war will come, a better war than this. Fought not with anonymous bullets fired by francs-tireurs, but in duels, man to man. An orderly war, where days proceed according to the rules. Let me tell you, I have never slept as soundly as in a bivouac. It is the essence of order in the midst of chaos, the regularity of a well-prepared night after a day in which everything was unpredictable. Within these walls, sleep is hard to come by. They are as cold and damp as the cheeks of the woman who has betrayed me, and whose name I will not dignify by committing it to paper. Her last letter was stained with teardrops, or perhaps they were just ordinary drops of water. She is an actress after all. Sometimes, in this place, I press my cheek to hers and feel the mouldering chalk, the white powder on that treacherous face, and I wonder if it is the wall or my bones being ground away, the dust of my crumbling sanity? So much for the ramblings of a madman … Fidèle, let us talk about her. Where is she, Jacques? Are you looking for her? Under the circumstances, surely it is the least you can do.

**4**

A gust of wind tore the letter from my hands and a page tumbled off across the grass, staying just out of reach. The last traces of summer had vanished. Bridal veils of mist trailed up from the lake and along the wall, where they evaporated on the backs of the tethered horses. Everything had changed colour. Life slowly faded from the leaves, like ink from a page left too long in the sun. Only the apple trees with their triumphant fruit were in clear focus. Heinz emerged from the mist and was greeted with a loud whinny from Megaira. She swayed her head and kicked the fence she was tied to.

'Easy, girl!' I heard him say as he brushed her flanks with long strokes. 'Watch out for those hooves and they'll carry you far. You've got a whole world to conquer, running faster than wildfire, so people will know to fear the cavalry.'

Perhaps he had said something else entirely. The wind snatched the words from his mouth and chased them away. You could make of them whatever you wanted. I wanted him to speak these words to the horse that looked like another horse, a shadow that had refused to be captured, never mind be led off on a halter. Fourteen years ago von Bötticher had abandoned his search and purchased a doppelgänger in readiness for a war that was coming no matter what. By the look of it, Megaira was ready. Those twitching ears of hers already seemed to be tuning into an historic future.

I slipped and lunged across the grass. Got it! A corner of the page was wet, but one sentence continued to stand out from the rest: *I will claim my right of attack.* Those words had been pressed into the paper. The right of attack is a rule that infuriates many a fencing novice. The fencer who launches their attack first has priority and any hit by the opponent is discounted as long as the attack is in play, which can force them on the defensive until they are able to respond. Talk about spoiling the sport! Countless times I had hurled my mask to the floor when the president dismissed my sublime hit and rewarded my opponent's pathetic efforts just because they had extended their arm a split second earlier. But one day, mid-match, I formed an instant attachment to that strange rule. My opponent was my superior in every way: a man three times my age who towered head and shoulders above me. When he shook my hand he had the nerve to purse his lips slightly as if he found me endearing. My vision clouded with rage, I fought like an animal, snarling at the air around me when I failed to read his moves. I was trailing by ten points when suddenly, through the mesh of my mask, I zoomed in on how he was holding his weapon: nonchalantly, three fingers barely touching the grip. The man was bored! Even before he decided to attack, I had decided to beat down on top of his blade. The match ended in a draw. This revelation didn't lead me to abandon fencing on my reflexes: the best attacks are seldom calculated. At most they work their way into your system through experience, just as a bear learns to perform a trick.

'Hey, Fräulein!'

Heinz waved. He had untied the horse and was leading her across the field. She walked alongside him good-naturedly, as if checking her stately stride to match his plod, unsurprised by his puniness or that of humans in general and how awkwardly they move on their two stilt-like legs. She could easily pull the rope from his hands with a single tug but she refrained, the urge having been patiently wiped from her horse's brain. Why rock the boat? Yet just once I would have loved to see a surge of anger force her up on her hind legs, to watch her rear up with her velvet underbelly on display.

'Do you know what breed she is?' Heinz shouted as he approached. 'A Trakehner. The noble steed of the Prussian soldier. King Friedrich Wilhelm I began rearing them two centuries ago, and there's no hardier breed to this day. A hussar couldn't wish for a finer horse. Tough and lean, look at those haunches.'

Megaira was staring blankly. Horses apparently sleep three hours a day, the sum of minutes snatched between taking to their heels and having to keep half an eye on where they are going.

'Look how squarely she's standing,' Heinz said. 'That's training for you. Four legs planted firmly under her body. Tall and correct. You'll never see a horse like that in the wild. They straggle by nature. A superior breed, the Trakehner, but if her legs had been crooked we'd have had her put down. No point wasting time on defective foals. We have to be as cruel as nature, otherwise we are doomed. And you know who said that, don't you?'

I shook my head. I could feel the water seeping up through the grass under my bare feet and had no desire to be stuck here sinking into the ground while Heinz kept chuntering on at me.

'The Führer. A state should not be an economic organization but a living national organism that keeps its own kind in order. Look at Megaira here. What a magnificent specimen she is.'

She buried her nose in his chest, not caring that it was hollow, that his ribs were as crooked as the rest of his body. How often do you see magnificent creatures—dogs, horses—being led along by an unsightly master, yet there's never a hint of shame. Not so the other way around. Dog owners apologize for the shortcomings of their four-footed friend, joke about putting the mutt out of its misery, but in the still of evening, when no one's around, they whisper into those big, soft ears that he's the sweetest, most beautiful animal in all the world. What a nasty piece of work is man! Could Megaira sense she was only the echo of another horse, selected for her likeness to Fidèle?

I thought of the twins and their steadily fading likeness. Only in sleep were they still truly identical. The previous day I had crept up on them as they lay entwined on the divan, in a carefree slumber that made them look no older than twelve. Friedrich woke first and looked at me, stretching and yawning. I would have kissed him if I hadn't noticed Siegbert glaring at us from beneath a fretful frown. Nothing escaped his notice. I was startled by his stare, just as you jump when you are caught unawares by your reflection and, without the chance to straighten up, you see yourself as you really are, shoulders drooping as you slouch through life. For a fleeting moment, in Siegbert's eyes I saw the Janna other people saw, and I didn't like it one little bit. I rose abruptly to my feet and left them to drift off into another shared nap.

'What have you got there?'

Heinz pointed at the page I had rescued from the wet grass.

'Nothing much.'

'The ink is running. Look, your fingers are black.'

And then, without so much as a by your leave, he grabbed the letter from my hand. The cheek! His eyes, beady and sickly as a pigeon's, bulged from a clutch of pink wrinkles as they shot back and forth across the page. He examined the paper back and front and then—heaven preserve us—began reading the final paragraph aloud, complete with running commentary. His swallowing and stammering were enough to turn my stomach.

'A new war will come, a better war than this. Well, that's as plain as the nose on your face. Fought not with anonymous bullets fired by francs-tireurs ... what are they when they're at home? Just like him to chuck in some French. It's the master's handwriting, all right. But who's this fellow Jacques? Some frog or other, no doubt.'

'He's my father. Give it back to me.'

He obeyed without even thinking, as if he wasn't in the least bit interested. But as he stood stroking the horse, he was clearly chewing over what he had read.

'You know what it is? Herr von Bötticher acts like nothing's changed, when there's a national revolution on the go. There's a new war coming all right, but not one with him as the hero. Now it's the people's turn. It's just like Hitler says, the generals act like knights and nobles, while he needs revolutionaries. Von Bötticher's not listening, of course. That's what comes from having nothing to do all day. Wealth makes you hard of hearing.'

With a click of the tongue he commanded the horse to move on. I watched them till they disappeared into the stables, the majestic Trakehner and her ragtag groom. There was no doubt how the roles were divided. If I closed my eyes I could hear the horse enunciate: 'Little man, do you honestly think your kind has advanced all that much over the past few centuries?'

Later, I had to close my eyes before I realized that the aromas my pitifully human sense of smell had picked up on were coming from the kitchen. It was the maître doing the cooking, I knew that much. At breakfast he had placed pots and pans at the ready and produced knives from drawers, whistling as he dragged them across the whetstone. For men, cooking is showmanship, all grand, superfluous gestures and liberal sprinklings of herbs. My father would come into action for nothing less than a roast: carving notches, wrapping things in bacon, rolling and binding lumps of meat, tucking bay leaves, mace and God knows what else in every crevice. My mother looked on benignly. The result was edible but she knew better.

As soon as I entered the kitchen, I could smell the raw meat on the chopping block, cutting through the fug of stewing apples and sauerkraut. To my disgust, Gustav the rabbit was sleeping next to it, dead to the world but for his pulsating nose. Without warning, the maître pressed his palm to my face. 'Smell ... the first deer of the season.'

'More like the last,' I said. 'It stinks like an old corpse.'

'That's just what it is,' he said. 'Flesh from a corpse. Which is why you have to wait till rigor mortis has passed or you'll end up chewing till you're blue in the face. A deer should be left to hang till it's falling off the hook. The proteins break down and the meat becomes tender. Turn up your nose all you like. Eskimos fill a slaughtered seal with dead birds, without even plucking them, and leave it lying for six months until it has fermented.'

He had a seemingly endless supply of these stories. I was sure he only told them so he could relish the sight of me swallowing hard at every gory detail.

'They say the flavour is wonderful. A wonderful, decadent rotten taste, not unlike French blue cheese.'

'My father throws cheese away once it's gone mouldy.'

He shook his head, grinning. 'If anyone should know how useful mould is, it's a doctor. Take a walk in the woods. Wherever you look, you'll see new life springing from decay. Mosses grow on mouldering tree stumps, animals eat mushrooms. Nature seldom starts from scratch. She's always putting something old to good use — a ruin, an old carcass. But people pay no heed to nature. They'd rather listen to a gaggle of other people telling them everything has to be constantly renewed and reinvented.'

He began to cut the meat into chunks. 'Do you know what makes me smile? What really excites me ... where's that damned peppermill?'

He shoved Gustav off the chopping block. The rabbit landed on the kitchen floor with a smack, only to shake his ears and hop off as if his entire being—body and disposition—were driven by his ears alone. Egon laid his hands on the peppermill and began grinding furiously. 'I love to see nature going about her business, laying to waste the works of man and carrying on as if they had never existed. Put a man-made object among the trees, a piece of furniture for example, and it'll be overgrown, eaten away, rotten in no time. Better still, leave it to the animals. They like nothing more than to destroy things. Give a dog, a horse or a cow a product of our labour and the next day you'll find it kicked or smashed or chewed to pieces. Nothing remains intact once they get at it. They're especially fond of tearing at clothes. Perhaps it's because they can smell us and want to get close to us, perhaps even want to *be* us. You are what you eat. It's the only option left to them: devour our regularity, crush our urge to manufacture, all those rules we've invented to cut death off at the pass.'

'Rules? Like the right of attack?'

'The right of attack ... ' He shook his head. 'The right of attack, now there's a thing.'

Without warning he pinched one of my vertebrae. A sharp, disturbing pain that makes you lash out instinctively. I was getting sick of this twisted pantomime of his.

'That's how a bear kills a man. Did you know that? Grabs us by our hopelessly long backbone and pulls us apart, just as we might fillet a fish.'

I turned to face him but he looked at me as if I were a stranger and I put all thought of kissing him out of my head. There had been a few such moments. At night we shared a secret pact, agreeing that no words needed to be spoken, but in the light of day even a knowing glance was too much to ask. Left empty-handed, it was little wonder that I grew more cunning.

And so it was that I burned all his letters. I went to work as he slept, absorbing his words before they went up in flames. I burned everything, even the big Poste Restante envelope. The only one to escape was the letter he had written in his cell. I couldn't get enough of it! He was lost, that was how it began. On the brink of madness, losing control, like in those fleeting moments with me. But better yet: there was no place for her in his cry of despair. My literary hero in his dungeon never once mentioned the name Julia. The Count of Monte Cristo, who took instruction in the sciences from his fellow prisoner yet never let himself be deflected from his revenge, what would my father have made of him? By then, had Egon read the letter in which my father wrote:

Those animal passions of yours, do you modify them if they turn out to be of no use to you, the way people do with the knowledge they acquire?

The tone my father took in his attempts to lift Egon's spirits was brisk, the briskness of a medical man. It was the same lack of compassion nurses display when they whip open hospital curtains, blinding the patients in their slumbering half-life with the cloudless world outside.

Your soldiers have *Gott mit Uns* engraved on their belt buckles. God is with us. Without optimism you won't get far, it's true. But poor old God had to stand by the Belgians, the French and the British into the bargain. Your lot were all too sure of your cause.

My father's letters were blind. He was feeling his way as he wrote, never knowing whether his words would be read. Perhaps that was why they betrayed so little emotion. Yet even when he had admitted to being stripped of his certainties, to his fears that science was all for nothing, a reply had not been forthcoming. Egon had read every word, even my father's disillusionment as he witnessed the exchange of the prisoners of war; the letter had been stuffed back into its torn envelope. What had gone through his mind as he read about the British soldier without a face?

... his entire lower jaw, including the lateral section of the maxilla and the palate, had been blown off. The field doctor had tried to use the remaining skin to close up what was left. The wound had dried well but the tissue was beginning to fester. Had he been older, he would have been less prone to hypergranulation, but by my estimate he could not have been more than twenty. Interesting how we first look for a person's age in their eyes. His gaze was still that of a boy, a farmer's son most likely, plucked straight from the countryside and hurled headlong into war. Still a virgin, no doubt. And what woman would kiss him now? No lips to pucker, no smile, no whispers. Doomed to spend the rest of his life staring out at the world in horror. You are so afraid of losing face, Egon, but your fate could have been so much worse.

One night Egon asked, 'Do I repulse you?'

I straddled him and ran the tip of my tongue down the uneven crack that began at the corner of his eye. It was a perfect fit. He shuddered briefly—the thin skin was sensitive—then abruptly pulled his face away. War wounds are not for licking and yet it had excited him. I climbed off his lap and left him to his state of arousal. I did not want to feel pity for him; such feelings never last. That mutilated young soldier, what was his life like now? Immediately after the war perhaps a girl had waited for him and licked the tears from his lashes, telling him over and over again what a hero he was. But now, twenty years on, surely she had left him, her devotion no match for his speechlessness.

'Perhaps I should take up the épée,' I said, handing Egon the butter. My look was a challenge, knowing full well he would protest.

'The épée? Nonsense! An unwieldy weapon for old men. Your strength is your speed.'

'With an épée, at least there's no stupid right of attack to worry about.'

'There is nothing stupid about the right of attack,' he said. 'A duel that results in two corpses, *that* is stupid. Grant your opponent the right of attack and you grant him his life. One death is more than enough—even a dying man can understand that. If wars are played out by the rules, all sides can live with the outcome.'

He shook the roasting tray over the fire and watched silently as the butter melted. For a moment I saw how old he was, hunched over the low stove. This was no hero, no revolutionary, but a wealthy man who was hard of hearing, just as Heinz had said. It was not a sight I wanted to see. But as long as he kept his curtains drawn, I knew I would wind up back in his bed.

# 5

Watching the Otter eat was enough to whet any man's appetite. Before each mouthful he turned his plate, debating whether to spear a gleaming chunk of venison with his fork or go for a stewed apple. Choice made, his gaze settled on the far end of the fencing hall as he chewed. Sitting next to him, I heard him grunt contentedly.

'The finest hunters cook their own game, Egon. This is delicious.'

With candles in only one chandelier, the light in the hall was muted, as were the voices of the two students who had not joined us at the table but raised their glasses from a dark corner of the room. This first Saturday in October had been reserved for the Mensur. Through the window I could see autumn chasing its tail beneath the lantern in the garden. The summer had disintegrated into snapped twigs, shredded leaves, grit and dust, animated briefly by gusts of wind. Once they had abated, Raeren would slide into a deathly silence. For now, the whinnying horses railed against the forces of nature and a spider clung gamely to its trembling web in a corner of the window. Perhaps it was time to return to the city.

There were eight of us at the table. In addition to the Otter, the maître had invited the four duellists of the day, two of whom had bandaged heads, the others a modest dressing on the cheek. Between them sat the Arbiter, the same stumpy little man who had presided on the previous occasion. He tucked in even before a toast had been raised and continued to shovel food into his mouth while one of the duellists murmured grace. The twins sat there wide-eyed. It was the first time they had experienced the Mensur and they were on their very best behaviour, though during the duels they had gnawed anxiously at their knuckles. The Arbiter cleared his plate before the rest, straightened up with a condescending smirk and elaborately undid his napkin, poking a duellist's jaw in the process and freeing his hands just in time to cover a belch. Egon pretended not to notice. His feet encountered mine and, much to my surprise, stayed where they were. A wrenching sensation rose up from between my legs. Afraid the doctor sitting next to me would diagnose my condition, I pulled my legs back, but he merely glanced at my décolleté and gave another grunt.

'A Dutch beauty, Herr von Bötticher. Tread with caution.'

Egon paid him no heed. He sat there enjoying his self-made dinner and would have preferred the conversation to centre on that and nothing else. The point had been made several times: this meal was *his* work, not Leni's. Her little hands were suited to Rhineland dishes, the pauper's kitchen. He meant nothing by it, of course; transforming leftovers into food fit for the gods is an art in itself, and one she had mastered, but this was noble fare. Presenting his dish, he had smacked his lips and slammed the roasting tin down on the table with one thumb in the sauce: red deer with chestnut boletes, a royal stag from his own land, feel free to inspect the antlers in the kitchen. They had shot the animal early in the rutting season, another month of incessant bellowing and he would have wasted away to nothing.

'You recall Mata Hari, don't you?' the Otter continued.

'Her fatherland was pure as the driven snow during the Great War, but she on the other hand ...! A spectacular woman. Did I ever tell you I saw her dance in Vienna? Dance mind, nothing else. That was impressive enough. It was an act involving a veil, which culminated in her dropping to the floor like a lemming. Stark naked. Could it be, Herr von Bötticher, that *this* young lady has been sent our way by the French? Look, she's blushing already. Maastricht, wasn't it? The time is ripe for such stratagems, as ripe as this glorious Berlepsch.'

He laid his arm briefly on my shoulders and I lifted my chin with an enigmatic smile. Mata Hari? That was fine with me. If I had been sent here on a mission, I could honestly say I had given it my all. My father wanted answers, and didn't he have a right to them after all these years? Egon chewed on regardless.

'I'll be damned, Herr Reich, you have a nose for these things.'

'I beg your pardon?'

'Those apples are indeed Berlepschs. My orchard is full of them. Feel free to fill a bucket or two before you leave.'

This response perplexed the Otter, who had been hoping for a nudge and a wink, one man to another. Once again his arm snaked around my shoulders.

'It was only my little joke, of course, but nonetheless disgraceful of me to compare you to that courtesan. Look at you, pristine as a young ... pear.'

If only he knew, I thought. I wanted to say something coquettish, but the Arbiter cut in with the disdain of a tramp who, invited to a table above his station, believes the host's riches are rightfully his. His eyes glinted with envy as he totted up the value of everything around him, the corners of his mouth drooping.

'Gentlemen, I have heard and seen it all. You, Mata Hari,

when will you be returning home?'

I squeezed a crystal knife rest in my hand and stared straight ahead. This odious little man's tone was even more presumptuous than the Otter's banter, yet in passing he had asked a question everyone had been avoiding. In honesty, I had no mission. I had simply been sent away. Suitcase packed, clean pinafore on, and off I trotted down to the station with Father. Our conversation had been strictly outward bound, no mention of the return journey. We had discussed the practicalities of the trip down to the last detail: which platform the train would depart from, whether it was worth paying a surcharge for a forward-facing window seat, whether I had enough biscuits to last me the journey, my reading material, the merits of the scenery along the way. My father held forth for at least an hour about a forty-minute journey. As a parting shot he warned me about the high step, in case I stumbled. It had been a farewell like so many others: amid the haste, the hubbub and the steam, all that counts is the departure itself. The destination fades from view and what you are leaving behind only enters your thoughts when the train chugs into motion. The past rolls out of sight on the platform, waving and surprisingly small, one high step below the traveller. I had resolved to return as the best female fencer in Maastricht. One month later, my resolve had been dashed on the waves of love and had run aground on a riddle. Perhaps it was the riddle I had fallen in love with. In any case, how I would return home had become a matter of indifference to me.

'In two weeks' time,' Egon answered suddenly. 'Then her training will be at an end.'

The twins nudged each other. I looked down at my plate and saw too little food there to distract me. It would be empty in no time and I had no say in anything. The Arbiter scraped back his chair and began striding around the room, asking questions to which he expected no answer. Were the Dutch planning to remain neutral in the next war?

'Ultimately such a declaration is nonsense, you understand. Neutrality in the midst of warring parties does not result in a life lived in peace but in anticipation of war. One cannot remain inviolable for ever. You do realize this, don't you?'

'Oh, leave the girl alone. What does she know of such things?' the Otter muttered.

'Probably more than any of us here suspect,' the Arbiter said. 'When the next war comes, they will have to take a stand. And I trust that they, fellow Germans after all, will be wise enough to choose the side of progress.'

'I am curious about this war of yours, Herr Raab,' Egon said casually. 'Herr Hitler has never been party to a duel. Bismarck fought twenty-two, no less.'

The Arbiter puffed his cheeks and let the air escape very slowly. Then he picked up the hussar's hat, which Egon had placed at the corner of the table. No one said a word as he spun it around on his finger. Not even when he dropped it and flipped it back up with the point of his shoe.

'A word to the wise, von Bötticher: watch what you say. I have heard you make unpatriotic remarks of this kind before. You make no secret of your criticism of the fatherland. I for one would like to know what troubles you so much. Here, catch!'

With a sweep of his arm he flung the hat toward the students at the back of the hall. The skinny boy caught it and put it on his head, much to the hilarity of his companion. They had nothing to fear from their host, who was lighting a cigar at a safe distance, the length of a fencing piste away.

'What troubles you so, Herr von Bötticher? The fact that

the Führer has the guts to treat Locarno with the contempt it deserves? Unheard of, I agree. It would, of course, have been so much better to leave the Rhineland to the French. Better for Bohemians like you, that is. The cognac swillers and garlic eaters. All Greek to a simple student like myself.'

The sniggering grew louder. In front of the mirror, the skinny boy straightened the skull and crossbones on his head. The Arbiter threw an arm around his shoulders and addressed their brotherly reflection: 'Let me see, let me see. If it's not the Rhineland, what then? The new citizenship law perhaps? The *Reichsautobahn*? Could it be the Four Year Plan for the armed forces that troubles you so? I just can't figure it out. Help me, if you will.'

'Artillery is a poor way to restore an economy,' said the Otter. 'It would be better to invest in increasing our store of knowledge. No one can take away what's in a man's head.'

The Arbiter shot him a pitying look. 'Do you seriously expect me to fall for that old line? Your economy is not mine, Herr Reich, as well you know. I spit on your Masonic lodges. You claim to embrace mysticism while dancing to the tune of the Jews, the same Jews who control our newspapers and our universities, poisoning our culture in the process. But not for long, gentlemen, not for long. My, how you cower in fear of your own people!'

His shoes creaked as he circled the room. I pictured him tying his laces in the morning, cheeks flushed because his arms were too short for his body. I felt sure that he placed his shoes neatly side by side before getting into his miserable single bed, that he lay awake for an hour before surrendering to sleep, and that there were nights when he lay there sobbing with rage and loneliness. And I pictured a darkened trail, twenty years on, where Egon would stop his coach for a vagrant who wrung his cap contritely. But for now the vagrant continued to walk in circles through his host's house as if he were the only bidder at an auction. He stopped in front of a hunting scene on the wall.

'Is it fear, Herr von Bötticher, that keeps you ensconced here in your old money, far from the plebs? Were they not your equals when they perished as cannon fodder in your vanguard? Isn't that the reason you came back alive and they did not?'

'Put the hat back on the table,' Egon said in a restrained tone.

The student was about to obey, but the Arbiter held him back.

'Are you aware that this emblem belongs to the ss and has done for ten years? They wear the skull and crossbones now, because they truly are prepared to die. The commanders are all excellent fencers, to a man. And they are bringing about the revolution you wish to know nothing about. You sit here amid the plush of your own variety theatre with your back turned to the world stage. I can no longer keep your views from the Party. Please excuse me, I must go. Convey my thanks to Leni for this nourishing meal. Anton, Leo, Willy, and anyone else who feels called upon to do so, follow me. This place reeks of antique wax. *Heil Hitler!*'

Six men marched out of the hall. One of the duellists mumbled something about needing a lift and disappeared after them. The door closed with a bang. Egon tapped the ash from his cigar, clamped it between his lips and strolled over to retrieve the hat from the middle of the hall. I admired the way he had calmly sat there smoking. Not even blowing rings, simply inhaling and exhaling smoke. The doctor broke the silence with a rattling little cough.

'My apologies to the young lady. I was mistaken. The real spy in our midst has just left the room. We should no longer invite him as Arbiter, Egon. What an insolent lout.'

The remaining duellists exchanged nervous glances. The great day intended to unite them in a band of blood brothers had ended in a rift and they already appeared to be regretting their clandestine flirt with disfigurement. Perhaps they too were wishing they had gone back to the city rather than being stranded here at Raeren in its days of long ago. The maître sensed their doubt.

'Let me tell you something about this symbol,' he said. 'The skull and crossbones. Nowadays we no longer live with death, it is considered unhygienic. Just ask Professor Reich here. He teaches his students that a body has to be removed as quickly as possible, deposited in a drawer like the leftovers of a failed operation. The deceased's mortal remains. But we hussars live with our dead, they give us the strength we need to avenge them. In modern warfare you no longer need to wait for decay to do away with the individual who once was. One mortar strike and your old chum is instantly unrecognizable. I remember ...'

He walked away. What had he wanted to say? Had he seen death at close quarters before he had been wounded and removed from the front? It was a memory that would remain unshared.

'Herr Reich, I have a question for you,' he continued. 'In your capacity as a doctor, tell me why death takes some of us and spares others. Do you have an answer for me? What or who determines the inviolability of the few?'

While the Otter pondered an answer, Egon continued to stand at the window. All he could see was his own reflection, but the storm raging outside was making itself felt, the wind and rain so fierce that we had not even heard the Arbiter's car driving away. Perhaps he had not left at all and he and all his enmity were still here within Raeren's walls. Perhaps he and his companions were having tea with Heinz, venting their mutual aversion to Egon. I shuddered at the idea, without fully understanding why. With hindsight, it's tempting to claim that I chose the right side instinctively, that even then I suspected who would turn out to be good and who evil, but the truth is I was simply in love. The way he stood there at the window, melancholy and unyielding: it was not exactly a difficult choice.

'You see him on every battlefield,' he said. 'The inviolable soldier. Usually from behind, as he walks on ahead of you with a calm and upright tread, bullets whizzing past his ears. He knows they will not touch him. With your surprise dawns the realization that you are not him. You are not one of the inviolable. And that is the moment when the first bullet hits you.'

A sudden silence. The dust spinning beneath the lantern settled, the howling in the chimney died away. The twins looked at each other. I knew what they were thinking. Something told me their pale skin would not remain undamaged: perhaps it was the vividness with which I pictured their red blood running over it.

'Inviolability,' the Otter began, quietly. 'I once read a most interesting study on that very subject. Are you familiar with Girard Thibault?'

Egon frowned. 'I know the name from somewhere, but it's odd, I can't remember where.'

'His training method, *Académie de l'Espée*, is probably the most comprehensive work ever written on the martial arts. Seventeenth-century, during the Dutch Republic. It leans heavily on the principles of the Spanish School.'

Egon headed for the door. 'I'll be right back. I have something I think might interest you.'

Only when he had left the fencing hall did I understand that he had gone to fetch the engraving. Thibault—I had recognized the name more readily than he had. Dear Lord, not now!

'You must know of him,' the Otter asked me. 'Your compatriot, Thibault?'

'I've heard of him,' I said in a whisper. I knew Egon would now be in his room, hunched over the drawer, seeing for the first time that the green envelope, the entire Poste Restante of his own letters, was missing. Perhaps he had kept everything in a particular order and would know I had also rifled through the rest. He would see the hands—my hands—that had churned up his past, deciding on a whim what would continue to exist and what would not. None of the guests had an inkling of this crime. The twins were sitting there without a care in the world. Why wouldn't they, with all their decisions made for them? They had no mysteries to unravel, or debates to be caught up in. When you are two sides of the same coin, the taking of sides becomes an irrelevance.

'He studied mathematics in Leiden, old Thibault,' said the Otter. 'And went on to found a fencing academy in the heart of Amsterdam. Every Dutch dignitary of the age was under his tutelage. Now barely anyone knows it existed. A Dutch friend of mine had a number of engravings at home and explained some of the salient points to me. If you genuinely want to follow Thibault's method considerable patience is required, but eventually you will reap the rewards. We shouldn't underestimate his work just because it was written in the seventeenth century. It could still serve us well. Now more than ever. In these days of ... '

Egon returned and fixed his eyes on me immediately. I saw no anger, but neither had I seen any when the Arbiter had insulted him. To be on the safe side, I smiled. He narrowed his eyes to slits and turned to the doctor.

'A gift from her father. Along with his daughter.'

The professor took off his glasses and examined the engraving at arm's length.

'Yes! Good Lord! This is from Thibault's school! Well, I never ... There are many more like this one, hundreds in fact. A whole book of them. From the girl's father, you say, the doctor from Maastricht? That comes as no surprise. Hippocrates, the father of all physicians, once said: the human body is a circle. We doctors understand such things.'

He traced the geometric figures on the engraving with his finger. Looking over his shoulder, I saw the male figure was holding what looked like a rapier in front of his half-dissected body. The grip was level with his ribcage and the tip of the blade touched the circle in which he stood. From that point lines were drawn, dotted with a trail of footsteps. The words EX HOC CICULO ICTUS MOTU TOTIUS BRACHII VIBRATUR were written along the circumference.

'Everything in our bodies goes around in circles,' continued the Otter. 'Our movements, our breathing, even our thoughts. Our joints don't shuttle back and forth. They rotate.'

He extended his hands and for the first time I noticed the wedding ring embedded in the flesh of his left hand, like the collar of a mating cock pigeon. A long marriage. He must have made a charming bridegroom.

'Look, what a perfect union of geometry and arithmetic we are,' he said. 'Man is the measure of all things: well said, Protagoras old boy! We *are* the number ten. Ten fingers. Two hands of five. Four fingers and one thumb on each. A finger has three sections, the thumb has two. One, two, three, four, five—ten. The principle on which the temple of Solomon was built, not to mention the Ark of Noah. It's all there in the Bible: Noah's Ark constructed according to the proportions of the human body—three hundred cubits long, fifty wide and thirty high. Divine proportions running through all of Creation.'

'Your point being?' frowned Egon. 'We were talking about inviolability.'

The Otter grinned. 'You want to cut straight to the chase, but that is the crux of the problem.'

He began to walk in circles around the hall, eyes fixed on his feet, as if he were taking his first steps. 'It all comes down to proportion. Balance, symmetry. More than any other creature, humans have to be keenly aware of balance, walking as we do on two legs. We are born into this world comparatively unarmed. No spines or fangs for us. Instead, we have the power of reason, which develops gradually and recognizes the weapons of others. A man of true courage is aware of his own strength and does not attack in order to defend himself. He watches and he waits. This time around, we Germans should show more patience. Not dive in head over heels like last time, bawling soldier songs at the top of our lungs.'

'In 1914 everyone was in the mood for war,' said Egon. 'You know that as well as I do. I'm still not clear what you're getting at.'

The men were drinking plum brandy, and somewhere between the fourth and the fifth glass they dropped the formalities. The rest of us listened in, mouths parched. The Otter leaned over the twins.

'Will the two of you stand over there? Facing each other. No, not in the fencing position. Yes, that'll do.'

Friedrich stood there looking bewildered but Siegbert had been listening intently, with the same concentration he had shown when burying the mole. He wanted to study, to survey the land, while Friedrich was merely miffed that his brother knew things he didn't understand. As they stood there facing each other, I saw differences that were lost on the Otter.

'Two perfectly identical human beings,' he said, 'but in

essence every human is the same.'

Egon threw his arms in the air. 'Christ, what an evening! Are you about to spoon-feed me socialism too?'

'No, you misunderstand me. The proportions of every healthy human being—excluding those who suffer from dwarfism or acromegaly—are the same. There is no difference between the body of an aristocrat and that of a pauper once they have been bathed and dressed in a hospital nightshirt.'

'Nonsense.'

'Once you realize that the enemy does not in fact differ much from yourself, the reach of his movements can be predicted with a simple calculation. So why go charging in like a wild animal attacking its prey? Reason alone makes a man inviolable. No amount of flag-waving, raised feathers or forest singsongs will compensate. It's nothing short of disconcerting to lay eyes on these words of wisdom from the seventeenth century now that we are being plunged back into an animalistic age.'

'And what's wrong with animals?' Egon asked. 'You should cherish the animal inside you. Only a predator is completely free, to roam the land, to fight, to win, to devour. An excess of culture leads to degeneration.'

'Perhaps you're more of a National Socialist than you think, my friend.'

'Nationalist, possibly. Socialist, never.'

Grinning, they raised another glass. I slid the engraving toward me. On the left was a fencer, dressed to the nines, standing opposite a man in rags who was trying to kick him. Wisdom versus brute force, in terms even a child could understand.

'As far back as the seventeenth century,' the Otter resumed, as he walked back over to the twins, 'people knew it made no sense to lash out like an animal. After all, one well-placed thrust was enough to suck the air from your opponent's lungs.'

He let his hand rest on Friedrich's chest, where his shirt was unbuttoned. The mother turned her boys out well. They had far more clothes with them than I did and apparently they were even capable of dressing themselves. Unless, of course, they dressed each other. Every day they appeared in a fresh, finely woven shirt under a woollen waistcoat or knitted vest. Sometimes braces, never a tie. In the past few days they had seemed less inclined to wear identical outfits.

'Although medically speaking that is incorrect,' said the Otter. 'Incorrectly formulated, I should say. A lung collapses when punctured, not because the air escapes but because it becomes trapped between the pleural membranes.'

Friedrich looked from his chest to me, and neither of us was able to suppress a smile. He was beautiful, outrageously so, and worst of all, he knew it. The Otter lifted Siegbert's right arm and pointed his fingers at Friedrich's chest. I don't know why but I looked away. Perhaps it was the look Siegbert had given his brother when he saw our eyes meet. I had no desire to be drawn into this pointed engagement.

'A collapsed lung,' continued the Otter, drawing imaginary lines between one twin and the other, 'is the result of a thrust that makes all others superfluous. Thibault's theory was developed with only the gentry in mind. Exclusive knowledge made available to men whose bodies had to be closely guarded. Nowadays farmers drive tanks, but in those days the lower classes had no access to the martial arts, and just as well. It's all a matter of learning, Egon. Victory is algebra. Algebra for the privileged.'

Egon sat at the table with bloodshot eyes. This was not a position he could ever accept. He had told me himself, the best fencers fight without thinking, driven by emotion, basic urges. The brain lags behind instinct, a dog bites the hand that feeds him before he can regret it. Now his red eyes made him look rather like a dog himself, a wolf resigned to human company. And still those eyes would not reveal whether or not he knew. He turned to face the Otter, who kept nattering away as he traced an imaginary circle around the twins.

'There is nothing magical about Thibault's circle. Its radius is determined by the length of the weapons of both fencers, relative to their height. For the finer points, I suggest you read the book for yourselves. I believe that the libraries in Amsterdam still have copies, as do those of Barcelona. Therein lies the secret of inviolability. You may return to your seats, boys.'

Siegbert was first to walk back to the table. He pushed his chair some distance from Friedrich's, whose brazen attempts to catch my eye continued unabated. I ignored the pair of them.

'On the battlefield you cannot permit yourself the luxury of treating your enemy as your equal,' said Egon. 'That's exactly what I told Jacques—her father—all those years ago. He worked for the Dutch Red Cross, whose pledge was to help everyone, everywhere, always. But how can such a principle ever be applied in conflict? If we're all the same and we hate our enemy, it amounts to self-hatred. If we're all the same and we love our beloved, it's narcissism.'

Leni came in to clear the table and to point out that it was midnight. I could hardly believe my ears. It was as if the clocks had only started ticking again once the storm had subsided. Through the window I could see that the Arbiter's car was gone, but his threats still hung in the air. The duellists took their leave without looking us in the eye. I received a warm handshake from the Otter.

'So you'll be leaving in two weeks' time? We will miss you.'

'My father is coming to collect me,' I bluffed. Nothing of the sort had been arranged. Nothing had been arranged at all.

But my father knew where to find me. I remember his amazement when he discovered that Egon was living in Aachen. Quite by accident, though my aunt always insisted there was no such thing. She had brought me a copy of *Die Woche* featuring an article on stage combat. A maître from the Aachen region had helped the actors prepare for the fencing scenes in *The Three Musketeers* and they were deeply indebted to Herr Egon von Bötticher. My father had lowered the magazine and stared blankly out of the window.

'Two kilometres,' he mumbled. 'Two kilometres a year. That's all.'

He could see the railway masts over the roofs of the neighbouring houses. At the end of the line lived the friend he had lost twenty years ago. A straight line that stretched for forty kilometres, dissected by a border. Two kilometres for every year. It was beyond his comprehension.

**6**

A voice was calling my name but I was paralysed by sleep.

'Little girl.'

Was it German? I did my best to make it out but the words turned to gibberish. A couple of fierce, incoherent cries. My legs were still heavy under the bedclothes. I didn't want to get up. I wanted to stay here. I had the right to stay here, in this bed, in the attic room at Raeren. Permission had been granted.

'...'

'What?'

My voice rang hollow in the darkness. I had no choice but to open my eyes.

'What did you say?'

He came closer, one fragment then another, a picture that refused to complete itself. Only the left half of his body was clothed. The other half was naked. My eyelids grew heavy. Sleep.

'3.14159265. *Ratio vincit.*'

Reluctantly, I crawled out of bed. This kind of thing had to be resolved without delay or it would continue to drag me from my sleep. There was a vicious draught. I wrapped the blanket around my shoulders and fumbled for the light switch. All the while he remained standing there, eyes bulging. Yes, I know who you are, I said. Now bugger off. He gave no response at all, as if the words had never been spoken. Bugger off, why don't you? What else do you want from us? Where are your cronies? Did you let them drive off by themselves while you spent the whole night here, chewing the fat with Heinz? He stepped toward me and his penis swung flaccidly to and fro. Disgusting. The rags that covered one side of his body appeared to be a tattered military get-up, with tassels on the chest. Only when he stepped into the moonlight did I realize what I had been looking at: half man, half corpse. One half of his body was bare bones. Only one side of his face was flesh and bone, the other side was a skull. I screamed and, knowing now my voice was real, I kept on screaming as he rattled closer. Something was coming from his precisely dissected throat: not words but numbers. I couldn't understand how. They materialized without crossing his lips and filled the space.

'3589793238462643383279.'

I woke up on the stairs, in a pool of candlelight. It was Heinz, carrying the sconce. We jumped when we saw each other.

He was first to speak. 'What are you doing here?'

'I should be asking you the same question,' I said, surprised at how matter-of-fact I sounded. 'Your room is further away than mine.'

'Less of your cheek. I'm doing my rounds, as I have done for years.'

He looked me up and down. I folded my arms across my chest and he lowered the candle.

'They're here.'

'Who?'

'You can feel it too. I see it in your face.'

His voice was monotone, but the blood pounded in my temples just the same.

'It was a dream,' I said. 'I've had sleepwalking episodes

like this before.' He smiled faintly at my admission that I knew what he was talking about.

'Dreams aplenty at Raeren,' he said. 'The air here is thick with them. Feel for yourself.' And he took a deep breath.

'I couldn't find the light switch, Heinz. Just now, in the bedroom. Perhaps you ... '

'No need to be afraid. There's a perfectly logical explanation. Did anyone tell you the history of this house?'

I wasn't at all sure this was the time to find out. Why couldn't he just lead the way back to my bedroom, turn on the light and leave it on till I fell into a carefree slumber? But no, he continued whispering on the step below me.

'They set up a hospital here during the war. The wounded were brought in downstairs, where the fencing hall is now. They lay there screaming and bleeding in rows of fifty. Many people died in that hall where the three of you play musketeers. Too many.'

He began to descend the stairs. With each step the creaking grew louder and the candlelight dimmer.

'You're scaring me,' I hissed. 'You're doing it on purpose.'

'Not at all,' I heard him say. 'The spirit world is something to cherish, not to fear. No use clinging to logic. It won't be much use to you on your deathbed. That's the domain of the spirit. Nothing but pain, sorrow, fear, and hope.'

I woke the next morning in a state of confusion, unable to believe that so black a night could end, that the sun could ever shine in this room. The bells from the village sounded close by, one emphatic stroke after another ringing for all to hear, even for us, the strange folk of Raeren. When I opened the doors to the balcony, it turned out to be warmer outside than in. I looked out onto a landscape of finely woven brocade and swaying greenery, but there was a mouldering scent to the view. More keenly than ever I could smell the rotting, the bark and the moss of the pine forest, the apples left lying where they had fallen, the steaming dung heap and the creosote Heinz used to coat the stable doors. A procession of ladybirds toddled along the window frame like a string of jasper beads. Eight of them. When I tried to steer them through a crack, they gave off the sour scent of cold sweat. They're here, Heinz had said. You can feel it too. I looked at the wall lamp where my daydreams had brought all kinds of characters to life—the little girl with the straw hat had appeared more than once, a grey lady, a fat man with a broken nose, a very pale little boy. Nothing ghostly about them. My father would have called them loose ends, the frayed edges of dreams knitted together into something plausible. The brain ticking over, always needing to keep itself busy. My mother begged to differ. Narrow-minded she called it, to degrade the world's mysteries to however many ounces of grey matter. 'Anything between one and one and a half kilos,' my father would reply. 'Without its fluid, the brain would collapse under its own weight. That's how great its mass is.'

I felt the sting of tears. Was this homesickness? Home didn't enter my thoughts very often. Perhaps my parents actually talked to each other now I was no longer there to be a buffer between them. I didn't miss those evenings, didn't even miss my friends. They had faded like the cover of a magazine that had been read one time too many. I would never be able to tell them what I had experienced. How lonely that would feel! I wanted to be the way I was back then. That's real homesickness: when the traveller is beyond longing for home and starts to long for himself, everything he was and thought and knew before he left. Back then things were bright and clear, my life as self-evident as a circle. I was much too young to know what these past months had revealed to me—wars, bloody duels, ghosts, the skull and crossbones, *sexual intercourse*. Like the time he had grabbed me by the shoulders and shoved me down into the bed, tugging at my hips as he mumbled 'Yes, like that.' Janna, the poacher's prize. He had stripped me hurriedly, in a crisis of conscience, just as I had torn open his letters. Indiscretion lay in wait all over this house, taboos in every corner, secrets and riddles at every turn. Heinz had known this all along, had warned me on my first day here: these are matters that do not concern you. And hadn't his wife urged me to keep my father's letter to myself? If only I had listened. If the seals on all those envelopes had never been broken, I might still be in one piece myself. Damn it all.

I stepped into the basin and poured a jug of cold water over my head, jumping up and down as I dried myself off. I pulled on my fencing gear, not only the jacket and the flannel trousers I had worn in recent weeks, but the full kit. I had given up braiding my hair weeks ago, but now I sat at my dressing table and carefully teased out the strands. I still had two weeks left. For the next two weeks I would conduct myself admirably, even if no one else did. The maître had said it himself: then her training will be at an end. In that case it was about time it began. The letters had all been read, there was nothing more to be done on that score. No need to pay those wretched twins any heed at all. It would be another three years at best before they learned to fence properly and at least as long again before they grew up. Leni, Heinz—since when was a guest supposed to concern herself with the staff? Two more weeks. I would show them.

I ran downstairs, where the day was clunking into gear. Leni was in the hallway, rattling milk churns. Heinz was out on the terrace knocking the straw out of a brush. All the doors were flung wide, banging back and forth in the draught, while from the fencing hall a pitiful wheezing rose up, a groan of sheer desperation. Briskly I pushed open the door to find the twins bearing down on the old sow, her four trotters on the parquet. Was five minutes of normality too much to ask of this place?

'In the name of the Black Hussar!' Siegbert declaimed, pointing his blade at the sow's body. They had somehow managed to squeeze her into a fencing jacket, zip half open and sleeves trailing around her legs. Siegbert poked her in the side.

'Leave her be,' I said. 'You can see she doesn't like it.'

'Yes, leave her alone,' Friedrich said. 'Sigi, we should get her out of that jacket.'

The sow let herself be undressed, squealing all the while, then hobbled over to the other side of the hall with a deafening clatter. There she remained with her backside up against the wall. Compared to other animals, pigs seem to make a show of their emotions, not unlike humans. They begin to screech long before they are slaughtered. When the maître marched in, the sow stared him straight in the eye with a grisly look of common sense.

'What's going on here?'

'We were playing, maître.' Siegbert lowered his weapon. 'The Black Hussar.'

'What in God's name are you talking about?'

'*Der schwarze Husar*, you must have seen that one!' said Friedrich. 'It might still be on somewhere. Mama said we mustn't miss it and she was right—we nearly died laughing! It's set during the Napoleonic Wars and troop captain von Hochberg forces his way into the Polish king's castle in all kinds of disguises ... '

'Enough!' the maître shouted, raising his fist. 'God only knows what kind of rubbish you gawp at in those cinemas. As if there isn't enough to experience in the real world!

Judging by your idiotic pranks, it's clear you haven't a clue. You came here to fence, not to terrorize pigs. I will take this up with your mother presently. Take a good look at yourselves for once: a pair of sickly good-for-nothings. All you ever do is get in the way.'

The brothers looked at each other in confusion. They were not accustomed to bearing the brunt of someone's anger or they would surely have burst into tears. Could anything make them cry? Would they always go through life unmoved? If the maître was trying to goad them into becoming normal boys it hadn't worked: they asked no questions and edged closer together. Get in the way? They never foisted themselves on anyone. It was always other people who wanted something of them. They lived a life of needing no one. We watched as the maître steered the sow toward the door. Her tail began to wag contentedly as soon as he placed his hand on her back.

'I didn't hurt her,' Friedrich whispered in my ear. 'At first she wanted to play with us but then Siegbert had to go and pester her. He's so aggressive these days, sometimes I hardly recognize him.'

'Get to your fencing immediately,' the maître said. 'In silence. Not another word, and as little noise from your weapons as possible.'

We had trained like this before. For every noise we made, a point was deducted. We did our best to fight, but in avoiding making a noise we mainly avoided one other. The circles we made as we parried were larger than necessary to ensure our weapons did not touch. We crept over the piste, backing away from each other and even pulling back a few times in the middle of a direct attack. We shuffled to and fro like puppets on the strings of a mute puppeteer. When we understood that the maître had left us to our own devices yet again, we grew angrier but said nothing, keeping our words behind our masks. Only the stamping of our feet grew louder. During my final match against Siegbert, I could hear myself panting. He was continuing to improve. I knocked his weapon aside too forcefully and lunged forward to hit his lower abdomen. Friedrich broke the silence. 'That's it, Janna. Finish him off. Make him feel it.' Siegbert tore off his mask. 'Go to hell! Don't think I can't see what you two are playing at. Be warned, Janna, those who come between us disappear never to be found. There have been others.'

He marched off and left his threat hanging in the air. We stared at each other open-mouthed till we heard the slamming of one door after another. The hallway filled with voices. I heard Siegbert, Leni and the voice of another woman.

'Mother,' Friedrich whispered. Alas, it was true. She was back, but why so early in the day? He put his foil in his bag and walked over to me. I could tell what he was about to do. We were still trying to avoid the slightest sound and now there was silence. Our tongues were otherwise occupied. I clung to my foil for dear life as his hand forced its way under my fencing jacket in search of skin. I closed my eyes, followed the rhythm of his breathing against my cheek, and as my lips found his again, his grip tightened and I yielded to him. Our fingers intertwined, a pleasing fit. In the wild, we would have made a lovely couple: both young, glowing with health, the male blond and a little taller, the female darker and slighter, yet strong. At one with the natural order. So why was I bent on pursuing a man who was far too old, who was lame, disfigured, perhaps even malevolent? Why could I smell nothing now, while in Egon's arms I breathed in scents that both troubled and contented me? Did nature care for beauty? Wasn't there enough harmony in the world? The petals of flowers, I had learned, grow in perfect proportion and all capture an equal amount of sunlight, but a magnificent stallion will just as soon mount an unsightly nag. I averted my eyes, afraid Friedrich would see that our harmony left me cold. He turned abruptly as his mother entered the room.

'There's my baby!'

That cloying tone. Your baby is a man. Seconds ago his fingers were feeling their way under my jacket and, for the record, there was no breast protector to get in their way. He is a man and you have no idea how well he can kiss. You receive a peck on the cheek, he walks away, you act as if you haven't noticed a thing and make small talk with me.

'And? How was today's lesson?'

I shrugged. She blushed and tucked a stray lock of hair behind her ear. A beautiful stone glinted in its silver setting. Aquamarine probably. I could smell alcohol on her breath … so early in the day. She had driven drunk to Raeren.

'I heard there was no lesson again today,' she said. 'That he was nasty to you.'

'Not to me.'

Her skirt rode up as she sank to her haunches. It amused her that I could see her garters. 'Have you heard the term *Sippenhaftung*?'

I shook my head. The inside of her thighs reminded me of whitefish. At the market in Maastricht there was a man who sold smoked mackerel. All day long he shouted, 'Fatty thighs, fatty hips.' Straight-faced. Honest missus, it's just the fish I'm on about.

'How little you know of the world,' she said. 'It's when children are made to suffer for the sins of their parents. Guilt runs through the bloodline. Polluted blood must be spilled till it runs pure. The old Germanic tribes did it. The Jews too, we can't have them pleading innocence. "And the king commanded, and they brought those men which had accused Daniel, and they cast them into the den of lions, them, their children, and their wives; and the lions had the mastery of them, and brake all their bones in pieces or ever they came at the bottom of the den.'"

She looked me deep in the eyes. Aquamarine. Though she narrowed them to slits, those cold stones remained piercing. 'You smell of sweat,' she said.

'And you smell of booze.' There, I'd said it. To hell with the consequences.

'Listen here girl, you can calm down. I'll not stand in your way for a second. Do whatever you like with my sons, sample one and then the other. Let people despise them, spit on them, rape them. The sons of a whore, they call them, the fruits of treason. Do whatever you like in the little time that's left before those barbarians drag them off to some war or other. Then they will be lost to me anyway. Truth be told, they were never really mine.'

She stood up and adjusted her skirt. She was more slender than I was, her hips as narrow as mine should have been. They were not the hips of a mother.

'Or do you have another man in your sights?'

I snorted. One step backward and she would be standing on my fencing bag, and I was poised to push her off it and watch her darling legs slip out from under her. As I stood waiting for that one step, she heaved a sigh.

'Don't tell me you're in love with your maître? Oh child, you really are a walking cliché. The pupil and her teacher. But what is he teaching you exactly? Another day has gone by without a lesson. Not that it's any of my business you understand, but ... '

She paused for effect. The feigned deliberation of an inveterate gossip.

'You are not here to learn fencing, you know. You have

been invited so that he can settle an old score. With your father.'

Was I, now? What did she know, the drunken trollop? And boy was she drunk! There were tears in her eyes. She began to pace the floor, but unlike the Otter's measured circles these were furious, ever-decreasing circuits, enough to make your head spin.

'Are you disappointed?' she asked. 'Egon collects people with whom he has a score to settle. Blood feuds, honour killings—they're all he thinks of, from morning till night. Like an old Teutonic warlord. There *is* nothing to fall in love with, my dear, not any more. You should have seen him in his prime. Oh, he was beautiful when he went to war! Everything about him was bright and new. His tight gamashes, the shining lance with the flag wrapped around it, the seat of his riding breeches ... even his cock was brand new. I hadn't touched it, in any case. Not then. He may even have gone to the front a virgin. We behaved ourselves in those days. Don't you believe me?'

She looked in the mirror and shook her hair loose. It was thin and dyed. She clamped the hairpin between her lips and made a double parting.

'The rot only set in when the war turned sour,' she continued. 'That's when we let it all slide. It's the way of the world: death comes to the villages and reason takes flight. What good is decency when men are returning without flags, without legs? We womenfolk surrendered all, regardless of class. Farm girls and ladies of high standing, they all went to the tavern alone. In they went and out they came with any old drunkard on their arm. From their expression you'd have thought they were lugging a laundry basket. The pickings were slim, but as long as the flagstaff was fit for purpose ... Fidelity? What of it? In a war where so much has been wasted, what is there left to be faithful to? Your country? The soil slurping up all that waste like the drunkard on your arm? But then an officer came to the village, one whose body was still intact. Lieutenant von Mirbach was on leave, but he looked as if he had just been woken from a three-year beauty sleep. Ha! He was the way we all used to be. Perfectly conserved. So pure, so honest, so handsome, it was downright offensive. Our eyes followed him wherever he went. I threw myself at him before anyone else could. If I had a shred of dignity left, this was my last chance. With complete abandon, I let him get me pregnant.'

I could not bring myself to look at her. Why was she telling me all this?

'A woman has to fend for herself in wartime, Janna. Don't underestimate how tough that can be. Even a front-line soldier has someone to take care of him. He gets his orders and his grub, while we are left behind with the livestock. In East Prussia, the Cossacks ransacked the villages. Rumour had it that the bodies of the women and children were left hanging from the trees, like diseased cadavers. We began to act accordingly. Determined to reproduce, no matter what.'

I looked at the sinewy back of her hand, her pert, symmetrical nose, her thin hair and pale ears. The only image that sprang to mind was that of a bird. She took out a long cigarette but left it unlit.

'Don't let anyone saddle you with blame, Janna,' she said. 'No one had it easy. Sometimes it's less of an ordeal to undergo something than to watch from the sidelines. What your father did ... '

'My father did nothing wrong.'

She waved my words away. 'We're all innocent, myself included. I thought Egon was dead. One year came and went without a word, then another. Later I found out the censor intercepted all letters sent from the internment camps. The words he had intended for me ended up in the clutches of other women. Yes, they left that job to women. It seems we have a talent for it. How would you like it, reading declarations of love meant for someone else? It would make me sad. Jealous too.'

Perhaps Egon had blurted it out as soon as she walked in the door: 'The girl has been reading the letters.' How many had he sent her? It couldn't have been many, given the two postage stamps a month he had mentioned to my father.

'Did you ever receive them?' I asked.

'No. Perhaps it's just as well. I felt guilty enough. Love letters are part and parcel of war, but there wasn't a woman in my village who opened an envelope without feeling uneasy. All those words, scribbled in trenches, wet rags salvaged from the pockets of the dead, they were not addressed to us but to the angels. We were no angels. We did not know what we were, so what chance did those boys have—boys we barely knew? The censors decided I did not have to wait for a boy I barely knew. Thanks to them I was free to marry a hero. My husband has more medals than I have jewellery. I was six months pregnant when he was decorated for the first time. We both had something to show off. He defeated the Russians at Tannenberg, then he fought in the Alsace, and at the Somme. All that time Egon was out of action in the internment camp. *Der lieber Leibhusar.* I might as well tell you, Janna. He wanted to be a hero but he was stranded on the sidelines. That is the grudge he bears. Time and time again I've tried to tell him you don't have to do anything to become a hero. All you need is a little imagination. It's something he doesn't possess.'

'He is my maître,' I said. 'The best I've ever had.'

'I'm not trying to take him from you,' she said. 'Your

hero, I mean. I shouldn't have told you all this.'

'Then why are you crying?'

She shook her head without drying her eyes. 'A woman who has been betrayed doesn't cry because she's afraid of losing her husband. She cries because she's afraid of being left behind. A gruesome fate for any woman.'

Sobbing, she ran out of the fencing hall. I jumped up and shouted after her, 'The betrayer becomes the betrayed!'

What had got into me? I hoped she would jump into her car and leave. But when she reached the hall she stopped. To my horror I watched her feel in her pocket, produce a key and, sniffing and spluttering, open the door to Egon's quarters. That did it! I threw down my foil and sprinted around to the side of the house, smooth soles slipping on the wet grass. Where did I get the nerve to hurl abuse at a lady of good standing, old enough to be my mother? Before I knew what I was doing, I was hammering on the window like a thing possessed, two grown-ups staring back at me. It was one of those fleeting moments when you convince yourself that you will never again care what anyone else thinks of you. Egon's eyes were wide as saucers as she sank her face into his collar, inhaling the scents I loved.

'Let me in!'

Behind him I could see the corner of his writing desk. On it was a box, a crate perhaps … No, I'll be damned—it was a drawer pulled from the chest! I banged on the window-pane. He spoke to her. I could not hear his words. She pouted and shook her head. He whispered something in her ear and she walked away. As casually as a prison warden, she turned the key and let herself out, locking the door behind her. I pressed my forehead to the glass. Egon walked back to his desk and sat down. I could only see his hands. They disappeared into the drawer, pulled out a card and struck a match. They held the card as the flames leaped higher. Smoke curled up from the ashtray and remained hanging under the lamp above the Thibault engraving. He let a burning cigar hover above the antique paper and then smoothed it out, like a miser with his last banknote.

# 7

At the stroke of midnight, the door was ajar. One hour earlier it had still been locked. I took in every detail as I walked down the hallway to his room. Through the windows I could see the trees bend in the wind, groaning like the sow had the previous morning. Why was the wind here so much fiercer at night? In his room a flickering candle was giving off smoke; it would probably last another fifteen minutes. He was sleeping, or pretending to be. At the foot of his bed a hulking shape rose to its feet and stared at me placidly. I whispered to it to lie down and it obeyed with a hearty smacking of its chops. The cold room filled with the smell of its coat. I would have liked nothing more than to lie down next to its master, a comforting presence as long as he slept, with a chest to rock to sleep on. But there was a desk to investigate. The Thibault engraving lay in the middle and the space around it had been tidied with obsessive precision: three equidistant sharpened pencils, a compass directly in front of them and half a notepad positioned squarely on the left corner, a rubber placed between two lines of the top page. This, I understood later, was the desk of someone who was at a loss, someone exorcizing confusion by ordering items of stationery. His fist had crumpled page after page into a ball and hurled them into the wastepaper basket, and now he was lost in mournful sleep. I held the candle over Thibault's half-dissected figure. Its right hand pointed upward, his skinned left hand pointed down at the words *Concavitas musculorum Femoris* and above them: *perinaeum, penis, anus*. Seventeenth-century perversity! There should be nothing sexual about a half-corpse. I ran my hand across the surface of the notepad and felt the indentations of the compass. Egon was still lying on the bed, eyes closed and hands clasped over his crotch. *Circulus no. 1, 2, 3, 4, 5*. In the wastepaper basket lay more of the same. Circles, numbers, lines, illegible scrawls, furiously shredded paper. I was about to stand up when my hand brushed against something hard. It was a piece of cardboard, charred around the edges, probably the card he had set alight the previous evening. A stamp was visible among the sooty remains, *Calvariënberg Hospital*, and a handwritten name, *Officer Cadet E. von Bötticher*. How could I have overlooked this? I flipped the card.

16-08 Debris with musket, buccal. Femur shaft fracture ... cerebral contusion ... connective tissue ... vascularization severely compromised. 17-08 Br ... t's traction. 18-08 Black necrotic buccal, granul ... debridem ... 1-09 High fever and shock ...

There was a fold in the cardboard along the crumbling edge where a note had been inserted. It all but turned to powder between my fingers.

... dissociative disorder ... worthy of closer examination. Patient suffering from the delusion that he is his own doppelgänger. Signs suggest he has an emotional but no cognitive sense of his identity. On seeing his reflection he becomes severely confused, convinced his eyes are deceiving him ... Nervous condition probably due to the impact of a horse's hoof above the right temple ... patient does not respond to stimuli directed at the left side of the body. Motor f ... I am firmly convinced that this case could help us build on Ramón y Cajal's study of the hippocampus or Janet's findings on the sense of reality and psychasthenia. For this reason alone, the advancement of scientific endeavour in our fatherland, I ask you, while by no means wishing to diminish the seriousness of the war and the purpose of this hospital, to keep patient E. von Bötticher under observation here for a few months more, especially since this region does not anticipate a major new influx of war-wounded in the foreseeable future.

'Need any help deciphering the contents?'

The card fell from my hands. He sounded alert, but in the shadows I was unable to gauge the expression on his face.

'An activity at which the Dutch excel,' he said. 'Deciphering. You never rest until it all adds up.'

'My father wrote this,' I said, clutching at a flimsy excuse.

He nodded. 'Correct. He sent it to me after the war, at my request. I had hoped it might exonerate me but it contained nothing of use. A man of towering ambition, our Jacques. A mere medical student, yet already seeking to emulate the famous Cajal! Nothing much came of it in the end, wouldn't you agree? Without my body he didn't stand a chance. What a disappointment I must have been to him. In the end I wasn't disturbed enough. And he wasn't talented enough.'

I looked through the open door. I had to get out of here. 'I'm sorry, I should never have ... '

I had almost reached the hallway when he grabbed me by the wrist. He grinned as he pressed my hand to his head, so forcefully that I could feel his pulse beneath his temple.

'Not disturbed enough after all,' he whispered. 'I was not hit by a hoof. My horse was not to blame. It was flying shrapnel, a blast that sucked the air inside out. It was the monstrous, deafening void.' He moved my hand. 'This ear was defunct from then on. And as for this … '—he pressed my palm to his scar—'they had to slice it open again. Scrape death out of it. Necrosis, my cells were dying, just like one half of my mind. What did your father expect, that the human consciousness could ever fully recover from such a blow? But I became a better human being. To live, you need to have tasted death. Here, taste it.'

I pulled myself free of his grasp. As I ran off down the hallway I heard him chuckle and swore never to go near him again. Never!

I lasted two days. He refused to leave his room and we all began to worry. Leni complained he hadn't eaten a mouthful and collected the trays of untouched food from outside his door. Heinz had not seen a light burning in the master's quarters for at least a day and remarked that, while he had always been one to mope, von Bötticher had seldom taken this long to come to his senses. The twins took advantage of the situation and no longer felt obliged to do anything. Every time I saw them, they were lying down. On the divan, on the carpet in the salon, soft cheeks glowing in front of the kitchen fire. I trained alone, with Girard Thibault as my brother in arms. Could human beings really be deciphered? Surely his method was doomed to fail? No two people moved, thought or dreamed the same. Thibault assumed everyone would stay within the lines, but the point of the weapon was still aimed at the lungs. I doubted I could ever remain so obedient while looking such a breathtaking death in the eye. The temperature in the fencing hall seemed to rise suddenly, as if my breath had been joined by someone else's. I spun around with my foil at the ready. She flew back, stumbled, and would have fallen without the doorpost to cling to.

'Oh, Leni! I didn't realize it was you.'

She looked smaller than usual and stared deferentially at my quilted torso. She soaked our uniforms in soda every week but she had never seen us fence. Since fencing was something she did not understand, she had decided the fencing hall was forbidden territory, worthy yet somehow suspect, like a strange place of worship or a university. In the mirror I saw that I had not relaxed my fencing stance. I towered above her like an angel in white as she plucked nervously at her apron.

'I wanted to ask you … I've received a telegram, you see. If it's not too much trouble, and if I'm not disturbing you, would you be able to help me out in the kitchen?'

I put down my weapon and she relaxed. 'Tell me what you need, Leni. I'm finished here for the day.'

'I need help. It's a buffet for twenty persons and it has to be a surprise. Von Bötticher mustn't know anything about it.'

She bustled through the passage ahead of me; it was thick with the aroma of butter and onions, and her shuffling steps revealed something close to gleeful anticipation. 'Only last week I warned him that I'd have to visit my sister in Köln. A long story, Janna, and not a happy one.'

When we arrived in the kitchen, she dragged her little black hearth chair from the nook in the corner, where it fit snugly thanks to its broken back. Its seat could only accommodate half the bulk of her thighs. Leaning forward to maintain her balance, she whispered, 'My sister's been bed-ridden for a while now. Going from bad to worse, my brother-in-law says. Von Bötticher promised I could leave for Köln tomorrow, but then this telegram arrived.'

She fished a sheet of paper marked *Deutsche Reichspost* from her apron pocket. 'Addressed to me personally,' she said proudly. 'See for yourself.'

DEAR LENI FIFTEEN STUDENTS TO ARRIVE AT RAEREN
TOMORROW AFTERNOON
SURPRISE FOR HR EGON. KEEP THE PARTY A SECRET —
DR REICH

'You see my problem?' she asked. 'It's a surprise. I'm not allowed to say anything.'

'And you're going to obey, no questions asked? This might be the last thing the maître wants!'

Irritably, she snatched the telegram out of my hands. 'It's from Professor Reich with orders for me and I'll see to it they're carried out. I said to Heinzi: if the master doesn't want them here, let *him* show them the door and I'll pack up the food for their return journey. I suspect it's to do with his birthday. If memory serves he had visitors this time last year, and the year before that. In fact, I'm as good as certain of it. He's not one for celebrations but I've no mind to ask him, not in his present state. Long story short, we'll make three meat pasties and three cream pies. And I'd very much like you to help me if it's not putting you out. I still have my luggage to see to.'

Impatiently she lifted the lids from pans that contained carrots and potatoes stewing in lard, with red onion and bay leaf. It was an aroma that made me hungry, the smell of food with the potential to become any number of meals, but she was planning to add pork and fill pie dishes with it. It was my job to top them off with the lard pastry rising on the windowsill.

'No word from Madam Julia, but then she's always been one to turn up unannounced,' she shouted as she gave the chops a good seeing to. 'Forgive me, Janna, but I thought ... I couldn't help overhearing the two of you. Would you mind telling me what you were arguing about?'

She pulled the face of a naughty child. It wasn't just the

meat mallet she was brandishing that unsettled me. She was the wife of an embittered servant, and the only way she could attract his attention of an evening was to feed him gossip about the man he hated. I wasn't about to tell her anything.

'Do you want me to ask him if it's his birthday?'

'Hmm?' She was staring absent-mindedly out of the window, where the twins were pulling the sow along on a rope. Boys and beast seemed to be on the best of terms again, and the sow was happy to tag along with them, albeit at her own pace. When they reached the grass, she sat down and spread herself out like a courtesan.

'Not an ounce of sense between them,' Leni said. 'What do you reckon? Are they *his* children?'

'What?' Had she really asked that question? 'What did you say?'

'Not an ounce of sense,' she repeated. 'They worship each other, but then again they don't. They make my skin crawl, it's like they're always up to something. A few days ago I heard a scream and rushed into their room to see what was the matter. The tub was in the middle of the floor and there was water everywhere, the two of them covered in soap ... I mean it's not like they're little boys any more.' She blushed. 'One of them was sitting on the bed with his face in his hands, the other was sucking blood from a cut on his hand and asked me to bandage it up.'

She looked at me expectantly. Tell me.

'They are von Mirbach's sons,' I said. 'I know for a fact.'

Her expression turned stony. Pointing at the pastry under my hands, she said, 'That could do with being thinner.'

I don't have to do this, I thought. Ask that scraggy old husband of yours to help you out. But at that very moment he breezed into the kitchen looking so peculiar that any thought of asking him went straight out of my head. Heinz was all scrubbed up right down to his fingernails, and was sporting a pair of plus fours held up with a belt, second-hand most likely. He strutted about the kitchen like a scrawny pigeon.

'And ... did you speak to him?' Leni asked, clearly unimpressed.

'Not a chance,' he said. 'I bumped into him on his way to the privy and told him his horse needed riding, but he was having none of it.'

He swaggered over to the window, clasped his hands loosely behind his back and stared out at the sky. Another storm was brewing.

'A neglected horse becomes a dumb animal,' he said. 'Unless you ride them, they get sluggish, forget what they've learned and dry up like their saddles. Unlike people, who wake up when they are ignored. They get angry, sharpen their tongues and then their knives.'

'Shhhh,' Leni hissed.

Outside, beneath a sky that was swiftly turning a dark shade of green, the twins had come to blows. They rolled on the grass, tugging at each other's arms and slapping each other in the face. The sow was trotting around them, like the referee at a boxing match.

'Do something, Heinzi,' Leni said. 'Get that animal out of harm's way.'

Heinz put a cigarette in his mouth and started hunting for light. 'That pig is ripe for the slaughter.'

'We've meat enough.'

'This kind of nonsense won't make her any more tender. Confound a pig and its blood runs thick. People mollycoddle an animal like that and think they're making her happy, but they couldn't be more wrong. My grandmother once told me a tale about a pig, one she'd heard from her grandmother before her ... '

He filled his lungs with smoke. Behind his back, one twin was pinning the other to the ground with his knee while the pig snuffled at them. I could see the first drops of rain on their faces.

' ... about the innkeeper's pig,' Heinz went on. 'It took place after the year without a summer, when the people went hungry. 1817. The innkeeper was expecting distinguished guests but had nothing to offer them. The storehouses were empty, the land was bare, the farmers could only look on idly as their children perished. Now, the innkeeper's wife had a pig she loved, a lean old sow that warmed her bones. She could see what was coming and that night she tied her sow to a tree in the woods and told the innkeeper the creature had up and fled. The innkeeper was at his wits' end and started moaning and wailing. They had a good marriage and his wife couldn't stand to see him in such despair. She promised to conjure up a feast for the guests and set off into the woods to shoot some game. But the year with no summer had emptied out the woods too. So she ended up back at the sow and decided on a horrible deed ... '

'Get a move on,' huffed Leni. 'We've had enough of your fairy tales.'

'Well, she brought the sow back to the sty and sliced open a vein in her neck. Lengthways, with surgical precision. And once she had drawn two pounds of blood, she stitched up the wound with a needle and thread. She mixed the blood with rye and onions and baked a splendid *Möppkenbrot*. The dish pleased the distinguished guests so much that they stopped at the inn again on their way back home. This time it was the innkeeper who got hold of the sow and repeated the same process, and then again for other guests who had heard tell of the fine food at the inn. Time and again the clever old creature succumbed to the knife! Before long she knew what was coming and ran off squealing in terror as soon as a coach drew up at the gate. But try as she might, she could never escape the bloodthirsty innkeeper. It got to the stage where his wife no longer recognized her own husband and couldn't stand it any more. Hanged herself, she did. A grisly tale, don't you agree?' He inhaled again and began to laugh. 'All for the sake of a *Möppkenbrot*. And the moral of the tale is: never get too sentimental about livestock. Pigs have to be slaughtered. Quickly and expertly.'

'Who has to be slaughtered?'

Egon was standing in the doorway, hat in one hand and a small suitcase in the other. He looked dazed, like a helmsman who has spent too long staring at the waves. Most likely he had been reading non-stop, perhaps the same way I had read, ploughing through letter after letter in the hope of reaching my destination safe and sound, only to discover I had learned nothing along the way.

'Pigs,' said Heinz, tugging sheepishly at his plus fours. 'You shouldn't let them wander around too long. In the end it's the meat that suffers.'

We all looked at the sow, shaking raindrops from her skin as she trotted around outside.

'In that case there's no time to waste,' Egon said, putting on his hat. 'I'll slaughter her as soon as I return.'

'Return?' Leni asked. 'But where are you going?'

'I'll be off as soon as the storm lifts. You'll have to manage without me for a while.'

'Without you? But you can't! I told you, I'm off to see my sister!'

'You can go as we agreed,' Egon said. 'By the look of things, you're making plenty of provisions. The girl can fill in as long as need be.'

'But you can't just … ' Leni burst out again, on the verge

of tears. 'People might come to call ... what about your birthday?'

'My birthday? Don't be absurd, woman! Heinz, I wanted to ask you to take steps to protect the young roses. Something tells me there's a severe ground frost on the way.'

He picked up his case and walked out. Leni flew through the kitchen like a chicken fleeing the hatchet, lifting lid after lid, as if a solution might be simmering away in one of the pots. 'What am I to do? Oh Heinzi, what am I to do? We have to stop him. Perhaps the weather won't clear and the storm will rage until Professor Reich arrives. What do you think, Heinzi? Say something, man!'

But there was the sound of the engine, faltering and much quieter than you would expect of such a bulky car. I threw the pastry down on the board and ran after him.

'Don't let him leave!' I heard Leni shriek. 'For God's sake, tell him about the party if you have to!'

He saw me in his rear-view mirror, screaming at him as I skidded across the wet lawn in my fencing shoes. He remained unmoved.

'You can't just leave without telling us where you're going! Is it my fault? I'm sorry!'

Its pitch-black hood raised against the rain, the car resembled a hearse as it disappeared into the storm. I blinked raindrops from my eyelashes. The smoke from the exhaust seemed to have a life of its own as it turned invitingly on the air before vanishing around the corner after him. I was left behind with all that water streaming down my face and into my mouth, diluting the tears on my cheeks and seeping unpleasantly into the collar of my fencing suit. I didn't notice the cold. Once again I felt someone else's warmth, just as I had in the fencing hall that morning. Helene, I decided. Weeks had passed without a single daydream and now my imagination came back to life with a déjà vu that, like all déjà vus, evaded me as soon as I tried to trace its source. Where had I seen my giant Helene before? Flames shooting out of her head, her laurel crown, her red-hot hand reaching out to me. I knew her from somewhere and knew what came next: 'An Olympic torch,' one man said. 'No,' said the other, 'the Blessed Virgin.' It must have been a dream, a flaw in the temporal lobe. She was already starting to speak, telling me to leave this place, telling me there was nothing to learn here, though that was why I had come. I nodded. Daydream or not, my giant Helene was right.

Real life intruded in the shape of a whinnying horse, peering over the stable door with her nose in the wind. When I entered the stable, she bumped her fifteen kilos of olfaction against my jacket, but though her soft lips were flapping, they weren't about to tell me how to saddle her up. That was Heinz's job, but what I was about to do was no business of his. Entering his domain, I laid the heavy saddle over my left arm while I took the bridle down from the wall with my right. I found a felt saddlecloth on the heater. That should do it, I thought, but when I presented the bit to the horse she clamped her jaws shut with the unreasonableness of an animal that looks smarter than it is. I had once seen Heinz poke Loubna's teeth with his finger until her jaws opened, but the sight of Megaira's yellow grin horrified me. My grandmother's village was home to a man who had lost two fingers to a black devil of a horse. The thought of it still made me shiver.

'Help me out, you old nag.'

The look she gave me was proud and playful. This animal was in no hurry. I had hoped she would set off in pursuit of her master even though I did not know the way. That heavy nose of hers could sniff him out at a distance of a hundred and fifty metres, but by the time I had saddled her up, half an hour had been lost. When I opened the stable door she came to life and began to turn, so that I found myself hopping along behind her with one foot in the stirrup and the reins in my unsteady hand. If Heinz caught me we would need to make a quick getaway, but as it turned out I didn't even have the chance to give her the scent. As soon as I landed in the saddle she was off and running. I looked down in horror at her thrusting neck, a furious turbine no man could stop once she was in full flight. Taking a tight bend, she flew through the gate and headed straight for the woods. It was already getting dark. What on earth was I thinking! If I fell now I would come crashing down and God knows where I would land ... Playing it safe, I crouched in the saddle, but not deep enough. A branch caught my hair, my legs turned to jelly and the last thing I saw was the white of her eyes and two flaring nostrils. I knew, decided perhaps, that I was going to fall. With the horse gone, I felt the earth take me. More than anything I wanted to lie there in my fencing gear among the leaves, but the horse galloping through the woods could not be allowed to escape, damn her. She was a devil with a promise to fulfil, a war to win, a warrior and foreigner, as Herodotus would have it. Head still spinning, I began to walk. The woods had become a diorama of cut-out trees propped up in front of a twilit backdrop. Not a single leaf in the tree-tops, only a jagged weave of branches lit up by a moon I could not find. Tiny lanterns danced above the path ahead. I blinked hard but they would not disappear. If I had known they were fireflies, it might have calmed me down. Then I might have realized that the strange whistling coming from the bushes was the sound of frogs. For a second I thought I heard a panicky thrum of hooves. I held my breath but the sound died away. My shortcomings weighed heavily: the dullness of my meagre senses, the impotence of my asymmetrical limbs and—'Megaira!'—the pitiful range of my voice, while the animal could tune in from afar with consummate ease. The initiative was all hers. She could decide to return and forge an opportunistic alliance in exchange for a mouthful from the fields, as her ancestors had done six thousand years ago. There she was. A majestic steed, grazing with her head bowed, still smelling of the summer that had been stripped from the land and lay drying in the hayloft. She picked up my scent too and registered my relief. After this wordless exchange we turned back toward Raeren, where we would remain till our master came home.

20 SEPTEMBER 1917

Dear Egon,

There are few places as peaceful as a battlefield after the
battle, when the dust has settled, the blood has seeped into
the soil and the bodies have been carried away. No sign of the
implacable sun of three years ago, when the stench had us
gnawing on our knuckles. (Limburg cheese, Gerard, my Red
Cross brother had said, keep telling yourself it's the stink of
Limburg cheese and you'll get through it.) The sky was
cloudy, the air a little damp, yet in the distance I saw a couple
of men reaping wheat with sickles. Good on them, I thought.
The earth is not in mourning so why stand on ceremony? Of
course, I had no idea what was going through their minds as
they bowed over the soil. I can only speak for my own, which
was recalling that sunny day in 1914.

   We had decided not to head out to the battlefield but to
wait for a German truck to bring the wounded to us—until
we received word that it had broken down. We reached the
truck in question only to find that the officer lying in the
back was already dead, upon which all the medics except for
Gerard made a swift about-turn, having been assured that
anyone we encountered further on would be beyond our
help. Gerard stuck around because he was in the mood for an
adventure, the fool! I stayed to help the men dig. They had
brought a shovel with the patient, expecting death to turn
up like a bad penny, but everything about them told me they
did not have the strength to take the dead officer back to the

crammed mass grave they had filled in behind them. 'I ain't diggin', one of them kept repeating. 'Not me.' He looked at me without looking and his swollen eyes did not meet mine as he handed me the shovel. Gerard and I took it in turns. By the time we had finished digging, another soldier had the engine running again, but at first they did not want to return to the battlefield. They insisted there were no more casualties to be found, only the Grim Reaper staggering around in search of the last dregs of life like a drunk at closing time peering into near-empty glasses for one last gulp. Yes, if I had listened to the others, to my brothers from the Red Cross or your brothers in arms, you would have been left to wait for death alone.

When we arrived there the stench was horrific. Perhaps there were no more wounded to be found, but my God there were wounds aplenty! The stinking battlefield, nothing more than a pasture in front of a smouldering farmstead, was littered with horses. Those that were dead lay with their swollen bellies upturned, but some were still in their death throes, hooves twitching, nostrils flaring ... I walked hurriedly from one body to the next, and although their uniforms were handsome and their helmets still shone, they themselves were ugly and stiff as lumps of wood. But not you. You were lying quietly in a ditch, like a child put out to nurse. It did not seem to bother you that worms were already crawling from your wounds, nor did you complain as we carried you to the truck. The journey to Maastricht was a long one, yet you lay there quietly between us with a faint smile on your bloodied face. All four of us shared your silence. I don't think the Germans had it in them to dig another grave. They must have thought: at least let this one make it. All their hopes were pinned on that still-breathing body of yours. They also knew your body was mine: a case of finders keepers. You were my buried treasure, mine to examine and investigate.

War is a boon to the medical world. We have the war of 1870 to thank for the invention of antiseptic, and now the halls of academe are resounding with news of the work of Jan Esser, our own Dutch surgeon who did such wonderful work in Brünn. He has given a face to so many mutilated soldiers who could no longer eat or speak. I read that the never-ending stream of wounded enabled him to try out new techniques and that working under pressure sparked his creativity. In peacetime, with all its prescriptive considerations, many of the problems he tackled head-on would have been sidestepped for the sake of convenience. He gave one soldier a left foot for a hand. For another he fashioned a nose with tissue cut from a cheek. The tutelage of war is bloody. In this light, let me impress upon you that your war has by no means been in vain! While deconstruction was most likely your aim, the inevitable objective of the soldier, reconstruction would turn out to be the purpose. Your recovery, which began on that oppressive day in 1914, would herald the recovery of many civilian patients who came after you. That was my resolution when I found you. We cleaned and bandaged the injuries to your arms and legs as best we could. I had already diagnosed your leg fracture, but my main concern lay elsewhere. Something in that head of yours must have put that peaceful smile on your face. You lost consciousness once you reached the hospital, but even then your smile remained. Localization theory had been a major part of my studies and, brain addled by the stench of death and decay, my thoughts ran away with me. Astonished by your smile, I wondered what had happened to the deep thirst for war to which your battle-dress attested. Might it be possible to remove such senseless belligerence with one simple procedure? Would it not be so much better if the war coffers were emptied and their contents devoted to studying the brain, to locating the exact spot where peace-loving sentiments reside within the human nervous system?

Of course these idealistic considerations disappeared as soon as we arrived at the hospital, where speed was of the essence. But these days I often think of my celebrated compatriot Esser, who worked under the same pressure and cemented his astounding reputation with a masterly demonstration of brain surgery. His neurological expertise enabled him to remove a bullet from the head of a soldier who had almost been given up for dead, without any damage to the brain tissue. Why then did he go on to pursue a career in plastic surgery? What was it about the science of the brain that scared him off? Every explorer of that secretive landscape fears the effect his discovery might have on how we see ourselves. For instance, we now know emotion and reason each inhabit their own hemisphere. Our brain's symmetry, a beauty we are all so keen to achieve, has turned out to be purely anatomical.

As I have already told you, symmetry was the only thing with the power to calm you when later you woke in a state of utter confusion. The objects on your bedside table had to be arranged just so, the curtains had to be closed in a particular way; it was a stubborn quest for the order that had been so dramatically disturbed inside your head. By the time you— my archaeological find—were deemed cured and had to leave Calvariënberg, I had decided to dedicate my life to the study of neurology.

Perhaps this account is of little interest to you. If so, please know that my only aim has been to formulate an apology in an attempt to ease your situation. Once again, I must leave you disappointed. You sent me out into the world with a question and, I regret to say, my answer is that I did not find your horse. I made inquiries of the blacksmith in the village, and described her appearance and brand to a number of farmers in the neighbourhood. They knew nothing and probably could not have cared less, even if the horse had been French or Belgian. Two permitted me to inspect their stables but the only creatures there were draught horses: Limburg shire horses or the like. If it is any consolation to you, on the battlefield we asked the soldiers to put dying horses out of their misery on sight, since we carried no weapons ourselves. They complied with our request without hesitation.

In hope of reconciliation I remain,

Your friend, Jacques

**8**

They arrived the next day, claxons honking. Ten men with one case between them jumped down from a Benz, caps at a rakish angle and hands thrust into the pockets of their riding breeches. They were not drunk, but their bearing suggested an eagerness to embrace inebriation once they were inside. This was more than an intention; it was an entitlement born of following the Arbiter, the man of my nightmares, now clad in a military coat. He was the only one to keep his hands behind his back. Leaning forward stiffly, like the stump of a dead tree, he eyed the knock-about antics of the students. They laughed, he did not. He spun around to face the kitchen window and I had to hang on to the net curtains to stop myself falling. They advanced on the house, trudging feet in riding boots. The driver locked up his vehicle and I realized I had reason to be afraid. The Otter was nowhere to be seen.

'Perhaps he'll turn up later,' said Heinz, blowing out the match he had used to light the oven. Early in the morning he had harnessed Loubna up to the carriage and taken his wife to the omnibus. Leni had been immaculately turned out, so much so that she chuckled at herself as she climbed into the carriage, tapping nervously at the veil of her hat. The sad purpose of her journey did not seem to worry her. What mattered most was that she was leaving to attend to her own affairs, having left everything shipshape for us.

Though she knew better, she still held out the hope that the maître would return that same evening to savour her pies in the very best of company. It was simply a matter of heating them up in the oven. And while she expected nothing of her husband—even a little help lifting her suitcase appeared to be too much to ask—she seemed to have the fullest confidence in Professor Reich, the good-humoured man of medicine who would transform Raeren into a haven of calm and well-being. She believed all this as firmly as she had placed the hat on her head. A sense of foreboding seized me as I watched her veil dancing in the wind like a fulmar on the wing before the storm breaks.

Of course the Otter was not coming. The uninvited guests thumping on the front door were the ones behind the telegram. While Heinz trotted off to let them in, I went in search of a hiding place. There was no way I could make it to the stairs unnoticed. My only escape was through the small door to the side room off the kitchen. I stumbled up the steps in the ink-black chill, fingertips brushing the preserving jars and the rough-skinned onions. They smelled and felt strangely comforting now that my eyesight was out of commission, and I was doing my best not to hear the threat contained in the approaching din. The kitchen door slamming into the wall, bellowing voices in the hallway and then another voice bleating just an arm's length away: 'Cooking us up a treat, my good man?'

'Certainly not. My wife has prepared everything. All I have to do is pop it in the oven. How many of you are there? Any more on the way?'

'We can discuss that later, my good man. I say, even cold this doesn't taste half bad. What can you offer us to drink?'

The kitchen door slammed again and a yodel rang out somewhere above my head. My kneecap collided with the trunk and I sank to the floor, fists clenched. Familiar outlines began to take shape—the coat rack, the broken mirror that had reflected back the Kaiser's daughter in her death's-head hat—only now they left me unmoved. The dinner service clinked in the cabinet, a yelp of pain was greeted by the roar of men laughing in unison. I had never heard as much racket at Raeren. Of course the crescendo of our weapons had sliced through the quiet of the morning and we had stamped our feet in victory and cursed our defeats. Of course the gramophone had wailed through the house, as off-key as Leni's half-remembered songs. Of course voices had been raised in anger. But this agitated din had an edge to it, the overture to a manic outburst.

'Sir!'

'Anton! You lot get started in the fencing hall. I have a thing or two to discuss with the lord of the manor. We should let the lads blow off a little steam first, don't you agree Herr Kraus?'

'Of course. Call me Heinrich.'

'You were once a young lad yourself, Heinrich.'

'But unfortunately I am not the lord of the manor.'

'Ah Heinrich … who knows what tomorrow might bring?'

'A drink first?'

'Yes, a drink.'

I could feel the cold rising up through the floor and began to worry my bladder might start playing up. Right now, I was the only lady of the manor. Please God, let them leave and soon.

'So he stole off like a thief in the night.'

'No, in the afternoon.'

'Did he say where he was going? Someone must have tipped him off, there's no other explanation. And yet, if he has a clear conscience, what is there to fear? People never cease to surprise us in these times. Don't you agree? Fascinating times we live in, Heinrich. Let's drink to that.'

'To the future.'

A long silence followed and, like a dog abandoned in a strange farmyard, I tried to sniff out its meaning. The two men were probably sitting there with the bottle between them, chewing over their thoughts. They must have spoken to each other before, no other conclusion was possible. Plans had been hatched and thwarted, and now it was time to look each other in the eye and come up with a solution. But a third person entered the kitchen and their thoughts ground to a halt.

'I left something through there.'

A voice as smooth as oil. Friedrich.

'Well, be quick about it boy. Here.'

The two men sniggered. I flattened myself against the wall in disbelief. Christ Almighty! He was heading my way! As the light stretched into the room, I ducked behind the trunk.

'What are you doing in here?' he whispered, too loudly.

'Close the door!'

He lit the lantern and put it down in the corner, then crawled toward me on his hands and knees.

'Did you know there are all kinds of secrets lurking here? I can show you if you like.'

I suppressed a grin. Delectable ephebe, don't think for a moment you are the only one to nose around in the treasure chambers of your paedotribe ... 'Not now. Let's wait till those two have gone.'

'You'll be waiting a while. Heinz is on the bottle with that little man, you know, the oddball who stormed off after dinner.'

'The Arbiter.'

'He's sitting there in his full regalia getting plastered. Why didn't Heinz ever join the SA or what's left of it? Von Bötticher wouldn't let him is my guess. Anyway, my father says it's nothing but a rabble nowadays. Plebs the lot of them, just like our Heinzi. Father says you're better off going straight into the forces.'

He fell silent and in the yellow light I saw a watery film in his eyes. He shuffled closer and I smelled the alcohol on his breath.

'May I kiss you?'

The ephebe had hair on his lip but not on his chin, which was as it should be. Before the meeting of the demots he was required to swear by the gods and the olives and figs of his fatherland that he would fight to protect all that was pure. But would he? I pushed him away. 'Only if you will fight to protect me.'

He nodded eagerly. 'Always.'

From the kitchen came the clearing of throats. The two men did not put their decision into words. Were they keeping the doors to their leery minds closed to one another or were they conspiring in gestures, sensing that they were in the company of eavesdroppers?

'We're here now, let's make the most of it,' said the bleating voice at last.

'There's plenty of food.'

'We did not come here to eat.'

'Perhaps he will return this evening.'

'If he does it will be clear enough where he stands. Fine, we can discuss all this later. First, another drink.'

Friedrich put my hand on his chest. He felt red-hot and I shivered. No, I wasn't really cold, I whispered, but he slid his hands under my buttocks, cupped his fingers around the mound in my tights and pulled me to him. A consignment of womanhood ready for the taking. I put my hands around his neck and kissed him. He could hardly breathe. I inhaled his warmth. In the kitchen more drink was being poured amid mumbled words of agreement. I pushed my tongue against his. His hands explored below the belt, mine above the collar.

'No one can work him out. I remember when he came back from visiting the garrison in Aachen ... '

'Von Bötticher? Does he know them over there?'

'Yes, he came back drunk. Told Leni they were a hopeless bunch. That the French could come galloping in whenever they felt like it and chase our lads back over the Rhine and beyond without breaking a sweat.'

'Insolent bastard! I suspect even the French admire the Führer for all he has achieved. Wiping his arse with Locarno. Now there's a toast worth drinking to.'

Whatever they were drinking, there was no slackening of pace as they knocked back half-filled glasses at a single gulp. Friedrich leaned over me. He seemed more muscular, though perhaps it was just the tension gripping his body. In the dim light, and the silence we were forced to keep, he felt what had to happen as if the instructions were written on my body in Braille. With some satisfaction I noted that my tights were holding his wrist firmly in place. We would see how far this was going to go.

'Von Bötticher's a swine! What German would say such a thing? You know, Heinrich, I was there this spring when they marched across the bridge in Köln. A magnificent sight. Uniforms sober, jaws set. I don't mind telling you I shed a tear that day. And I wasn't the only one. It had been so long since we'd seen our soldiers in action. Courage, there's one thing they cannot take from us.'

'I remember the hussars back in 1914,' I heard Heinz say. 'What a joke! Dressed to the nines, I'll give them that, but there were men among them who had never so much as shaken a fist at the enemy. Fat, cheery blokes who liked their Bratwurst, and academic types with those little spectacles perched on their noses. You couldn't help but wonder if they'd last ten minutes over there.'

'Academic types? Jewish conspirators, more like. Not easy to finish them off. They'll slip through any crack. Like cockroaches.'

The strangled strains of a foxtrot wailed from the gramophone upstairs. Enough to smother any fit of passion, except that of my ephebe. Poised to storm the bastion of manhood, nothing was about to distract him from me, the first woman. From our dank and feverish Eden he would always remember the touch of my sealed-off little pussy, pulsing with anticipation beneath his fingers.

'Tell me, Herr Raab, does Professor Reich strike you as one of them? A Jewish conspirator?'

'Why do you think we left him out of this? Your boss is the only man who still fraternizes with that stateless vermin. He's lucky he still has friends in high places, we should tread carefully where he's concerned. But that's for another day. First of all ... '

'The men with brains,' slurred Heinz. 'Scientists. Not a month goes by without them dreaming up some new contraption, but nothing to lighten the working man's load. When I worked at the factory, they had to hire people who could operate the machines. But did things improve? Did they hell! The machine got in the way. No one understood it. No one understood what they were working for any more ... '

His rant ran aground on a coughing fit and the bottle was knocked over, triggering a salvo of curses from the Arbiter.

'I'll fetch us a new one,' Heinz wheezed. 'Plenty where that came from.'

I heard him shuffling around close by and prayed this sudden flurry of activity would not jog his memory about Friedrich's whereabouts. I tried to edge further out of sight, but that was Friedrich's cue to yank down my tights and thrust his penis clumsily between my legs. I wasn't about to show him the way. I pulled back from the light of the lantern in order to gauge his expression. From the shadows I watched his troubled passion dissipate as soon as he forced his way inside me — his heat was intense, that was something at least. From then on, it was simply a matter of drawing conclusions. His: I am the one who is doing this. Mine: I should never have done this. Where was his beauty now? I tried to stretch myself to get a better look but all I saw was the haste of his movements in a tangle of hurriedly stripped-off clothes.

'The worker no longer understood what he was working for, damn it!' Heinz shouted, alarmingly close. 'He grew lonely! Damn, we were lonely then, lonely for years. Each and every one of us, in the years after the war … '

'Those days are over, Heinrich. We have a leader now.'

'To the end of loneliness! *Heil!*'

'*Heil.*'


When we emerged, they were slumped over the table, heads resting on their arms. It was not yet seven. The Arbiter's ear lay on the made-to-measure pillow of his swastika armband. There was something animal about the way they had nodded off with the pie in front of them on the table, having broken open its crust and clawed out its contents without warming it up. One and a half bottles of apple gin had washed it down. All their open mouths could do now was snore, a cheerier conversation than they had managed with words. Friedrich fished two scraps of meat from the cold pie dish and placed one on each tongue.

'Corpus Christi.'

They looked ridiculous, but the embarrassment I felt had nothing to do with them. It was the way Friedrich strolled through the kitchen and lit the cigarette he had found, the deliberate way he left his shirt hanging open. I had thought he might leave our little hidey-hole feeling something close to awe, want to be alone for a while and wander through the garden gazing up at the sky. At the very least, I had expected him to avoid my gaze. This is how woman-izers are born, I thought bitterly: donning their top hat on the threshold of the brothel and leaving all sense of shame and wonder behind them in the darkness. He flashed me a smile as he smoked, the same affected smirk his brother wore when he won a match and cast aside the mask behind which he had just died a thousand deaths. I was not a sore loser but I despised fencers who, after the fact, kidded themselves that the victory had always been theirs for the taking.

'What do you say we take a little look upstairs?' I asked, filling two glasses to the brim. 'Sounds to me like all hell's broken loose.'

He needn't think I was going to tag along in his wake. I kept him waiting while I braided my hair in front of the mirror and made sure I entered the fencing hall ahead of him. Sure enough, all hell had broken loose. I saw ten gap-ing mouths, eating and drinking without tasting, moving without forming words that had any meaning, blaring along with the gramophone without singing. Yet it was still a pleasing enough sight. They all wore the same crisply tailored student uniform with buckled belt and bright-red armband, as if to emphasize how absent the swastika had always been at Raeren. Before it had entered the fencing hall swinging on the sleeves of this bunch, the emblem had led a grey existence on postage stamps, banknotes and anniversary spoons, on Heinz's song pamphlet and the delivery van that belonged to the butcher, the only vis-itor to do his patriotic duty and greet us with the Hitler salute. But until now I had never seen the swastika in glorious colour, spinning in black, red and white.

'A woman! At last!'

He was by far the biggest of them all, and probably the oldest. He stood there, gin bottle in one hand, *Mettwurst* in the other.

'That's the Dutch girl,' someone said.

The colossal figure filled a second glass next to his own. They had probably brought their own sausage, but I recognized the mess of cream and crumbs as the remains of Leni's pies. Back home we were under strict orders never to mix sweet and savoury. My mother decried it as the behaviour of pigs and my father insisted it would give you a stomach ulcer. Eating was to be done at set times and according to fixed rules. On that at least, they both agreed.

'A Dutch girl,' mused the Colossus. 'No problem there, Willy. The Dutch are Germanic. Didn't you say we should be uniting all Germans in a single bond? A communion of the people? Wouldn't she be a good place to start. How about a spot of communing, Fräulein, you and I?'

I took the glass from him. 'First things first—I like to dance.'

Hoots of laughter. As I walked to the middle of the floor on the arm of the Colossus, I saw Siegbert skulking by the window, pale and stiff as a board. He did not deign to look at us, he only had eyes for Friedrich. Could he smell something in the air, like an animal? Had he felt his brother's euphoria as he forced his way into me? It was a subject on which I had no desire to dwell.

'Enjoying our company?' said the Colossus, laboriously taking the lead. 'It's a shame the master of the house has not seen fit to join us. I suppose you've no idea of his whereabouts?'

His beautiful green eyes were the extent of his charms.

His nose had taken a stiff knock from the right and was smeared across a good deal of his face, a face so fleshy that his head must have outweighed the average by at least a pound. His full lips had the kind of primitive shape a child might cut out of a potato. The overall effect was endearing.

'And what about these nephews of his, or whatever they might ... '

'Pupils. Sabreurs.'

'Fascinating. Do they fence each other?'

'Every day.'

'I don't see how they could hit each other fair and square. Don't they say identical twins feel each other's pain because they shared the same placenta? It must make fighting each other impossible, like giving yourself a good thrashing.'

All at once, I was gasping for air. In the mirror I caught sight of a circus bear and a diminutive clown labouring under the delusion that they were dancing. Someone closed the curtain to shield us from the setting sun and now we were condemned to one another. I mumbled something about needing to eat and he threw his arm around me, so tightly that the steel button on his breast pocket scratched my cheekbone.

'Your wish is my command. Leo, find us some other tunes, will you? We can hum these ditties backward by now. I'm sure the girl can tell us where our host keeps his record collection.'

I was about to tell him the master was not a music lover when to my astonishment Friedrich announced that von Bötticher had a whole stash of records. Better still, he would show our guests to the master's quarters, where they could be found. Heinz had the keys, but since he was out for the count it was a problem easily solved. That was when I should have intervened. I should have stayed one step ahead, hidden the keys, or found a way to deter Friedrich from his plan. Von Bötticher's room was my lair, its red velvet bedspread at the heart of the fire that consumed me. But I did nothing. I played the aggrieved ballerina in the arms of what passed for a *real* man, a bear of a Nazi who sliced sausage and plied me with drink without taking his hands off me in case—did I even believe it myself?—I might swoon. With age one comes to view such youthful grievances with tenderness, but at the time I did not feel a shred of sympathy for myself. All the more reason to drain one glass after another.

'It still gives me the creeps,' said the Colossus when Friedrich had left the room. 'Two in one—there's something twisted about it. If you're not unique, how can you ever give yourself completely? I could never trust a twin to be loyal. Would you marry one? Not me. Two for the price of one would be another proposition altogether, but then they'd have to legalize polygamy again. Not such a bad idea seeing as the population needs to grow.'

'That's what they did after the Thirty Years' War,' one of the students interrupted. He had unusually thin hair for his age and peculiar features: a face I had seen before. He put his glass in front of mine and emptied the bottle. 'There weren't enough men around, so they allowed it. Those bastard children brought our nation back to full strength. The last war has left us with a shortage of men too. The Party doesn't condemn single mothers, nor does it want to see good seed go to waste. That would be a sin, demographically speaking.'

The Colossus unleashed his belly laugh and uncorked a new bottle. His wrists had to be at least ten centimetres in circumference. I had more than enough on my hands with him for the time being. Another hour of dancing and then I would climb the stairs to my pigeon loft—alone, let's be clear about that. Then they could all clear off, damn their ugly mugs to hell.

Did I say that out loud, drunk as I was?

'Willy likes his theories,' said the Colossus.

'But he's not so keen on doctors and their offspring,' said the balding student.

At that moment the Colossus fished the locket of the Virgin Mary out of the front of my dress with his little finger. I had no idea why; that thing meant nothing to me. 'Looky here, Willy,' he grinned. 'She's Catholic.'

And then it began. Leo kicked open the door, his hands full of more than just the case of records. He had brought books with him and a pile of trinkets, which he proceeded to lay out earnestly on the table. Friedrich had returned with a large bottle of Ahr wine and was keen to pour it for the students but they showed no interest, gathering instead around the corpora delicti on the table. I recognized the painting of the horse's head and the jacket of Egon's uniform. The miniature Doric pillar and the snake eating its own tail, I had never seen before. The mood changed when Willy began to fling the records through the hall. One slashed a painting, another came to rest in the chandelier. Hoarse shouts rose up instead of the howls of laughter I had been expecting. Banned music! American-Jewish trash! Look, Billy Murray, what did I tell you? Irving Kaufman. Hah! Get this! Louis Armstrong! Friedrich looked around skittishly and took a gulp from the bottle, red liquid dribbling down his chin. One of the buffoons pulled on the officer's jacket. The pillar was smashed to pieces, the uroboros disappeared into an inside pocket, while the horse's head was paraded around until someone stuck their head through the canvas. Last of all came the burning of the books. One smouldering title did raise a laugh or two: *The Future of an Illusion*.

No one came after me, thank God. That at least made some kind of sense. The way I staggered out of the room was not exactly seductive. Drunk, they call it, but my mind was sharp as a tack. Sharp enough to register that my limbs were well beyond my control. Now for the stairs. Oh, if only I hadn't grown up—I had said it as a little girl and I would say it as an old crone. And for the rest of my life I would think back to the stairs I now began to climb, in my clear-headed state of bewilderment. There was no one else to blame for what I had done, and that alone made me sick to my stomach. I reached my room without resorting to all fours—there was still some hope for me. Lying on my bed I continued to spin in my drunken haze, listening to the same strange sounds I had heard that morning, interspersed with deathly silences that became ever longer and therefore more disturbing. Later I woke in a panic and threw up. In the pitch-black, with my basin between my trembling knees, I noticed that the acoustics of Raeren had been restored. Off in the distance I could make out cheering and the clanging carillon of crossed swords.

Leni. Yes, it really was her. One clap of her hands and it was late morning, while I had been convinced the night still had a long way to go. Now there could be no doubt as to who was the lady of the manor. Sensing something was wrong, she had returned early from Köln and chased the yobs out of the house. From my balcony I watched them stagger around the garden. The Arbiter, his coat hanging loosely from his shoulders, was helped into the Benz by a student who was wearing Egon's hat. I looked for the Colossus and saw him standing, legs wide and hips thrust forward, leaning against a tree with one hand. When they had gone, I helped Leni clear up. We had barely exchanged a word and our silence continued as we swept up fragments that could never be glued back together. Behind every door lay another shambles that kept us speechless. Raeren turned out to contain far more than we had ever thought possible. I found myself looking at the tatters of paintings I had never seen whole, the smouldering remains of clothes I had never seen anyone wear, torn newspapers, books and letters I had never discovered. We threw away everything that was broken—why keep something that catches your eye simply because it is defective? Only when we came to the end of this trail of chaos did we discover the twins. They were lying next to each other out on the terrace, dressed in their fencing uniforms. Their feet were limp, toes pointing inward. Weapons abandoned, their hands lay across their chests with fingers intertwined, a child's contentment on their sleeping faces. Identical once more. They, the sky and the ground were pure white, as if it had been snowing. The only colour was on Friedrich's collar, a red rim of spilled Ahr wine.

## 9

The big clear-out began the following day, when Egon returned home with the look of a lover. On greeting his master in the hall, Heinz mumbled, 'From the twinkle in your eyes, I'd swear you'd found love.'

'Indeed I have,' Egon answered, producing a large, fragile book from beneath his coat. 'I came across this old master in Amsterdam.'

Jealous? You bet I was. Of a book, an inanimate object, of anything that did not involve me. I had been lumped together with the servants and the twins, the naughty children in the hallway of the ravaged house, though he seemed oblivious to the damage. He really was as blind as a man in love. We held our breath as he headed for his room, but the feared outburst never came. He did not ask what had happened to the painting of the horse or why the window was broken or why the curtains and the wallpaper were ripped at the seams. He emerged from the room with his gratified glow undimmed, lit a cigar and announced that all of Raeren was in need of a clear-out. Leni's floodgates burst. It wasn't our fault, she wailed, we had done our best to clean up, but there had been ten of them and they had led her poor Heinzi up the garden path—well, plied him with drink in any case—and of course the girl and the boys had been powerless against such odds but she, Leni, had come all the way from Köln on a hunch that there was trouble afoot.

'It's all because Professor Reich failed to turn up and left us at the mercy of those ruffians. You see that don't you? Doctor or not, he's not to be trusted.'

She fired a look in my direction, so fierce I felt the urge to parry. The kind of look that stops you speaking before you even knew you wanted to.

'Poor Heinzi has even taken some of the things to his workplace to see if there's anything he can salvage,' she continued, looking up at Egon again. 'Isn't that right, Heinzi?'

Heinz gave a crooked nod. He hadn't been able to straighten his neck for two days and Leni's words were fired into one ear and rolled out the other. Since his drunken evening, his face had shut down and it was clear that no words would be forthcoming for the time being. Egon gave him a pat on the shoulder, or perhaps he was just looking for something to lean on as he took the oval mirror down from the wall.

'Everything of no use has to go. Too many things in this house serve no purpose. I'll point out what's to be got rid of and you can decide what happens to it. As long as I never have to lay eyes on it again.'

'But it's a shame to throw that out! I can put it to good use!' exclaimed Leni, a protest she would repeat often in the days to follow. Egon pointed out scores of household items, so many that Heinz had to fetch the wheelbarrow. The wheel left long trails of muck through the house, but Egon was unperturbed. Manure, after all, had the decency to fade away all by itself, while rubbish made by human hand clung on like genuine filth. All anyone ever talked about was things, he said, yet what mattered was the thought that preceded the invention. 'It's not the wheel that's important but the thought that led to the wheel. This ... and this ... and this ... are mere by-products.'

Off they went, the bashed-up chairs. We ditched them without a second thought, like birds driving the weakest chick from the nest. But the Bavarian nutcrackers proved more difficult to part with, and why the mantle clock had to go was anyone's guess. Heinz tried to set aside as many items as he could in the hope of selling them, while Egon took delight in smashing things to pieces by hurling them directly into the wheelbarrow. There went the mocha coffee set. Books were exempt, as were weapons and the collection of worn-out shoes we discovered behind a curtain in the attic. 'I've no idea who they belong to,' said Egon. 'By the look of them, the owner took to his heels and ran.'

He's lost his mind, Leni kept repeating. He'll rue the day, just you wait and see. We were ordered to put chalk marks on the pieces of furniture that had waited like jilted brides under sheets in the bedrooms. A bunch of brawny men would be brought in to cart them off, enlisted along with a couple of good painters and decorators. Egon had more than just a clear-out in mind. At the close of day, Heinz built a bonfire in the garden. We looked on as he slotted items of furniture together and stacked them to make a tower sturdy enough to live in. Just as painstakingly, he set them alight; his torch was the magazine with the portrait of the Kaiser's daughter, rolled up and doused in methylated spirits. 'Here's one decision I can live with,' he said as blue flames shot out of Victoria Louise's head. 'Won't lose any sleep over this one.'

The girl in the picture seemed to writhe as the fire took hold. That's me: the thought flashed through my mind. A girl no one will lose any sleep over, however hard she tries, however much she dresses up, or undresses. A girl too unremarkable to keep. The fire took on the shape of the objects it encountered. Each time I recognized something I was seized by the urge to save it, but once it had been swallowed by the flames I could no longer remember why. If Egon was right and it was thoughts not things that mattered, what had become of those thoughts? All part of the unstoppable march of progress, my father would have said, a firm believer in forward momentum fuelled by reason. But once the fire had done its work, all of us, even Egon, found ourselves staring vacantly at the flames like dumbfounded cave dwellers, not a single thought between us. All those lost civilizations had been ablaze with ideas. If only they could be brought back by destroying new things. If only the end of one thing was always the start of an impassioned plan. If that had been the case, I would have thrown that big book of his into the flames without hesitation.

The bonfire was still smouldering the next afternoon. Through the kitchen window we saw black flakes leap from its remains like persistent vermin. Heinz slammed his fist down on the windowsill. Egon had just told him that, in addition to the decorators, a farmer was on his way with a tractor and plough to 'restructure' the garden.

'The master wants an orderly view,' he fumed. 'Only a man who has never put a spade in the ground could take such a decision. Gardening is a matter of cultivating trust between garden and gardener. When I first came here, this was barren woodland. I fed it as I fed my ailing father, one spoonful at a time. And what does the master do? He brings in a tractor!'

I wanted to tell him it was the most beautiful garden I had ever known and that I felt I had truly got to know it during those late-summer months, right down to the roots of the tall grass that swayed before my eyes and the grains of soil in my hair. But instead I said that the ugly always outlasts the beautiful, and all you could do was hope people had a good memory and would live to regret their deeds and admit how beautiful everything had been in the first place. I heard Heinz smacking his lips as if he were trying hard to swallow something. I looked up and saw it was his tears.

'Something took possession of him there in Amsterdam,' he said. 'God knows what he got up to in that capital of yours. I've heard talk about what a damnable place it is. Nothing more than a den of Jews, with a bunch of dock workers and their whores thrown in for good measure.'

I thought back on my summer trip to the Olympics in 1928, the only time I had ever been to Amsterdam. We had shared a taxi with two strangers—it was cheaper than taking the tram—but as we approached the stadium, the traffic ground to a standstill. I was sitting next to a blonde woman who chewed tobacco. When the street vendors passed by hawking their wares, she wound down the window and spat her tobacco at a bloke playing a squeeze box. 'Give it a rest will yer,' she squawked. 'It's bad enough we can't get to the stadium without listening to your racket!' Without batting an eyelid, the hawker reached into the taxi and pulled out a blonde wig, which he dangled between thumb and forefinger. 'Now then darlin',' he grinned, 'how much for a tune?' We didn't know where to look, but the woman, bald as a coot except for a little black tuft, screeched with laughter. That's Amsterdam humour for you, said my father.

Heinz did not move a muscle when the engine that had come to destroy his work appeared.

'A Lanz Bulldog,' he observed, staring red-eyed at the hot-bulb engine that peeped out over the gate. When Egon finally opened up, it drove in, barking on its one cylinder, and made a few circuits on the lawn before lowering the plough onto the rose bushes with a gruesome rattle. Heinz stalked off and it took him three days to return, by which time the garden had been levelled and Raeren had come to resemble a sanatorium, with only the barest of necessities clinging on amid the ash-grey wallpaper and the white-glossed doors.

'The master has finally taken one sensible decision,' he said to Leni. 'About the pig. The slaughterman will be here any minute.'

The village slaughterman was so immaculately turned out, it was hard to believe he had driven his cart eight kilometres through the rain. He stepped into the kitchen where the water was already heating in cauldrons on the stove, slid his tool bag under the table and plumped himself down as if he was about to order a drink at the local pub. That wasn't far off the mark, since the schnapps Leni served him was a perk of his profession and, in observance of the principle 'you can't stand on one leg', he wasn't about to refuse a second glass either. All the same, there was nothing uncouth about him. He was clean-shaven, had an air of wisdom and better table manners than the twins, who were wolfing down their food across from him with their elbows on the table. They had no idea why he had come, not even when Heinz presented him with a sledge-hammer.

'Here, you can borrow this.'

'Blow to the head? No bolt?'

'We've done it that way for centuries. Blow to the head, blade to the throat.'

The slaughterman shook his head in amazement. 'I'm not having it. Where's the master of the house?'

'Use a slaughtering mask and it won't bleed out properly,' said Heinz stubbornly. The slaughterman removed a cylindrical instrument from his bag and put it on the table in front of Siegbert, who still suspected nothing.

'German-made. Pyrotechnic. Hasn't let me down yet, whether they weigh one hundred or two hundred kilos.'

Half an hour later the sow was shooed out of her pen. For a pig, her cries were very tuneful, a loop of three descending tones to jangle all our nerves. The twins stood in the doorway crying, with their hands over their ears. Leni lugged straw and pans of boiling water, as if someone were about to give birth. The maître signalled to us to leave, his limp more pronounced than ever now that a sheath containing a butcher's knife was strapped to his thigh. Only Heinz was smiling as he hovered around the sow. She refused to keep still, eliciting cries of 'Halt!' from Heinz, as if he were refereeing some kind of match. Eventually he managed to tie the sow's back leg to the stable door. All the while she continued singing, ears flat against her head, which swayed from left to right as she clocked the slaughterman sneaking up from behind, till the bolt gun was aiming at her forehead.

'Halt!'

The sow collapsed in spasms on the concrete. The slaughterman turned on his heels, like an athlete not wanting to see the result of his throw. Heinz grabbed her jerking hind legs while the maître shoved a basin under her neck. He unsheathed the knife and a pitch-black wave dragged me under.

Some time must have passed before I opened my eyes again and saw the silhouettes of three men standing in the empty grounds, forcing the creature to its knees and cleaving it open along its backbone. Leni sent me to fetch salt to stop the blood clotting. That night I knew I was not the only one to hear the old sow cry, drawn-out wails echoing across the wasteland that surrounded the house.

# Part Three

To the distinguished and most gifted gentleman Gerbrand
Adriaenszoon Bredero,

My worthy and beloved friend, your affectionate and most
welcome letter did not reach me until yesterday. It does me
a power of good to hear that you are in sound health and
that you have seen fit to grant my request to pen a series of
laudatios for my work. Engraver Michel le Blon, with whom
you are well acquainted, has also pledged his services,
enthralled as he is by what he has understood of the theory.
The Académie de l'Espée is sure to be more accomplished
and more extensive than anything printed by my Spanish
instructors from the Destreza, whom I hold in the greatest
honour and esteem. It is my most fervent wish that this work
will protect our descendants from senseless bloodshed, for
we should not wish to pursue a course on which the thirst
for revenge will claim yet more young lives. If it were in my
power to do so, I would return to Amsterdam this very day
and at long last make haste with the printing of this work, all
the while rejoicing in my friendship with you, my most
extraordinary, dedicated and artistic pupil. Alas, I am duty-
bound to remain here to train the Elector of Brandenburg to
his satisfaction in the art of fencing whenever it pleases him
to visit his newly acquired lands. However, not a day goes by
but I yearn for the life we shared in Amsterdam. The land on
our south-east border knows no such conviviality, having
been mired in revenge and redress as long as any man can

remember. I sometimes think no man here capable of tracing his mistrust back to its root. The peace is still young, the treaty signed but eighteen months ago, while rancour runs deep, passed from father to son. The Elector, our margrave, has yet to make his own peace with this new reality. He makes little use of the entitlements granted him and the lives of his new subjects will carry on much as before, but Wolfgang Wilhelm is and will remain his rival until death. To this day the very thought of how his foe drove his troops from Düsseldorf for the sole purpose of celebrating Mass there fills him with rage. Such Catholic ostentation! I am wise enough to keep my own counsel whenever he inquires as to my Spanish ancestry.

My greatest fear is that we find ourselves at a mere way station and both of us will live to see the day when a new war erupts around Cleves. This enforced peace is as a malnourished child who turns his face from the spoon. Truces never hold long in these parts. Of course, the Spaniards were first to occupy Aachen and our prince, my illustrious pupil, was not to be outdone. To him I have sworn an oath only to use my art for the protection of the fatherland and not to abuse it by killing a man out of spite. But who gives a fig for such noble resolutions in times like these? Ah, dear friend, all this leaves me weary and once again my lungs protest at the lack of sea air. My theory must be printed as soon as possible, with fine illustrations, for my noble pupils are wont to ignore the words that trip from my tongue. Johan Sigismund, for instance, is a melancholy man of kindly disposition, yet stubborn nonetheless. He asked me how better to hit his opponent. I answered that he would be wiser to focus on the science of inviolability. You understand my words, we have spoken of such matters oftentimes before.

Geometry is the science best suited to the art of fencing. It teaches the fencer to think logically and methodically, without being hindered by emotion. A good fencer keeps a cool head, liberates himself from vengeful urges and views his opponent from a distance. In doing so, he is the spectator of his own battle, basing his judgement not on feelings but on absolute truth. He observes as the scientist ponders a calculation, practises as the mathematician makes the glorious art of measurement and formulation his own. You must agree that if man possesses the knowledge of how to remain inviolable, emotional attacks can serve no useful purpose? In allowing your fencing to be led by observing your opponent's intentions, you will find yourself growing closer to him. After all, you inhabit the same set of circumstances. Working well together is in your mutual interest.

It is my constant endeavour to bring these matters to the attention of the Elector in the idle hope that I might prevent a new war. It is always wiser to observe the situation before spilling blood. Every duellist needs to know how important their seconds are, the just onlookers who do not allow their vision to be clouded by the thirst for blood that consumes the two combatants but who instead take note for future generations. It is my humble hope that I may go down in history as the surgeon who healed us of the blind hunger for vengeance.

As for those who refuse to understand such things, I refer them to the slaughterhouse occupying the cellar under our beloved fencing school in Amsterdam, next door to the house on the Nes where you were born. At the time of my departure, that cellar contained no less than fifty slaughtering blocks, all of them in use. Our most esteemed master of mathematics, fencing maître Van Ceulen, was so proud of his premises above Leyden University library, little knowing that in fact he was pinning science beneath the sole of his shoe. At least we could lay claim to stamping on the blood of the butcher's block, launching every attack in the full realization that we are not animals.

Farewell, my exceptional pupil, and do not forget me.

Your most devoted maître,
Girard Thibault

# 1

Egon spoke of Thibault as if he had known him personally and talked about Amsterdam as if its Golden Age had never ended. He had sailed up the River Amstel by barge, waves foaming at his feet and a mackerel sky above him. A nursemaid had shown him the way to the library and somewhere in the warren of ever-narrowing alleyways she had lifted her skirts for him, but he had pressed on past gloomy households and backstreet squabbles. The librarian had pocketed the pouch of silver coins and hauled up his treasure from the depths of the catacombs with a toothless grin: it's all yours, our little secret. That was the Hollanders to a tee: a shifty bunch of prawn-guzzlers. Walking down the Rokin he had almost slipped on the discarded shells and peelings that lay everywhere. Everyone seemed to be gnawing on something as they scurried along, a nation of hucksters. The sugared brandy a barmaid had slipped him, though he had only wanted a bite to eat, had been just as sickening. A mussel-peddler had conned him by the light of a smoky oil lamp. But it had all been worth it in the end. What a triumph, what an honour to bring Girard Thibault back to the land of his Elector so that his mystic lore could at last be handed down to us coddled profligates! If we succeeded, the rest would follow. Of this he was convinced.

As far as I was concerned, this new von Bötticher was

a sorry sight. The humility with which he allowed his seventeenth-century maître to peer over his shoulder, the devotion with which he laid the great book on the table, the gloves he obediently donned before turning its pages. He had been reduced to an altar boy. If this was how he planned to carry on, I was no longer interested. In an effort to make my feelings clear, I laid it on so thick it made my eyes sting. I no longer cared for him, never had, yet I couldn't simply abandon the sad old soul. I still had a whole life ahead of me to become a good fencer, with or without that book of his. When he showed it to me, I snorted indignantly. Those ridiculous illustrations! Gentlemen in knickerbockers, copycat marionettes with identical faces striking cramped poses so as not to deviate from the diagrams beneath their feet. One engraving showed eight such figures lined up across from one another, sword arm extended, while angels wrote wise words in Latin and a lion held up a compass and a square rule. I ask you! Siegbert, our young geometrist, was enraptured of course, but Friedrich did what I wished I could have done. He walked out, declaring that all these niggly calculations left him cold and that he would much rather have an old-fashioned bout of swordplay with the antique *Parisers*, which for some reason had escaped the master's furious clear-out and were still hanging on the wall. At this, Egon had been unable to maintain his evangelistic poise. He grabbed the brat by the arm, dragged him back into the hall and set him in place like a chess piece. Resistance was clearly futile when faced with this antiquated shadow of our former maître.

Luckily for me, the twins bore the brunt of it. I was allowed to watch as they were forced to stand opposite each other for an hour, stock-still and silent, while Egon modelled them to the examples in the book. He stalked to and fro with the frown of a precision engineer, holding up a measuring tape to their weapons, which they had to hold in the same position till their arms trembled. 'Stand there and don't move,' he barked, pressing a notebook to his knee and filling page after page with his scribblings. Occasionally he examined their limbs as if they were deformed, mumbling, 'There's something wrong here.' They shuddered with humiliation as he tapped them with his pen. The atmosphere grew more ominous. None of us, Egon included, felt at home in this deconstructed Raeren, and yet none of us spoke a word about the old Raeren that had taken pity on our misdemeanours like a seedy landlady. Truth be told, it was only Siegbert who had nothing to be ashamed of. Perhaps that was why he was the one to throw down his weapon on the third day. It bounced across the floor on its tip. This in itself was an unforgivable infringement, one that would have earned us a hiding even back in Maastricht. But Siegbert proceeded to kick the foil across the floor. 'We want to fence again,' he growled. 'We want to hit, not just parry.'

The maître picked up the foil and looked at us at last. Tension hissed in our ears. But before he had the chance to answer, someone entered the room. A man of flesh and blood. We were ready to smile in relief, till we saw how much he had changed. Professor Reich looked as if he had returned from the dead, a journey that had sapped him of all his strength. He bore only the faintest resemblance to the carefree Otter we knew. His cheeks were drawn, his moustache cropped and the eyes that had always played second fiddle to his chomping and chattering mouth now dominated his face. They could not hide the fact that he had spent night after night watching and waiting. He took off his hat and looked around at the newly papered walls, stripped of their paintings, and the circles the decorators had been ordered to trace on the parquet.

'It's changed here, too,' he said. 'Everything has changed.'

Egon heaved a deep sigh, in mourning for his interrupted lesson.

'We have put our affairs in order,' he said. 'See for yourself.'

He pointed at the circles that had been painted on the floor. The Otter nodded, he recognized them, but what of it? Cautiously he sat down on the one remaining chair in the room and clasped his hands to stop them trembling.

'I am indebted to you,' said Egon. 'I was able to find the book you spoke of. The Thibault. You told me you had never seen the original?'

The Otter sat frozen to the spot, far from the book, like a wallflower unexpectedly asked to dance by an unattainable lover. Egon was not to be deterred. He steered the twins into position, ready to outshine the Otter's own demonstration that drunken evening. He circled them, making hurried gestures.

'As it turns out,' he said, 'it's mistaken to think in halves. Two halves of a fencing piste, two semicircles: wrong. A divided man is doomed to fail. Thibault's circles overlap but remain whole and move with the individual at their centre. As long as you observe the other's circle, you are safe. The fencers stand one pace apart ... '

'Like at the Mensur!' Friedrich exclaimed, earning himself a resounding clip around the ear.

'Not a bit of it,' said Egon. 'I am talking about the Spanish School. The masters of the Destreza, who always returned unharmed, no matter how often they went into battle. Imagine! At a time when the duel claimed lives every day, they did not sustain so much as a scratch. No one knew how they did it. All kinds of stories did the rounds, but the knowledge of the Destreza remained a secret. In the end, no one dared challenge them. To be feared to such an extent, that is what we must achieve! Whether you fight with a rapier or a tank, it's all about the myth of inviolability.'

He pushed Friedrich aside and tapped Siegbert's foil tauntingly, before spreading his arms in an open invitation. Siegbert brought down his weapon and lunged, but to his amazement the point of his blade flew half a metre wide of the maître's flank. Another tap. Quick as lightning, Siegbert responded yet his weapon still ended up in completely the wrong place, though he had clearly taken the right decision by coming in high. It was beyond belief. I decided to focus on the maître's feet, convinced that his footwork was the source of this trickery. On the third manoeuvre he took a step I would never have taken and once again Siegbert missed. Slowly the maître brought the steel of his blade against his opponent's neck. The Otter leaped to his feet indignantly.

'What are you doing to these children? Look at them standing there. You've drained them of every last drop of passion for the sport. It wouldn't surprise me if they never wanted to hold a sword again.'

'Not so,' said Egon, handing the sword back to Friedrich. 'These boys will lead the way for a new generation of warriors. As twins they can set the finest example, the embodiment of Thibault's identical figures. Perhaps I will bring other twins under my tutelage. I had hoped that, as a medical man, you might be able to help. Do you have any twins among your patients?'

The Otter sank back onto the chair, shaking his head. Egon did not pursue his line of inquiry; his conversation was with himself. For too long he had kept quiet about the scholarly insights he had carried back home under his arm. He had kept the book waiting for a time in his study while he had cleaned the house, as one does with unexpected guests of high standing, but now the house was ready and there were no friends interested in entertaining his guest. He had conveniently forgotten the one distant friend he did have, the man who had steered him toward Thibault in the first place. My father, the coward.

'Inviolable soldiers have always existed,' he said. 'At the front, I saw them with my own eyes. Men who were never hit, who ran rings around death. That gift was theirs by nature. They could never have explained how it worked. But Thibault deciphered the mystery of inviolability and now it can be learned.'

'I beg you Egon, stop this now,' the Otter whispered. 'We are no longer living in the seventeenth century. Terrible things are coming our way.'

'Some animals have the same natural gift,' Egon continued. 'An unshakeable conviction that protects them like a suit of armour. My horse Fidèle could not be hit. She ran to the front line and kept on running while everything around her was screaming and burning. Did she embody this myth? Absolutely. It did not occur to anyone to fire at her, while I lay dying in the sand, a failed hussar whose conviction went no further than the skull and crossbones on his hat.'

'The same skull and crossbones now worn by the Waffen-ss,' said the Otter, flatly.

'Outward show has no substance.'

'Then let me tell you that it chills you to the fucking bone when one of those skull-bearers looks straight through you and decides that the blood pulsing in your temples has no right to flow there. I tell you, Egon, terrible things are coming our way. I have come to say goodbye.'

The Otter saw that von Bötticher was listening at last and the agitation disappeared from his face. He pulled the book toward him, opened it and gave a sign of recognition.

'At the academy I was once given a book full of mysteries for my birthday. Romberg's *A Manual of the Nervous Diseases of Man*. It described many afflictions which were rarely seen but appealed so strongly to the imagination that lithographers never tired of portraying them. Progressive facial hemiatrophy, the degeneration of half the face! The case of Pauline Schmidt, half youthfulness, half decay. A century ago she was known to doctors throughout Europe. They wrote dissertations about her and did not shy away from the strangest questions. Were her thoughts divided too? Was she only half capable of love? In those days science was no stranger to desire. Nowadays everything has to serve a purpose, we no longer deal in the singular aberration.'

As he turned the heavy pages, the Otter's thoughts got the better of him. We could tell he wanted to let them out but was holding back, as if he had caught a rat by the head and was sure it would bite him as soon as he let go. 'Nothing is made with such attention to detail any more,' he said after a while. 'Why is everyone in such a hurry these days? We're like animals that guzzle down their food before it's taken from them. Entire forests have been chopped down and turned into newspaper, animals forced to flee, entire sections of humanity—like the Aborigines—all but wiped out because there's no profit to be made from them. Can we look at a waterfall any more without simply seeing energy? Is there no honest labour we won't mechanize? The organic succumbs to the organizers, but beware, for the rabid zeal behind their organization, the all-consuming frenzy, is most definitely animalistic! And what is your response, Egon? You teach these children to wait patiently within their little circle but step outside it and they will be devoured, bones and all. In this country, there's no turning the tide of what's to come.'

As his former self, on a lonely walk with his horse or messing about in the garden with his animals, Egon would have agreed with the Otter. His thoughts had so often tended in the same direction. But since returning from Amsterdam, his melancholy streak had made way for brisk planning and he was in no mood to have his new-found certainties swept away by a physician warning of tides that could not be turned. In the end he dismissed us. The twins dashed outside, foils in hand, eager for a fencing match in the garden. An icy wind swept in through the front door. I lingered in the hall, hoping to catch more of their exchange, but the two men found wisdom in silence. I headed for the terrace, shivering with cold and the audacity of my enterprise. They weren't going to shrug me off so easily. I knew the doors were ajar—Egon left them open after every session to rid the hall of the smell of our sweat, which seemed stronger now that the walls had been re-papered. Through the half-open net curtains I saw them standing face to face on the spot where I had waltzed with the colossal brute who had come to assign these men to one of two categories: victim or culprit. Who really knew the intricacies of it all? Heinz perhaps, who had avoided our gaze since his master had returned? At that moment, the wind changed direction and carried his name to me.

'Heinz.'

'Oh, that sad case does what I employ him to do.'

'I swear to you, they had taken my weapon. Loaded. It's a miracle I ever got it back.'

'Where will you go?'

'To Bordeaux.'

'Friends? Family?'

'Family. They are planning an ocean crossing, but I doubt it will come to that.'

The Otter slipped a hand into his inside pocket and took

out a slim book. 'These days a passport like mine won't get you far, so Erich arranged this one for me. I owe that young man my life.'

I saw him rub his eyes, but could not tell whether he was crying. Egon took the document from his hands and sniffed it. 'Gilt on leather. They have taste, I'll grant them that. The Weimar eagle has already flown, I see.'

'It's the new design with the national emblem. Not a sight I'm fond of, the swastika. There's something fishy about it. You know who first introduced it to Germany, don't you?'

Egon shook his head, frowning with concentration as he flicked through the pages. A gust of wind seized the net curtains and flung them together. As if he knew I could no longer see him, the Otter raised his voice.

'Our old friend Schliemann. When Schliemann discovered Troy, he found the swastika by the tomb of Agamemnon. Along with that mask.'

'Schliemann has been dead for half a century,' said Egon.

'Be that as it may, Kossinna and a flock of other archaeologists followed in his footsteps, claiming Greek civilization was in fact Germanic and Homer's heroes were Aryan. Schliemann's only objective had been to prove that the *Odyssey* was based on fact.'

I risked tiptoeing over to the doors. Through the gap I saw the Otter pacing across Thibault's circle, one foot in front of the other. My father believed that everyone who observes madness ultimately succumbs to it himself. He had seen it happen in the clinic, but he had also been afraid my mother's mania would end up being contagious. With the Otter caught in my cramped field of vision, I wondered if this danger intensified if you looked through prying eyes, just as everything becomes sharper when your field of vision narrows.

'That sign is cursed,' he said. 'You know how curses escape from tombs? Since Schliemann desecrated Agamemnon's burial site, a curse has fallen upon the German people. They've put a spin on it, rotated it a full 45 degrees, but the damned swastika will keep on spinning and drag us down in a spiral till we devour ourselves tail-first. The curse of Agamemnon and his golden lance; it will take more than a Dutch geometrist to put that right.'

Another gust and the doors were flung open. The Otter responded to the look in Egon's eyes, spun around and saw me there. Both men were dumbstruck. The wind did its best to veil my shame with the curtains, but there I stood fully exposed as an eavesdropper. The Otter spluttered a word or two and then shrugged. There was nothing to be done, I had heard everything. All at once he began to laugh, halting but steadily louder, his first taste of laughter in at least two weeks. 'Speak of the devil! Our very own Greek goddess with a flapping curtain for a robe!'

When eventually he said goodbye he was remarkably calm, almost back to his old self. He hummed a little tune as he walked to his car, doffed his hat as he climbed in and put it back on once he was behind the wheel. I felt a glimmer of hope as I watched him go. Perhaps a little of that old spirit had returned to Raeren. We might have forgotten what purpose it served, yet it was too familiar simply to be abolished. Somewhere on those pristine walls a useless knick-knack had reappeared, a little mirror hung too high to hold your reflection, too high even to be seen.

## 2

I was woken by a dream that refused to be pinned down. It was dark outside and the birds were no longer singing— my afternoon nap had stretched into evening. Fumbling fingers buttoned up my jacket. A spot of fencing, a bite to eat and I would soon feel better. I picked up my bag and headed downstairs, to be met by the comforting smell of roasted meat in the hall. Perhaps Leni had kept a pan warm for me. Bizarre dream images flashed before my eyes: a giant owl pressing its padded face against the window-pane, a blurry opponent who appeared out of nowhere clutching two swords and turned out to be a chrysalis. My appetite vanished instantly. Some dreams make the dreamer a stranger to himself, drench everything in a curious light and leave an aftertaste that lingers all day. I had woken up in a house where I was not wanted, a house occupied by strangers who did not care about me, and where I was casually passed over by intruders. These gloomy thoughts recurred endlessly, an inescapable loop of loneliness. The maître had said nothing more about my departure. Two more weeks, as I recalled, and they had almost passed. Of course I could ask him to take me to the station, but there was every chance he would jump at the invitation. I saw myself sitting on the train, wearing the same pinafore I had arrived in, with no photograph and none the wiser. A dismal ending to *War and Peace*. I would be better off asking my father to come and collect me from Raeren, without a word to the maître. That would shake things up and no mistake. But it would also mean dispatching Heinz to the village to send a telegram, and he was the last person I trusted to run such an errand.

I heard a cough. The door to the fencing hall was ajar and inside the light was on. Something about the situation made me uneasy. 'Is anyone there?' No answer. I put on my mask to strengthen my resolve, but as I did so another remnant of my dream leaped out at me: the chrysalis receiving a gold medal from the queen. Keep walking. 'Who's there?'

A woman was standing in the middle of the fencing hall; she too was masked. We drew our weapons at the same time. She was my build and jogged on the spot briefly, just as I always did before a match. A short run-up, then back, three little jumps on the balls of her feet and she was ready, striking the perfect position without a second's hesitation, from her heel to her fingertips. Who was she? I felt my breath grow heavy inside my mask. This promised to be a scintillating contest, as long as I kept my head. I felt the grip in my palm, inclined my wrist from *quarte* to *octave* and brought my arm back into position. I was ready. Who on earth was she? *What* was she? The speed at which her taut body sprang into motion was so inhuman I half expected to see a tail sweeping from her backbone. Her movements were not fluid but seemed to skip moments in between, the way birds move. She was upon me in the blink of an eye. I stumbled back, knocked her weapon aside and attempted a riposte. In vain—she backed off as quickly as she had advanced. The mesh of her mask was too fine, the light from the wall lamp too dim. I could not see her face but I felt her anger. Before I knew what was happening, she hit me full in the stomach.

In triumph she skipped backward to her position. Ready, fence! Effortlessly she extended into a lunge only Helene Mayer was capable of, with a reach that pulled everything out of proportion. To my amazement, the point of her weapon was already at my side. She attacked relentlessly, my nerves were jangling. I had learned to turn such rash behaviour to my advantage and to let my opponent wear herself out, seizing my moment like a psychiatrist restraining a frantic patient, but I had no idea who she was—that was the thing; perhaps I was the one who was mad. I swivelled my torso to one side and she lost her balance. With a high sidelong thrust, I jabbed the point of my weapon into her waist. Perhaps I was a match for her after all. I caught a fleeting glimpse of her face, enough to see that she too was smiling. We ducked and weaved over and under each other's weapons, clenched our fists when we scored and controlled our voices when we sustained a hit, though I was sure we were both longing for the release of crying out. It dawned on me that I had never fenced so well in my life. By the eighth hit I was two points ahead, but winning no longer mattered. I did not want this enthralling bout to end. No sooner had the thought materialized than she took off her mask.

I saw Helene Mayer, with her coiled blonde braids. A moment later I no longer knew who I was looking at, the kind of momentary incomprehension that comes over you when you taste something without knowing what it is. But then I recognized her bright blue eyes, the determined set of her jaw, her brightly painted lips. With her cheeks flushed from exhaustion, Julia looked younger than ever. She might have been my sister.

'Was he your first?'

'What?'

'Egon was not my first,' she said, her smile bitter. 'Nor

was my husband. He arrived too late as well. We fucked ourselves silly, you see. All the women in the village waited dutifully until it became clear what we had to lose. I can point them out to you, the ones who remained faithful and missed out. They look thirty years older than I do. In war, virginity counts for nothing.'

How did she know? Egon would never have told her. Perhaps the twins had found out and said something to their mother or, worse still, perhaps she did not mean Egon at all, but Friedrich. I ran my hand over my face as if my fingertips could tell me what she had read there.

'And now you're wondering how I know?' she said. 'I sense these things. I am the mother of twins after all. Halfway to being a goddess, if the natives of Africa are to be believed: to them, twins are gods, born to their mother without the need for human conception.'

She spun a good yarn, though of course she was acting. She spoke of twins emerging from the mist on the Nigerian border in search of a woman to be their mother. The father was of little consequence, she said, even more of an irrelevance than Joseph in the Bible, a role anyone could play—Egon, her husband or one of those men with the good fortune to turn up in a village where the women let themselves be taken as if their lives depended on it. What mattered was those picture-perfect children of hers, their young blood. The boys who looked with two eyes and spoke with one mouth. They had chosen her. She stepped lightly around the room, attempting to float on air, examined herself from top to toe and then turned from her reflection with a smile. The bitch. I wanted to tell her that Red Indians saw twins as a curse visited on a mother who'd had blazing rows during her pregnancy, that they believed her own children would end up killing her unless they drank her urine for the rest of their lives. Was that any less true?

I had read something of the sort and was about to tell her so, but thought better of it as she squared up to me.

'It's lonely as hell to be the mother of twins. As if they were never really mine. They love themselves above all else.'

So we were back to that old chestnut. I had a hard time believing this woman could awaken tenderness in anyone. Lonely as hell? Aw, bless her heart! She didn't need pity from anyone.

'And what of the girls who fall in love with them ... For, oh aren't they handsome? And oh aren't they perfect? But I can tell the poor dears that they will only ever have half a lover. The other half will always belong to his brother. And now it's time for my boys to join up and serve the fatherland without delay. Or as my husband puts it: serve someone other than themselves.'

Water broke the surface of her icy blue eyes. This was not an act, for at the same time her nose swelled up and her mouth creased into a clownish grimace too ugly to be part of her repertoire. Her palms were clammy as she took my hands in hers.

'Some say we all have a twin, you know,' she said. 'For the natives of Cameroon, twins are divine because both souls become visible at the same moment. But they believe every one of us has a soul that experiences everything directly and a shadow soul that tracks and observes us, standing aloof till we die and then passing on our experiences to our next body. Wouldn't that be lovely? A record kept by a kindred spirit?'

By way of illustration she pointed to her own shadow, a comical shape thrown against the wall. I mumbled that I had enjoyed our fencing match but that now I was going to bed. She shrugged and walked off through the balcony doors and into the evening air. Gone, just like that. No thrumming engine, no sound at all. Over by the oak, a flicker of something haughty and unmistakably feminine appeared, but it could just as easily have been one of Heinz's ghosts. The storm compacted the air around the house. The windows were drawn tight, as if to seal in the stifling silence that seemed to descend earlier each evening. Only a month ago, Egon would still have been playing cards with Heinz at this hour and they would have ended up arguing and uncorking a bottle to smooth things over. But now the kitchen stood empty, there was nothing on the stove and the ashes in the hearth had cooled. I no longer heard creaking as I climbed the stairs and there seemed to be no end to them, as if the attic had risen a floor. The sense of alienation was so strong that I stamped my feet and wished it were daytime so I could summon Egon to drive me to the station. I no longer wanted to go to bed without someone wishing me goodnight. I felt lonelier than I had ever intended to feel, and if I had a shadow soul it was keeping one hell of a low profile. Perhaps my life was not worth observing and I had experienced nothing much worth passing on. Or perhaps Raeren was a place no shadow could penetrate and they hung around outside its walls like hopeful beggars.

And yet ... as I entered my room, I sensed the recent imprint of someone else's palm on the door handle. On my bed lay a letter. Face-down, as if the sender had run away as soon as he had licked and sealed the envelope. My name was scrawled on the front in a hand I did not recognize. I made a quick circuit of the room. There was no one under the bed and the balcony was deserted. *Janna.* Yes, that was me all right. Here was one envelope that did not need to be hidden away or set alight; it was addressed to me and I had every right to open it. Yet I had no desire to. In the letter he had given me to deliver, my father had said he was happy this was one letter Egon would read since I would be there to make sure he did. He had no way of knowing that all his letters had been read; Egon had ripped them open and soaked up their contents. He had even answered them, only those answers had never reached my father. It all came down to a handful of practicalities—the licking of stamps, a trip to the postbox—mere details. More importantly, he had directed his words to my father, albeit out of earshot, and had saved them for a better moment. Until I came between them, that is. The fact that I was now being addressed directly troubled me; I felt like a beachcomber who meets a survivor from the shipwreck he has looted. I sniffed at the letter. We seldom leave envelopes unopened. It is an almost superhuman achievement not to break the seal while the contents are unknown. We walk away from spoken words but speak written words in our minds as we read, only to realize afterwards that we had no desire to hear them. My stomach turned as I unfolded the thin sheet of paper. Only a quarter had been filled, with frenzied, ostentatious strokes of the pen.

To the sweetest, most beautiful musketeer of all!

I will never forget the first dance we shared. Yes, it is true. We have danced together. I still remember every detail, the bird that sang when I stepped outside afterwards. And when I looked up from the garden to where you were recovering from the turmoil, this evil place took on a friendly disposition because it was watching over you. You have held your tongue ever since because you never fully understood what happened that day—you had fainted after all. But those who saw us then, who watched our steps as we came together and moved apart, steps people call dancing, know there was no question of combat even though we are both fencers, born and raised on opposite sides of a border. The enemy is elsewhere, the other, the one who has come between us, uninvited. I will defeat him, although I know you do not want me to. Forgive me for not signing this letter. While I do not believe the rumours about the reasons for your stay here at Raeren, I do believe that it is dangerous to put one's feelings into words in these troubled times, even feelings of love. If those feelings are mutual, they will find each other, just as passion reaches for the foil and the foil aims for the heart. Janna, I love you, do not deny me!

Good grief! I had to get out of here, and fast. It was a simple enough undertaking, it came down to a handful of practicalities—the packing of a suitcase, the purchase of a ticket—mere details. No time like the present. No need for goodbyes. I would smuggle my suitcase out of the house at the crack of dawn and wait for Heinz, my underhanded porter. I would ride to the village with him and as soon as we passed through the gate my unsuspecting shadow, which had been waiting for me outside the walls, would join me once again and I would arrive home with a conscience as clean as the one I had left with.

# 3

The day began with a scream. It rose up from far below, growing louder and louder only to trail off suddenly, like a whistling kettle lifted from the fire, and fade to feeble whimpering. Heinz had fallen out of the hayloft. His foot had missed the ladder and he had plunged four metres to land right next to the bales of hay he had just thrown down ahead of him. We found him curled up on the stone floor, clutching his ankle with both hands. The St Bernard stood next to him, sweeping his tail back and forth as if the scene warranted a chuckle. 'Broken,' Heinz groaned. 'My bloody ankle's broken and no one gives a damn.' Egon established that nothing had been broken, sprained at most, but Heinz hobbled to the kitchen leaning heavily on his master, insisting on a glass of plum schnapps as the bandages were applied and wasn't there still some of that spiced gingerbread Leni had baked the other day? After knocking back a couple of glasses, he ground his knuckles into his eye sockets though there wasn't a tear in sight and swore this would be the end of him. Egon sighed as he sat down beside him at the table and inquired how long it was likely to take, this end of his. Heinz shot him a dirty look to rival the grime under his fingernails and Egon stared back, leaning forward, hands flat on the table. There they sat, a pair of leery fossils face to face, till the twins came charging in to ask when the lesson was due to start.

I thought I had shaken off my doubts of the night before, but upon seeing the twins' finely pencilled profiles a sentence came back to me, word for word: *But those who saw us then, who watched our steps as we came together and moved apart, steps people call dancing* ... a sentence with three clues to the sender. A fencer I had danced with and who had grown up across the border. The only man I had danced with at Raeren was the Colossus, if a lark with the only girl at the party could be called dancing, the perfunctory prelude to a spot of communing. I hadn't made a lasting impression on him, that much was certain. True, he was a fencer and a German, but so were three of the four men at the kitchen table, all of whom were ignoring me; not even so much as a good morning from the twins who, having understood that today's lesson was cancelled, had laid claim to Heinz's gingerbread. Friedrich licked his fingers one by one. The letter had been written with a flourish, not the work of someone who had barely been stringing a decent sentence together for ten years. The long strokes of the pen reminded me of Egon's old letters, but would his handwriting really have remained so ostentatious after two decades in which he had penned countless other missives? Years pass and our grand gestures shrink along with our plans.

No, it could not be him. Besides, Egon had never danced with me. Julia had managed to lure him onto the floor and in her arms he had attempted to waltz, with the air of an animal that has been dressed up for a laugh. I doubted he would ever accept a dance from me. If he did, it would be up to him to lead and I would do my best to follow his stiff steps, maintaining the fiction that this dance was new to me. My gaze settled on the curve of his back beneath his cotton shirt and I thought contentedly that I knew how it felt: warm, soft and sturdy as a piece of furniture polished in the sun. If I ran my hands over its surface I knew I would have to lift them halfway to avoid touching the bump made by an ugly wart. Further down, next to his sacrum, he became warmer and the sensation of wood gave way to metal. If we ever danced, I would not hold him there.

They maintained their silence: brother to brother, servant to master, master to servant. Their suspicion was almost tangible, the stray doubts and rumours that had hung in the air all this time were spun tight across the table. I had no desire to witness these threads of recrimination being sliced through. I walked over to him and placed my hand on his shoulder.

'Take a walk with me,' I heard myself say, the most sensible voice that could have sounded in the kitchen at that moment. 'There's something I want to ask you.'

He nodded and got to his feet immediately, in a far more amicable mood than I had expected, certainly more amicable than those who remained silent at the table. When I looked back inside through the window they had not moved an inch, tempers simmering to the point where the air above their heads seemed about to ripple. The temperature outside was close to freezing. The grass remained hard beneath our feet and beneath the paws of the St Bernard, which ran on ahead in a carefree cloud of doggy warmth. Halfway across the field he found a stick and kept tossing into the air, shaking his head as he picked it up to kill his make-believe prey.

'I'd change places with him in a heartbeat,' said Egon. 'Wouldn't you? Running around in the here and now. Seems like a blessing to me. History separates us from the animals, but what good does it do us? I'd rather have had no history at all.'

He peered into the melancholy distance of his autumnal estate. I waited for him to tell me something, a tale to carry me along, but he did not say another word. I crossed my arms, since it was pointless to expect we might ever walk arm in arm.

'Why didn't you send those letters?'

He winked at me, so briefly that I might have been mistaken. What difference could it possibly make to him? I was leaving in any case.

'There would have been no point,' he said nonchalantly. 'Letters from the internment camps were sent straight to the censor. My letters would have fallen into the wrong hands. Filching fingers, black with ink, would have sifted through them in search of untoward phrases. It takes a certain type of man—they'll never be heroes but they're not bastards either. Lonely, anonymous characters who jump at a phrase that might be addressed to them personally. I wrote with the intention of sending my letters at a later date, but once the war was over I no longer saw the need.'

He paused, a sign that it was my turn to speak of practicalities. I obeyed, just as I had in the weeks gone by.

'I'm leaving.'

'I know.'

'Yes, but I'm leaving this week and I would like my father to collect me.'

He nodded. 'Do you still have that photograph?'

I held my tongue, dumfounded.

'The one you brought to the dinner table that evening. Of your father and the other man?'

'That other man was you.'

'No it wasn't,' he said with a rueful smile. 'I wasn't myself at the time.'

He quickened his pace, put some distance between us. When was he ever himself? Here he was, my first love. A man who would rather have had no history, with the stated intention of living in an all-consuming present, an example set by his dog. This man was nothing like the man I had spied on. There were no more secrets for me to uncover. Here he was, giving his past away unprompted, without a second thought, a past in which my father and I were sealed away like old harvest in forgotten jars. Anyone who wanted those dusty old stories was welcome to them. Newer, fresher ones were on their way.

'I was unrecognizable,' he shouted into the wind, 'a shadow of myself. Your father has probably told you about the disorder I was suffering from. A manic obsession with regularity and balance. Everything had to fit together, every hour of every day. There were times when I sat puzzling from morning till night to get it all to make sense. Only it never made sense! I was afraid to move for fear of wrinkling my sheets. At night I fretted that the moon would knock the universe off kilter unless it was pared into shape. A particular tree drove me to distraction because it was never in the middle of my field of vision. I tried to solve the problem by asking the nurse to move my bed, but she refused. Her right eye was larger than her left, so I kept my eyes shut whenever she was in the room. As time went on, your father would accompany me on wary walks past lopsided bushes, over paving stones, each one different from the next. The archway we passed under every day was missing a stone and I could not bear to look at the sloppy plasterwork that filled the gap. It wasn't only the things I saw. Birdsong turned my stomach if a trill broke off and the pattern was not completed. Jacques told me the name of my condition, a name I forgot instantly. I needed a diagnosis like I needed a hole in the head. It was all a logical consequence of what he had done to me.'

Egon shot me an inquiring look. He knew that I knew what he was going to say. I had read every word of it. All he had to do was clarify, annotate those letters with comments in the margins.

'They had taken me from my work, a duty I had been unable to fulfil, and confined me in a state of helplessness,' he nodded. 'I woke up to find myself stranded on the sidelines, in the vaudeville of Dutch neutrality, with its neat little cobblestones, twittering birds, crooked gables, the misleading props of everyday existence, while a few kilometres away real life was thundering on without me. I defy anyone not to go mad under those circumstances! Keeping me dangling at a loose end for months was bad enough, but taking a snapshot to immortalize me as part of that farce? It was one indignity too many. I tried to hide from the camera. If I had known then what was in store, that they were going to lock me away even deeper, I would have lost my sanity completely. At least in the photograph I was still a shadow but later, in the camp, I became completely invisible. Your father never understood that my mind would only ever be at peace in the war.'

He stooped to pick a flower from the frosty ground. Though the days were growing shorter and the sun more feeble, the snow-white petals still stood in the same relation to one another. What was it again? 137.5 degrees? All at once I was reminded of my parents stamping along ahead of me on our Sunday walks. I pictured my father's boots grinding down the brushwood as my mother dragged herself along in his tracks and I saw now that she could never really keep up with him, that perhaps she would have liked to walk arm in arm and it was my father who treated her as a stranger because she believed in fairy tales. Perhaps he should have told her a tale or two of his own, a miraculous account of the sacred geometry of nature with its logarithmic shells, hexagonal honeycomb and basalt pillars. Then she might have listened to him the way she listened to the priest, and if she started on about the hand of God, all he had to do was nod because in the end his explanations were not much nearer the mark. Perhaps then they might have had a good marriage. Egon chewed pensively on the stalk of the flower.

'People reckon war is chaos, but the opposite is true,' he said. 'I have never slept as soundly as I did at the front. There life is stripped back to its essentials, from boiling the potatoes over the fire to blowing out the candle before turning in. There's real comfort to be had in opening your eyes each morning and thinking it could be your last. A wonderful thought in all its simplicity. Being bored, feeling sated, that's what keeps people awake at night. Wealth is guaranteed to keep you tossing and turning.'

He began to skip along, the dog giving him an excuse, and it was surprising to see how naturally it came to him. When he skipped his leg seemed to give him far less trouble. 'It's beginning again,' he said pointing skyward. 'You can smell it in the air. Soon the stage set will be shoved aside and we can get back to what really matters. We can finally complete what we left unfinished.'

Then came the second scream of the day, followed by a salvo of astonished 'Oh's and 'Ah's. Leni came charging across the field, wobbling this way and that as if she too had a gammy leg, as if gammy legs were catching here at Raeren.

'Saints alive!' she panted once she had reached us. 'Heinzi's foot! What am I supposed to do with Heinzi's foot in that state! Who's going to take me to market?' Head, hands, belly and cheeks, everything was shaking as she continued to exclaim 'Heinzi's foot!' as if unable to get over the fact that this grubby part of her husband's anatomy had turned out to be the foundation of her entire household.

'We'll go together in the car,' said Egon calmly. 'It'll be like old times. And Janna will come too. We have a telegram to send.'

Half an hour later the three of us were in the car on our way to something that was not part of Raeren but not part of my plans either. The road to the village was strewn with dead branches and Egon swerved abruptly to avoid them. He had left the top down and all kinds of things were thrown in our faces, fragments of the woods we were leaving behind. I looked up at the stormy lives of the hovering birds and spinning leaves till the electricity pylons and telephone lines appeared.

I instantly forgot the name of the village, just as I forget the names of people I am introduced to if their features are particularly striking. The colours were to blame. The façades were like sugared almonds: pastel-blue, violet, lemon-yellow. We sped around a corner and had to brake for the red-and-white-striped awnings of the market and soon we were in among the crowd, the grass-green and burgundy hunting hats, the coloured feathers, corsages, black jute bags, suntanned noses, red cheeks, painted lips, nails, teeth, winks, shouts, whoops and roars, everyone full of life and relishing the prospect of more life to come. We lost sight of Leni, but Egon was unperturbed. He selected a wall to lean against and slotted a cigarette between his lips. This was a man I would never regret, a man worth remembering. I would always be able to picture his unerring fingers and above all his arrogant lips, the way he gazed into the distance with such damned indifference as he struck a match, knowing he could rely on touch alone. His warm, pulsing throat.

The other faces on the street looked foreign, so very different to Egon's and to mine. They were even different creatures to Leni. The sounds they made bore no resemblance to the words I was able to understand at Raeren, as if they had been whipped up into another language entirely. Behind one stall stood a butcher who looked so self-satisfied that he was ready for the spit himself, as well pummelled as his sausages and completely bald into the bargain: even his eyebrows were missing. He was serving a woman who was filling up her pram with groceries. A tub of honey occupied the baby's spot. Everyone seemed to know everyone else. The woman with the pram was embraced by an older woman and they laughed in each other's ear. The older woman gave us a nod and I realized it was Leni. Apparently Egon had signalled to her. I followed him over to the post office.

There they were again. The swastikas.

After what the Otter had said about the archaeologist who had unearthed the fateful symbol, I couldn't help but see the rank and file scraping a living while above their heads the curse of Agamemnon fluttered in the breeze. The cheery hustle and bustle became the sound of the sea churning in a whirlpool or the spiral of a shell, as the people around me were dragged under, groceries and all. There was nothing they could do to stop it. Dizzied by the swastika, they spiralled deeper into a fate that had already been decided. 'You look pale, are you feeling all right?' It was Egon's voice, a sound from far away. The post office was silent as a church. Sunlight streamed in through a high window. The chequered floor shone like a lump of back bacon, extending up to the polished wood of a counter at which only one position was open. '*Heil Hitler,*' the woman said. She did not smile, but frowned into the sun's glare, her complexion a mixture of brass and beeswax. Egon told me to wait on the bench and walked the length of the braided rope to the clerk, who nudged a form across the counter toward him. He wrote leaning on the wood while she remained motionless behind the glass, her eyes following the movements of his hand without reading what he had written. In her job it was the number of words that mattered, not their meaning. He hooked one foot behind the other, jotted down something else and handed the form back to the clerk. She tapped each letter with the top of her pen, as if sending a message in Morse. Other sounds followed: the echoes of the stamp and the drawer, the squeak of the trolley that took the form across to the telegraphist, the jingle of the Reichsmarks. Money, that was another thing: now I really did want to go home.

Was this home? I drank like a startled animal. Opposite me, Egon was playing cards with the twins. The boys had decided they were men and were insisting on beer instead of apple juice. The white pudding Leni had bought at the market was sizzling in the pan, and though it was making our mouths water, no one ventured to comment. The silence was anything but golden, unlike the roasted fat and the fried apples Leni served up. With a magician's flourish, she scattered a dusting of pepper from one hand and a pinch of salt from the other onto each of our plates. It was Egon who broke the spell, knocking a rogue playing card from Friedrich's cuff with a slap of his hand. He held the boy's wrist tightly and would not let him go. Despite the gloves we wore during the lessons, you could recognize all of us as fencers by the hard skin the foil had left on our fingers. Mankind has been wielding weapons since its earliest beginnings, archaeological digs have revealed. Our evolution from four legs to two is what set us apart from the animals, but without a weapon in its grasp the hand is a worthless instrument. The hand caught in Egon's grip had been reduced to a pathetic little paw.

Heinz came hobbling in. The first thing he saw was the untouched meal under our noses, then our expressions and then the paw. Realization dawned and he joined us at the table. Now we were all here together: the cheaters, the spies and the traitors. It was a situation primed to explode. Yet we all sat and waited for the maître to give a sign that everything was all right. The sign came: he started drinking with a vengeance. Instead of joining him, Heinz looked on—the very model of restraint—in the conviction that their roles had been reversed in recent weeks. His master had become his inferior. Egon drank so much that when he finally got to his feet I had to support him. We walked together along the hallway to his quarters, hurrying past the large windows, fleeing the immensity of the moonlight. The scent of animals pervaded his den. He kicked off his shoes and tumbled onto the bed in his drunken daze, whispering that my father must already be packing his suitcase.

'His word against mine,' he mumbled. 'Either my memory was abducted or I was.'

I undid the rest of his shirt buttons. On proper inspection, this man was exceedingly well put together. He resembled the anatomical models from my father's surgery, all men of Egon's build, never the gangling scarecrows or stocky little chaps you were far more likely to encounter on a daily basis. This body had been declared the standard model, a norm that made it easy to categorize other men in terms of extremes and averages. It was a body made to be described in Latin, to have its contours drawn on graph paper; the face above it, with all its wrinkles and expressions, kept vague for the sake of convenience. Emotions are not the point. It is all about organs and tissue, aspects the average person would rather ignore. Only doctor and patient fret about the likes of a pancreas, by no means a concern for my anaesthetized lover, who let himself be undressed without once losing his curious smile. I stroked and fondled him. If I'd had a pen to hand I would have noted: skin surprisingly soft but firm to the touch, very little body hair, including the area around the genitals, which are warm and content, like the rest of the man. It dawned on me that I could walk away and do with him what I wanted. He would have no say in the tale I would tell, as I embellished parts of him, concealed others and romanticized all kinds of things. I could transform him into a friendly fencing master and a licentious vagabond who loved me passionately. No need to bore anyone with the details: it would be a compact summary of the salient points, condensed to fit the back of a postcard and certainly more orderly than the chaos of the country, the history and the future to which I would consign his unconscious body.

The expression on his face was curious to say the least. Perhaps I should have turned on the light to see whether he was actually smiling, but that would have woken him and I wanted to go on gazing at this other Egon for a while, not the maître who had come back from Amsterdam in a state of confusion, but an amicable soul who returned my gaze with closed eyes. I slipped off my knickers, lowered myself onto him and watched his smile widen.

## 4

We were being watched. I could tell without opening my eyes. Reptiles see through a third eye in the back of the neck, one that registers the tension and heat of an attack from behind. I lay there still as an iguana on a warm stone, the sun on my buttocks. He saw us naked, my naked leg resting on Egon's leg, my arm around his back, his arm around my shoulders, and saw that this was how we had fallen asleep. He saw a man who was old enough to be my father, the passage of time etched on his skin like the rings of a tree: the war wound on his thigh, the flecks of pigment that spanned his shoulders, the hard skin that warped the contours of his feet. Next to them he saw the virginal soles of the girl to whom he had written a love letter. I have never been one to walk barefoot, something even tramps avoid if they can help it.

I continued to peer through my reptilian eye until I heard my admirer snap out of his shock. It came with a sudden movement, as if he were catching an object before it hit the ground. When I was sure he had turned to go, I opened my eyes. In the diffuse light I caught sight of his back in a fencing jacket, his hand clenched in anger or confusion, missing its hold at first but then slamming the door loud enough to set the whole house trembling. Egon woke up, became his old rigid self and looked directly at the spot where the letter-writer had turned on his heels.

Why the letter-writer? How could I be so sure that what I had seen—a shadow, an angel—was a glimpse of the person who had written me that letter? I couldn't, which was why I set off after him. I grabbed the sheet from the floor and wrapped it around me as tight as armour, for since the house had trembled there was a threat hanging in the air. I shuffled past the windows in the hallway, looking out at the bare ground, which looked back as if it were ready to turf me out. No need—I would be leaving of my own accord once this riddle had been solved. Out in the hall I caught another glimpse, his white jacket hanging loose, flapping like wings behind him. I headed for the fencing hall, determined to see his face, but a hand clutching a letter stopped me in my tracks. Leni did not say a word as she thrust the sheet of paper under my nose but stood there chewing, on her breakfast I assumed. Luckily there were no more than a few words to detain me, dictated by my father to a telegraphist in Maastricht: he would arrive by car around lunchtime, many thanks and kind regards. I nodded and Leni returned to the kitchen, still chomping grimly away. In a matter of hours I would have nothing more to do with her. But before then I had to know which of the two he was. I decided to go around the back way.

Perhaps the air outside was less full of malice than I would later recall. The lashing wind, the animal cries, the thick moss on the steps up to the terrace—all details that could easily have been dished up by my imagination in the retelling. As if the reality wasn't bad enough. It was probably nothing more than a nondescript autumn morning when I saw the twins standing face to face, ready to run each other through. They had taken the razor-sharp *Parisers* down off the wall and everything told me this was deadly serious. They stood there angry and unmasked, without checking distances or positions. Each waiting for the other to make the first move, and neither of them planning to wait long. Their jackets were half unbuttoned. Perhaps they had only decided at the last minute that this would be no ordinary fencing bout. They had taken the blades down from the wall with no discussion as to who should have which weapon. Consumed by curiosity, I waited. One of those sharpened tips was about to serve the purpose for which it had been honed a century earlier.

Of course, if this realization had hit home at the time I would never have allowed myself to act in the way I did. Later I had to invent reasons for not intervening, when people grew too indignant to go on listening to my story. One such reason was that the doors were closed. The net curtains had been pulled aside so I could see everything, but my way was barred. To be honest, the thought never even crossed my mind. I made no attempt to approach them, sensing that this duel needed no seconds. Who better to keep watch over their own jealous souls than the doppelgängers themselves? I stood there expecting a good match, a masterly display with weapons drawn to restore the balance between two sabreurs with a score to settle. But the threat hanging in the air was unleashed far too quickly. One moment collapsed into the next. At first there were two brothers, two swords, two steps. Then two became one: one victim, one culprit.

From the very start this had nothing to do with fencing. For a second the details were in place, the position of their hands, their first steps within the lines of the piste, but then the fabric of the scene unravelled. After a flurry of abrupt movements their bodies were pressed together in a sudden, cramped embrace. I did not see any blood. Their weapons hit the ground at the same time. They both sank to the floor but Friedrich was the first to double up, gasping for air with eyes wide open as if that might give him more room to breathe. I threw myself forward against the glass I had forgotten was there just as Egon stormed into the room, summoned by a scream I had not heard.

A deep silence had come from somewhere. Perhaps it had begun as I had set off in pursuit through the house, heart pounding in my ears, or when I had held my breath as I read my father's telegram, but I am sure the silence was complete when I saw that the twins were in earnest. It sparked a memory of the accident on the road from Maastricht to Kerkrade, when the passengers on the bus had all fallen silent. Men, women, children, ugly, oafish, fat, thin, wearing silly hats and other accessories, clutching bags full of useless junk, all sweaty armpits and bad breath— every one of them had achieved wisdom in one smack. Say nothing till you know. The silence they maintained when they sensed the man in the road was dead had nothing to do with faint-heartedness; it was an instinctive reverence in the face of destiny.

The memory triggered a rush of noise. One twin was sobbing while the other's gaping mouth seemed to take in no air, let out no sound at all. When Egon understood which of them had been hit, he slid his arms under the boy and let out a cry, raw and uninhibited from the depths of his being, a sound only men can make when all is lost. He held Friedrich's confounded body against his, lifted him up and howled like a wolf.

Time began to race. Heinz dashed outside and started the car. I ran from the terrace, tripping over the sheet. It came loose but I felt no cold, no shame. Nothing mattered, only time and air. If only there were time and air enough for everything in the world, but most of all for Friedrich. He was still breathing as they carried him out. Never had I been so keenly aware of someone breathing. Siegbert followed, holding Leni's hand, looking as if he had been cut out of paper. A red stain was stamped on his jacket, the imprint of his brother's blood. He briefly turned his haggard face toward me; I responded with a helpless gesture and watched as his mirror image was lifted into the car by Egon. Friedrich's head fell back and there was the first real blood, a pinpoint that ran like an insect along the edge of his jacket and over his shuddering chest. Heinz turned the car, patted his hat and began to drive away. Suddenly all three men seemed calm and consolidated. Even the victim, whose breathing had stopped. I squinted, searching for a change in the air, but it remained deathly still above the boy, not a hair moved in the wind. He had become an object. His body held none of the intense heat I had known.

As soon as they disappeared through the gate, Siegbert began to shake. Ever more violently, between juddering sobs, he sucked air into his lungs. Calm down, Leni pleaded, calm down lad. But he tore himself away, as if he had pulled a noose from around his neck at the last moment and decided to go on breathing.

**5**

Siegbert was to be taken to the farm down the road. He clung to Leni's hand like a child, his face turned away from me as she gave me my instructions: take the horses down to the meadow, keep an eye on the cake in the oven and above all, wait for me. She would be back in time to welcome my father. It was only a matter of taking the boy down to Frau Wolf's and then finding a telephone so that she could break the news to his mother. Leni was a pragmatic soul. Here she was fretting about a visit from my father, a man she had never seen, while a young boy had just departed, never to be seen again. I imagined her on her own deathbed, making sure her final cake had risen to perfection. Accidents occur when you least expect them, but a cake is the result of careful planning, measuring out the right ingredients and keeping track of time. It's a pity to abandon the things you can control just because disaster has struck.

'Now will you manage all that?'

She gave a wry smile and I saw her desire for Raeren to settle back into its old ways as of tomorrow. She wanted rid of him, this sickly creature with his hand in hers, ugly as a heron now with his ruffled hair and his flapping jacket, not to mention the sports shoes he had put on that morning, when he was still unsuspecting and in love ... Strangely enough, I found myself siding with Leni. Looking down at those neatly tied laces, I felt a deep revulsion. Who did he think he was? Get that boy out of here and let me see to the horses and watch over the cake: the only tasks remaining before I departed in the hope of leaving behind a house that was fit to remember.

'Don't worry,' I said as I saw them on their way. 'Everything will be all right.'

She nodded, in complete agreement. Distant bells began to ring. Only yesterday I had been to the place where those bells rang out, but now it seemed like a year ago. Though my visit had lasted an hour at best, I knew it was the memory I would recount more than any other: the colourful, crowded market and the polished hush of the post office were easy to talk about, while the story of Raeren would be one of disenchantment, like the mumbling that follows a dream, an attempt to share still-vivid experiences that founders on the listener's stifled yawns.

Leni gave the gate an extra push in preparation for my father's arrival in a little under an hour. Siegbert stood there passively in his bloodstained jacket and it struck me that Leni, who always made such a fuss about what others might think, had made no attempt to clean the boy up. If I had found enough time to get dressed, surely she could have tried to tackle the stain with a soapy cloth? No, something wasn't right. It was not my father she had opened the gate for. She was not on her way to Frau Wolf's. The boy was evidence. There were men who had been waiting a month to see such proof, men who had harboured doubts at first in light of the respect commanded by Herr von Bötticher but who had taken a growing interest in what the servant and his wife had to report. These men had jotted down the details and asked to be kept informed. And now they had enough ammunition to type a letter that would not require the intervention of a judge.

'Wait for me,' she called over her shoulder, but I already knew that I would not. First the swords had to be disposed of. They were still lying in the middle of the fencing hall, not exactly in a pool of blood but they still had to be wiped clean and thrown into the cellar. Then I carried my suitcase downstairs. The same luggage I had arrived with, as if nothing had happened in the meantime, as if experience weighs nothing. All the while, the cake had been filling the ground floor with its comforting smell and outside the horses were banging at the stable doors. There was no time to waste. I no longer knew whether I was wiping away the traces for the Gestapo or for my father. Loubna was filthy: with no regard for appearances, she had been rolling in the mud and, knowing it would take at least half an hour to brush her dirt-encrusted coat, I put her out to pasture as far from the house as possible. Megaira was in a more acceptable state, not because she was too noble for mud, but because a blanket on her back had sustained most of the damage. She rubbed her nose against my chest as if I were a tree.

'Don't worry, everything will be all right,' I said for the second time that morning, but the horse was not in the least bit worried. She looked right through me, holding my reflection in one inquiring eye. It was an ominous little portrait: my pale, round face against a background of naked trees. Horses see better far off than close up. Her eye tilted suddenly and my reflection made way for her own wild gaze. Her muscles contracted like springs and she stamped her hind legs, flexing them slightly as if she was about to rear up—God forbid, there was no way I would be able to hold her. Dung dropped from her rear end and she dragged her hoof across the sand. She had picked a fine time to treat me to her full hysterical repertoire. I could feel my anger rising and was ready to give the arrogant creature a good slap but then, in a corner of my reflection, I saw what she had seen. A car had appeared on the drive, a car as black as she was.

My father was always smaller than I remembered. He got out of the car, straightened his hat, peered in through the window and opened the door again to take out what he had forgotten—the bag he had carried with him every day of his adult life like a battered external organ. Within the walls of Raeren he appeared outlandish in all his formality. Everything about him was standard, well-tailored and pure new wool. More old-fashioned than need be. I took comfort in that, determined not to think of him as Egon's contemporary. Fragility was part of my father's constitution. For the past ten years he had adopted the bearing of a creature resigned to creaking joints and blurred vision. He did not see me until I called out to him. His whole body lengthened in surprise: 'What have we here?' I received a hasty peck on the cheek as he continued to square his disbelief with what his eyes were telling him. 'It can't be. Yet here she is!'

He was talking about the horse, which had settled down amid the distraction of our meeting. He stroked her and she snapped at a button on his coat. 'It's impossible, of course, yet I could swear ...!'

He shrugged, took off his gloves, tucked them away in an inside pocket and buttoned up his coat again. *Bon.* 'You're prettier than ever,' he said, with a hint of worry in his voice. 'Has your stay done you good?'

I nodded, thinking for a moment he might have sensed something. Many a mother can see in her daughter's face when a particular line has been crossed, but he was a man. He pressed his lips shut and gazed up at the house as if the answer he was looking for might be written on the wall.

'Where's the master of the house?'

I recounted the morning's events. He listened for a while, nodding and gazing off to the side in his doctorly fashion. 'Tension pneumothorax,' he concluded. 'The air could no longer escape from the pleural cavity. I doubt the perforation was deep, or he would have died instantly. I fear there was little I could have done for him.' Then the father in him resurfaced: 'For God's sake, take that blasted horse down to the pasture immediately and show me what's been going on here.'

When I returned, I found him standing outside the door that led to Egon's quarters, buzzing with nervous energy. Perhaps nosing around in other people's private affairs ran in the family. He withdrew his hand and slipped it surreptitiously into his coat, as if pocketing something that did not belong to him.

'So he let you practise using those antique weapons?'

'Of course not. They hung on the wall for decoration.'

Feigning nonchalance, he nodded toward the door. 'And this leads to the salon?'

'There is no salon. The kitchen is where we spend most of our time together.'

The kitchen was of no interest to him. He had already discovered it for himself and encountered Egon's dogs in the process. My father was not fond of dogs. He sighed; I was not exactly pandering to his curiosity. 'So where does this lead?'

'Von Bötticher's room.'

He vacillated between politeness and curiosity. It did not take long for the latter to gain the upper hand. I could tell by the little smile on his face, a hint of mischief that made a younger man of him. You know you have reached adulthood when you start to find your parents endearing.

'Would you like to see it? There's not much left since the

big clear-out. It was much cosier before.'

'Clear-out?'

'Ten days ago he suddenly decided to sweep the whole place clean. He came back from Amsterdam and announced that everything without a clear purpose had to be burned or thrown away. He had the walls repapered and the doors painted. It was quite a palaver.'

His expression clouded with concern. He stared at the stark white of the window frames in the hallway and I knew what he was thinking: the house looked like a sanatorium, the garden like a prison yard. 'My God,' he whispered. 'I've put you at the mercy of a madman.'

In Egon's room I hastily threw the bedspread over the sheets. My father saw this but I could not tell what he was thinking. He stared silently at the red velvet before turning to face the desk. In spite of all that had changed, the engraving was still lying there, along with the three sharpened pencils, neatly spaced, the compass aligned in front of them, the notepad in the corner and the rubber positioned between the lines on the paper. He smiled briefly on seeing the engraving but soon resumed his conspiratorial whisper.

'Perhaps I should never have told him about Thibault. I had hoped it would instil a more defensive attitude in him. I see now that he has relapsed into his old neurosis. Let me explain what I mean.'

He went on to tell me what I already knew: that Egon had become compulsively obsessed with creating order, a condition my father had explained as a natural side effect of a war trauma, though he had not been able to find anything of the sort in the scientific literature, not even when publications about shell shock began to appear. Egon had not suffered from tremors, there was no thousand-yard stare burning in his eyes. There had only been a brief period of dissociation and, once he recognized himself again, the obsession with order had begun and continued until the day they parted. Even then he had not been entirely cured.

'People have a natural desire for completion,' he said. 'Animals destroy things and think nothing of it, but we like things to be whole, to make sense. Yet look what happened here this morning, for heaven's sake. Try as you might to bring everything into line, passion can always come charging through and wreck it all.'

He sat down beside me on the bed. There were no chairs in my room at home and we had often sat side by side on my bed to talk. But this felt very strange. He knew no better than that this was the bed of a man he had not seen in a long time, a man who had become a stranger to him. Could he sense that I now knew him better than he did? A vague panic seized me and I stood up. If we drove home now, I would no longer be the carefree daughter singing along to the songs he always sang. He was bound to treat me to an ice cream from the little stand just over the border and I already knew it would not taste the same, that my attempts to remain a daughter would be awkward and pitiful, like a child who has grown head and shoulders above her classmates but still wants to join in all their games. I could no longer return to the past. This had been a one-way journey. I felt my stomach churn. At times we all become strangers to ourselves, and by the time we look back in shame at what we have become it is too late. Only Egon, after lying unconscious in a hospital bed, had not recognized himself in the here and now. A dissociative disorder, the doctors had called it, but was it really a testament to the incisiveness of his newly awakened consciousness? At that moment, I wished it was a gift I possessed.

I wanted my father to take me with him right away, but he continued to sit triumphantly on the devil-red bedspread, in the mood to pontificate. 'I came via Aachen. Ten years since I was last there. It was all astoundingly neat and tidy, as traditional and orderly as can be. It put me in mind of the home of an old woman who keeps scrubbing and polishing even though her husband has long since passed away and the children have flown the nest. Yet there is a certain beauty in ruins. You need them in order to start again. If anyone should know that, it's Hitler.'

He spread his hands on his lap and examined his finger-nails. 'With the National Socialists in power I would have expected a bold and manly city, not some folkloric haunt for old biddies. It's idealistic to think you can restore traditional values; once people have encountered science, there's no going back to primitive thinking. You cannot restore a woman to the innocent maiden she once was. At most you can hope to bolster her charms.'

He unbuttoned his coat again and took out the telegram Egon had sent him. Then he looked out of the window with a horse's gaze: failing to notice what was staring him in the face while picking out every detail from the distant past.

'Egon says he answered my letters, replies he kept but never sent. A long story. From long ago.'

'You don't need to tell me anything.'

For an instant, his eyes shot back to the present with a look of surprise. 'No, perhaps not. I have gone without answers for a long time. But there is also something he does not know. I too wrote a letter I did not send.'

From beneath the telegram he produced an envelope, stamped but not addressed. 'I wanted a fair exchange, on equal terms. Something he did not know for something I did not know. But he is not here. And as for his letters ... ' He glanced around the room.

'His letters are gone, too,' I said firmly. 'Let's go. I want to get out of here.'

To my surprise, those words were enough for him. 'I know,' he said. 'This is frightful. I am so very sorry.'

He rose to his feet and went to slip the envelope back into his inside pocket, but as he was leaving he turned and tossed it onto the desk. *Bon*. I followed him down the hallway. My neck was glowing. It felt like the warmth of a fatherly hand, but my father's hands were clasped tightly behind his back. Raeren had never been so quiet and it would remain so for a while yet, until all hell broke loose. It would be quiet when the master of the house returned to find no one there, only an old letter. It would remain quiet as he read, the silence you keep when addressed by your elders.

My father lifted my case from its spot in the sunshine and looked at me questioningly. Yes, I was ready. But as he walked on I remained standing with my hand on the doorpost, just as you hold a book by its final pages.

'One last thing,' I said, and went back inside.

Dear Egon,

I will seal this letter and keep it with me. A letter written but never sent—can it still be called a letter? Perhaps it is more of an indictment. When people bring charges they do not want to hear the arguments of the accused. Or is it a confession? In the confessional you indict yourself and would be only too pleased for someone to argue back, but they never do and you are left with an answer that is of little use to you. And so I fill this page with words, knowing they will not be contradicted. They are intended for you alone, my friend. An imaginary friend who is able to understand and find it in his heart to forgive me at last. Perhaps one day the imaginary will become real and these words will have been addressed to a future friend.

Why *do* we write letters? To justify the past? To do right by the future? They say Poste Restante keeps letters that cannot be delivered for fifty years. Written words carry more weight than the spoken, yet this hardly separates us from the animals. They too are more interested in the tracks a creature leaves behind than in its actual presence. It is misguided to suppose animals live only in the here and now. They too investigate the past and go in search of others, sniffing out creatures that once passed their way. It is only the future they care little for. They make no plans, have no desire to understand what it holds, entertain no notion of what life should be. They undergo change without worrying whether or not it constitutes progress. The one future they do know is death.

I cannot share your idealism and perhaps this attests to the animal in me. I want to heal people, not improve them. We like to see ourselves as an improvement on our ancestors but our organs still function in exactly the same way; the only difference is that now we are better at repairing them. I had the skills to repair every part of you, everything except your passions. If only we could cure the urge for vengeance. It would end this bloodshed once and for all!

Just now I sent you a letter in which I lied.

I wrote that you only lost consciousness in Maastricht. It is a lie you have always suspected. If word had got out that I had transported you to Dutch territory unconscious, you would have been entitled to lodge a protest and I would have been forced to let you go. Physical recovery would have been sufficient grounds, your psychological condition would not have been seen as relevant. I do not regret this lie but, for reasons you will understand, I am not able to own up to it until the war is over.

I wrote that I did not find your horse. This too is untrue. Your horse was the first living creature I ever killed. I took my scalpel and made an incision in her carotid artery. She did not resist. The frequency with which she snorted increased slightly and before long she closed her one eye, an eye that had seen so many things from which she could no longer run. The vet had made himself scarce by the time we found the two of you. You lay still, given up for dead like so many of your comrades, but she was scraping desperately at the sand, snorting, her legs jerking. She was the most beautiful horse I had ever seen. In spite of her wounds, her coat was shining. The blood had turned her belly black as pitch.

I have never cared much for animals, but your horse had an

instinct keener than that of most humans. She kept track of my every movement. In order to alleviate your own suffering, you need only look at others. In her eyes, I was the surgeon who divided her artery in two with one clinical stroke along its length: her blood flowed more freely, her muscles relaxed and the only future she knew came to pass. You sighed as she gave up the ghost, and it was then I understood that you were alive.

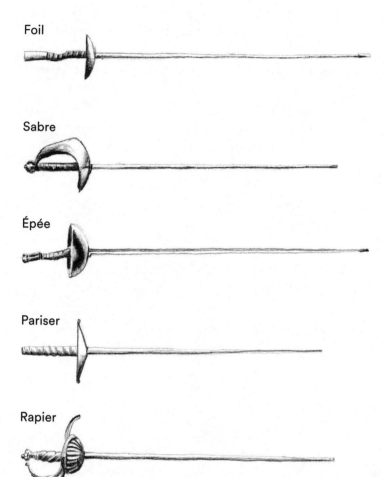

Foil

Sabre

Épée

Pariser

Rapier

## Thanks

First and foremost, I am indebted to Maître Bert van den Berg, who taught me the art of fencing, and to Maître Ruud van Oeveren for sharing his impressive expertise in this field. I am also grateful to Dr Job van Woensel (AMC Amsterdam), Evelyn de Roodt (author of *Oorlogsgasten*), Dr Krijn Thijs (Duitsland Instituut Amsterdam), Ankie van den Berg and Rolf Bergfeld for keeping me safe from mishits and slip-ups. Lastly, my thanks go to Mirjam van Hengel for her boundless faith in this book.

MdM
Mechelen, July 2010

The translator would like to thank Ed Rogers, Editor of *The Sword* (the magazine of British Fencing), for his extraordinary generosity and fascinating insights into the world of fencing; Rhian Heppleston for her invaluable and inspiring input; and N.C.M. Schluter, MdP, LdP, CC, for guidance and support above and beyond the call of duty.

## On the Design

As book design is an integral part of the reading experience, we would like to acknowledge the work of those who shaped the form in which the story is housed.

Tessa van der Waals (Netherlands) is responsible for the cover design, cover typography and art direction of all World Editions books. She works in the internationally renowned tradition of Dutch Design. Her bright and powerful visual aesthetic maintains a harmony between image and typography and captures the unique atmosphere of each book. She works closely with internationally celebrated photographers, artists, and letter designers. Her work has frequently been awarded prizes for Best Dutch Book Design.

The woman on the cover is Helene Mayer, who also features in the book as the sportswoman who inspires the protagonist to start fencing. At age seventeen Mayer won the gold medal for fencing at the 1928 Olympics, and quickly became a national hero. In 1935, due to her father being Jewish, she was stripped of her German citizenship and forced to resettle in the USA. Despite this, she returned to represent Germany at the 1936 games in Berlin where she won silver and, curiously, gave the Nazi salute on stage. The picture is taken from the Ullstein Bild archive.

The cover has been edited by lithographer Bert van der Horst of BFC Graphics (Netherlands).

Suzan Beijer (Netherlands) is responsible for the typography and careful interior book design of all World Editions titles.

The text on the inside covers and the press quotes are set in Circular, designed by Laurenz Brunner (Switzerland) and published by Swiss type foundry Lineto.

All World Editions books are set in the typeface Dolly, specifically designed for book typography. Dolly creates a warm page image perfect for an enjoyable reading experience. This typeface is designed by Underware, a European collective formed by Bas Jacobs (Netherlands), Akiem Helmling (Germany), and Sami Kortemäki (Finland). Underware are also the creators of the World Editions logo, which meets the design requirement that 'a strong shape can always be drawn with a toe in the sand.'